Also by Christopher C. Tubbs

SCARLETT FOX
Book 1: Scarlett
Book 2: Freedom
Book 3: Legacy

LADY BETHANY
Book 1: Graduation
Book 2: Betrayal

DECOY SHIPS
Book 1: Kingfisher
Book 2: Warley
Book 3: Farnborough

CHRISTOPHER C. TUBBS

Farnborough

THE DECOY SHIPS
BOOK THREE

LUME BOOKS
A JOFFE BOOKS COMPANY

Lume Books, London
A Joffe Books Company
www.lumebooks.co.uk

First published in Great Britain in 2025 by Lume Books

Copyright © Christopher C. Tubbs 2025

The right of Christopher C. Tubbs to be identified as author of this work has been asserted in accordance with the Copyright, Designs and Patents Act 1988.

This book is a work of fiction. Names, characters, businesses, organisations, places and events are either the product of the author's imagination or are used fictitiously. Any resemblance to actual persons, living or dead, events or locales is entirely coincidental. The spelling used is British English except where fidelity to the author's rendering of accent or dialect supersedes this. The right of Christopher C. Tubbs to be identified as author of this work has been asserted in accordance with the Copyright, Designs and Patents Act 1988.

No part of this book may be used or reproduced in any manner for the purpose of training artificial intelligence technologies or systems. In accordance with Article 4(3) of the Digital Single Market Directive 2019/790, Joffe Books expressly reserves this work from the text and data mining exception.

Cover art by Cherie Chapman

ISBN: 978-1-83901-615-8

This book is dedicated to all who serve no matter the country or the service.

Note to Reader

Farnborough is a work of fiction set against a historical backdrop. While the narrative features certain well-known figures and events from recorded history, they have been used in a fictitious manner for the purposes of compelling storytelling.

Preface

During World War I, after the Battle of Jutland, the German surface fleet was blockaded by the Royal Navy in German home ports and was thus rendered largely ineffective. This forced the Germans to further develop their existing submarine fleet into sophisticated and technically advanced vessels to carry the fight to the British.

At first, these advanced vessels — U-boats — targeted British capital ships, sinking the cruisers HMS *Pathfinder*, HMS *Aboukir*, HMS *Hogue*, HMS *Cressy* and HMS *Hawke*; the submarine HMS *E3* (in the first ever successful attack on one sub by another); and the pre-dreadnought battleship HMS *Formidable* in 1914 alone. From later that year, they were used to attack merchant ships as the navy developed tactics to avoid U-boat attack.

The U-boats' weakness was their poor underwater performance. Once submerged, they could barely manoeuvre and were virtually blind — periscope technology was in its infancy at this time. Consequently, they had to get into position on the surface and either attack while still on the surface or submerge and try a torpedo shot from there. Surface action at night was their preferred modus operandi, using either their gun or torpedoes.

However, British anti-submarine technology and tactics in 1914 and 1915 were equally primitive, with no means of tracking submarines under water and no way of killing them if they did (the first effective depth charges were not developed until 1916). The British relied on catching the submarine on the surface and either sinking it with guns or ramming it. One must also remember that radar did not exist; so, to find a U-boat you had to spot it using lookouts — which made it more a matter of luck than anything.

The First Lord of the Admiralty, Winston Churchill, proposed the idea of decoy ships to counteract the highly dangerous submarine threat Germany posed to Britain's supply lines in 1914. The idea, while not entirely original, got traction with the Admiralty and soon commercial cargo ships were being fitted out with hidden guns, the intention being to provide a submarine with a tasty morsel that it could take on the surface with its deck gun, and thus tempt it into surfacing. Once the bait was taken, the decoy ship would drop its disguise and open fire, hopefully sinking the enemy beast.

Queenstown, in Cork Harbour (now known as Cobh), was a British sovereign port by treaty. It had been named after Queen Victoria, who visited it in 1849, and was a valuable base for both British and American ships due to its strategic position close to the Atlantic trade routes. It became the main base for the decoy ships, which were named Q-ships in its honour. These ships ranged from sailing ships to disguised warships. Theirs was a hazardous duty and so the crews earned hazard pay as well as prize money.

This book covers (in Part One) the Q-ship careers of some of the brave and intrepid officers of the British Q-ship force, many of whom received the Victoria Cross for their efforts. I make no apologies for having additional main characters in this book apart from the primary two: all of the men featured earned their places in history and all deserve to be MCs. Some of their stories are longer than others, as Q-ships had notoriously short lives — even if they were not sunk, they generally had to be retired quickly because the enemy submarine commanders learned their identities or their descriptions.

Part Two of this book is dedicated to the Germans' decoy ships and focuses on the career of Felix Graf von Luckner of the *Seeadler*, whose descendant I had the pleasure of working with when I lived and worked in Germany. He was the exception rather than the rule when it came to officer conduct in the German navy as their submarine fleet became ever more ruthless as the war progressed. The Germans only had six decoy ships and only two of them were used, unsuccessfully, to hunt submarines. The other four were commerce raiders. I chose Felix's story because it is a standout "Boys' Own" story of dash, bravery and gentlemanly conduct.

A small disclaimer here. This is primarily a work of fiction and even though most of this happened, and most of these people were real, this is not a history reference book and some liberties have been taken.

This book is dedicated to the crews who sailed these ships and the officers that commanded them. They were beyond brave.

To help the reader:

British/Navy slang and terminology
Aye = yes
Aye-aye = understood and will do
(The) Andrew = the Royal Navy

Belay = stop
Cdr = commander
Chuffed = proud
CinC = Commander-in-Chief
Civvies = civilian clothes
CPO/Chief = chief petty officer
Dumb fire = practising loading a gun with spent shell cases
Fleet = fleet chief petty officer
Guns = gunnery officer
Knocking shop = brothel
Lt = lieutenant
Mid = midshipman
MTB = motor torpedo boat
Mufti = civilian clothes
NACB = Navy and Army Canteen Board
NCO = non-commissioned officer
Nmi = nautical miles = 1.15 miles = 1.852 Km
Oik = uncouth person
Pink gin = gin with a dash of Angostura bitters
PO = petty officer
Rating = ordinary seaman
Reeve a block = thread rope through a pulley
RNR = Royal Naval Reserve
RNVR = Royal Naval Volunteer Reserve
SNO = senior naval officer
Splice the mainbrace = get an extra tot of rum
Sprog = new recruit (or child)
Sub = sub lieutenant
Uckers = a variation of Ludo, played in the mess

U/S = unserviceable
Wardroom = officers' mess
Wet = a drink

Royal Navy officer ranks
Midshipman
Sub lieutenant
Lieutenant
Lieutenant commander
Commander
Captain
Commodore 2nd class
Rear admiral and commodore 1st class
Vice admiral
Admiral
Admiral of the fleet

PART ONE: THE BRITISH

The Beginning

1913 — The office of the First Lord of the Admiralty
Winston Churchill received a report from his staff on Germany's growing fleet of advanced submarines, and he was not impressed.

"This report is unconvincing. It claims that the Germans would use their submarines against merchant ships and civilians. Of that I am particularly sceptical. I do not believe this would ever be done by a civilised power," he later reported to the Cabinet. But he was wrong — and in 1914, as the Western Front degenerated into a muddy bloodbath, the Germans quietly slipped their U-boats out of harbour and into the North Sea and Atlantic to bring the war to Britain's waters.

By Christmas 1914, Britain had declared the North Sea a closed military area and any vessel could be stopped, searched and seized if it was suspected to be carrying anything that could aid the enemy. This included food, a measure that particularly outraged the German government. As Britain tightened its hold on European waters and effectively blockaded German-controlled ports, the Germans decided to retaliate. On 18 February 1915, Admiral Hugo von Pohl, the German Chief of Naval Staff, ordered that:

The waters around Britain and Ireland are to be treated as a war zone. Any vessel in that zone may be attacked without warning, regardless of nationality or flag.

With that, the submarine war started in earnest.

The Royal Navy was singularly unprepared for this development, lacking as it did the ability to detect and/or destroy submarines under water. Money was made available for research and development, but by then they were playing catch-up.

As early as June 1914, Churchill received a message stating that a submarine was sinking merchant ships off Le Havre. Churchill was a keen student of history, and his thoughts turned to the seventeenth century and HMS *Kingfisher*. She was built to solve a similar problem, namely that of how to get an enemy close enough to destroy him, when that enemy simply avoided any ship that looked military.

Churchill learned the lesson of history and responded decisively, telling his secretary, "Send a message to Sir Hedworth Meux, Commander-in-Chief, Portsmouth. To counter the threat of the submarine off of Le Havre, I strongly suggest that you arm and disguise a merchant steamer to trap the submarine on the surface and destroy her."

Initial attempts to use so-called mystery ships were unsuccessful, but the idea took hold and soon the navy was tasked with setting up a small fleet of decoy ships and an admiral put in charge of the project.

Admiral Sir Lewis Bayly was senior officer on the coast of Ireland and had his headquarters in Queenstown, where he had a number of officers and ratings working at desks and a large plotting table showing convoys in the Western Approaches and around the coast of Ireland. He was given the job of running the decoy ships and told to get a move on as this was a top priority. So, he called a meeting with the resident naval architect at Queenstown's Haulbowline dockyard in early 1915.

Queenstown was situated on Great Island in Cork Harbour and accessed from the Irish Sea through an inlet. The Roches Point lighthouse marked the eastern side of the entrance, which was protected by a sixteenth-century fort on the western side. It was the home base for British and, later, American destroyers that escorted the Atlantic convoys through the Western Approaches. Haulbowline Island lies opposite the town and is the location of the naval dockyard. Spike Island lies behind it and is home to Fort Mitchel.

Bayly set out the challenge. "The problem is this. To kill a submarine one must catch it on the surface and either ram it or shoot it to sink it. Of course, if the captain has any inkling that the ship is armed or is a warship all they have to do is submerge and get far enough away to then pop up to the surface and run away using their diesel engines." He paused as he collected his thoughts. "Churchill has had the idea that we use a trick that originated in the seventeenth century, when they disguised a warship as a merchant ship to lure in the enemy for destruction. We will turn that around and take merchant vessels, arm them, and disguise the weapons so that they can be deployed at the last moment."

"I see. They will be deck-mounted weapons?" the architect asked.

"12-, 6- and 3-pounder quick-fire cannons and Maxim guns. Whatever combination suits the ship. I want you to come up with ways to disguise them, and communicate your ideas to the navy's other shipyards."

The architect nodded. *This could be fun,* he thought.

The next thing Bayly did was summon to his headquarters a number of officers that were likely to command these ships, to discuss what types of ships they should requisition. It was a no-holds-barred think tank, and it came up with a list of ship types that naval inspectors were subsequently told to find and requisition.

Bayly and the officers also considered relevant tactics.

"Every German submarine is given a former North Sea pilot or sailor from the German merchant marine that has worked aboard or guided a British merchantman. These men are used to identifying targets and to deceive them will be no mean feat," said Bayly. They all knew that pre-war, many Allied merchant ships carried Germans among their crews.

"We have had a suggestion from Vice Admiral Beatty, or rather through him from the Paymaster, who has the idea to tow a submarine behind a trawler. The submarine can torpedo the U-boat when it surfaces near the trawler."

Lieutenant William Penrose Mark-Wardlaw looked interested and asked, "How would the submarine know when the U-boat surfaces or is approaching on the surface?"

Lieutenant Herbert, another former submariner, raised his hand.

"Yes, lieutenant?" Bayly said.

"We could run a telephone line down the tow and connect that to the submarine. That way the commander of the ship could talk to the submarine captain through to the point that they drop the tow to make the attack. The C-class has a connector available in the conning tower. When the tow is dropped, the wires will rip out and disconnect it."

"Excellent, that will be tried. Now, anything else to do with the surface ship?"

"The crew should look and behave like normal seamen. Are we keeping the crews on when we requisition the ships?" Mark-Wardlaw said.

"That is the proposal at the moment, not least because we don't have enough navy personnel to fully man the ships," Bayly said. "Only the gunners and overall commander will be navy men."

"Then those from the navy should dress like merchant navy — and behave like they do, as well."

The merchant navy was the collective name for all the civilian merchant ships registered in the United Kingdom, manned by civilian mariners and flying the Red Ensign. At the end of World War I, King George V made it an official title which is still in use to the present day.

That caused a laugh to ripple around the table.

"No saluting and calling anyone *sir*!" Lieutenant Commander Harrington Edwards laughed.

Bayly's secretary, June, an Irish girl who had blue eyes and dark hair that framed a pretty face, noted all of this down using Pitman shorthand. She would type it all up after the meeting. Perhaps that was why Mark-Wardlaw blushed as he raised his hand and asked his next question.

"A rather delicate subject comes to mind, sir. Naval-issue underwear. It is rather distinctive, and merchant navy crews hang their washing out on deck. A set of Royal Navy drawers hanging from the line would stand out like the White Ensign."

June smiled at him, which made his blush deepen.

"That's a very good point! June, make a note that all naval personnel are to be given a cash allowance to buy civilian underwear," Bayly said.

"Are we being given wireless sets?" Edwards asked, after the chuckles about the underwear had died down.

"Yes, all decoy ships will be issued with a standard Marconi set," Bayly replied.

"Then we need to conceal the antennae," Edwards said.

June noted this down and made a side note to herself for later, to sort the suggestions into things for the ship and things for the crew.

"What happens when a merchant ship is approached by a submarine?" Mark-Wardlaw asked.

Herbert explained: "Well, in general, the submarine approaches, fires a warning shot and signals for the ship to stop. At that point most merchant crews panic and abandon ship by taking to their boats. Once they are clear, the sub either sends over a boarding party to scuttle the ship or shoots the bottom out of it to sink it."

Mark-Wardlaw nodded and frowned in thought. Then he said, "That's what our crews should do. Only the navy men should stay aboard and man the guns."

"A panic party!" Hargreaves quipped and laughed. Little did they know that the name would stick.

The naval inspectors started delivering the decoy ships by the end of spring 1915. Trawlers, tramp steamers, colliers and cargo ships of all sizes were requisitioned and sent to naval dockyards to be converted in secrecy. A variety of methods were employed — larger guns could be deck-mounted and disguised as deck cargo or housings, the disguise fabricated in such a way as to fall away at the pull of a lever. Another way was to mount the big guns in the hold on hydraulic lifts that would raise them when they went into action. Lighter guns like Maxim machine guns had mounts installed around the ship so they could be optimally positioned as required.

QF (Quick-Firing) 12-pounder (3-inch) guns, QF 6-pounder (57-mm) Nordenfelt guns, QF 3-pound Hotchkis guns, and Maxim machine guns were all used. The 12-pound quick-firing guns could fire fifteen common pointed shells a minute, the smaller guns more than that, which would give the ship exceptional firepower. The common pointed shell they fired was made of cast steel and filled with a gunpowder bursting charge. Its long solid nose made it suitable for anti-ship work, but was not deemed to be armour-piercing.

At first they only worked the crews as teams to get them used to working together. Load, dumb fire, reload with each crewman doing his individual job as follows:

- Gun layer (controlling the gun elevation and firing it)
- Trainer (controlling the gun in the horizontal axis)
- Breech worker/gun captain
- Loader
- Ammunition feeder

Later, when the first fully naval crews had been deployed, men who could play-act and learn their lines were selected as general crew. An aid for this was the so-called *board of lies*, a blackboard bearing the ship's fictitious name, cargo, number of crew, port of registration and so on — all information that a submarine captain may want confirmed if he questioned the crew.

Crews of the Q-ships benefited by being based in Ireland and having shorter patrol times. Fresh meat was typical instead of preserved, potatoes instead of dried beans and peas, and fresh vegetables. Tinned sausages were a favourite with the crew and nicknamed *snorkers* (an old English name for a piglet). It was often said that their sleeping berths smelt less of dried pea farts than the regular navy.

The crews, whether merchant navy, fishermen or Royal Navy, had to be exceptionally brave as well. The panic party could expect to find itself in the crossfire between the ship and submarine at some point, or be machine-gunned by the submarine crew if they caught on to what they were doing. They could not surrender; the Germans, even if the British switched flags to the White Ensign of the Royal Navy, would treat them as pirates as they did not recognise this tactic as legitimate (even though they had decoy ships of their own) and shoot them out of hand.

The situation for the sailors and officers was made worse by the conditions of absolute secrecy the government and navy imposed on the whole operation. Civilians were made to sign secrecy agreements before they were allowed to crew the ships. Dockyards had to conceal what they were doing from general view, and if civilian dockyard workers were used, they had to sign the secrecy agreement as well.

Men had to lie to their wives or sweethearts — or, if they did tell them, they had to trust they wouldn't tell anyone else, as their lives depended on it. Sailors in mufti couldn't tell their former shipmates what they were doing if they met in a bar. Ultimately, this led to many misunderstandings and even fights.

Many senior officers in the Royal Navy thought that the very idea of using decoy ships was crazy. This view was particularly prevalent among the men who had served under Queen Victoria, many of whom ridiculed the little fleet of mystery or decoy ships and nicknamed them "Gilbert and Sullivan's navy". But the project had powerful backers, including Churchill and Admiral Beatty, Commander-in-Chief of the Grand Fleet, who managed to secure both hazardous duty pay and prize money for the decoy ships' officers and crews.

Prize money — or bounty money — of £1,000 was awarded for the sinking of a submarine, to be divided among all the crew as shares, whether Royal Navy or civilian. Each share was worth £1 18s 1d (therefore, there were 525 shares) and the number of shares a man received depended on his rank and whether he performed a significant role in the sinking. For example, an officer who had significantly contributed to the sinking might receive fifty shares.

However, if a submarine was sunk, no public credit would be given. Neither the decoy-ship crews nor their ship would be named in the *Gazette*. If they received any commendation, award or honour, it would probably not be announced, but if it was, the published citation would be heavily redacted. The men of the decoy ships would have to wait until after the war for the truth to be told.

Progress on the decoy-ships project was slow to start with; merchant crews were sometimes understandably reluctant when they found out how their ships were to be used. The means of disguising the guns so that they could be rapidly deployed needed some experimentation before suitable mechanisms could be adopted. This all resulted in various false starts and failed missions. Ships sank, crews were lost and not a single U-boat was sunk … until they finally got it right.

Harrington Edwards

The fishing trawler *Taranaki* was about to try something new. Her skipper and owner Geoffrey Couch watched as the Royal Navy modified his winch to take a towline with a telephone cable attached. He shook his head. *It's lucky they're paying me, 'cus there'll be no fish this trip,* he thought.

Lieutenant Commander Harrington Edwards, the officer who was now in command of his boat, came and stood beside him. "We will rendezvous with the submarine once they are done and the radio set is installed," he said.

"Just for my benefit, what are we doing again?" Geoff asked.

"We will rendezvous with the submarine and attach the towline and telephone link. They will submerge and we will tow them as if they were a trawl. If we spot a German submarine, we will lure it into range of the submarine's torpedoes and they will sink it."

Geoff was sceptical and it showed. "As easy as that."

Harrington smiled. "Well, not easy, but doable."

Geoff didn't like the sound of *doable*. "And where will all this happen?"

"East coast of Scotland."

That was a long way from Ireland and his home in Cornwall. But Geoff was pragmatic to his socks. "Oh. Better fill her up, then."

The coal barge was called alongside and the bunker filled to the brim.

Geoff had been approached by a navy shipping inspector and told that his boat was being requisitioned at port in Cornwall early in 1915. What he didn't realise at the time was they meant his boat, him and his crew.

He told his wife, "The *Taranaki* has been requisitioned by the navy. They want me and the crew to stay with her."

His wife was not impressed. "What for?"

"A patrol boat, is all they've told me. We'll be getting some regular navy men as well."

Cornish fishermen's wives were tough and used to missing their men for extended periods, but she didn't like the sound of this. "Why can't they put a full crew of navy boys on her?"

"That I don't know. Look, sailing around patrolling must be safer than fishing in the North Sea or Atlantic, mustn't it?"

She cuddled up to him; her belly was beginning to show that she was pregnant with their second child. "I suppose so."

Now he was in Haulbowline Island dockyard in Cork Harbour, having his boat refitted with the new winch set-up, a QF 3-pound Hotchkiss hidden on the foredeck and a Maxim machine gun on the prow. A Marconi radio set and the telephone to the submarine were installed on the bridge.

They wanted him to sail all the way up to Scottish waters in the North Sea and act as bait to catch a big grey shark with very sharp teeth. He looked at his charts and saw that Hargreaves had plotted the course for him. They would sail up the Irish Sea, through the Hebrides and around the north of Scotland to Dundee, where they would rendezvous with the submarine at dusk and take her under tow.

"You know we will only make, probably, four knots at the most with her on the line?" Geoff said to Harrington.

"That's perfect — we want the German captain to think you're fishing."

"For how long?"

"As long as it takes," Hargreaves said, and shrugged.

Geoff took out a packet of loose shag tobacco and rolled himself a cigarette. He licked the paper and finished it off before lighting it with a Swan Vesta match, which he struck on the bridge woodwork. "Well, if the U-boat captain knows his stuff he'll know something's up when we don't haul our nets every two hours or so," he said, the cigarette clenched between his lips.

Harrington frowned; they hadn't thought of that. He silently prayed that the submarine commander or his watchmen were not former fishermen.

A pair of workmen appeared on the foredeck and started fitting a large metal plate that formed the base of the gun mount. They drilled through the deck into the spars that supported it before inserting nine-inch bolts and screwing them down. The 3-pound gun was waiting on the dock, and Geoff nodded towards it.

"Are you expecting us to shoot that thing?" he asked after picking a strand of tobacco off his lip.

Harrington looked down at the gun. "No, it takes a crew of four to operate and they will be navy gunners. The Maxim needs two, a gunner and loader."

That explained why the hold was being converted to sleeping berths.

Farnborough

* * *

All the work was done by the beginning of May 1915, and they were fully coaled. The navy men had boarded and settled in. Geoff was still in command of sailing the ship. However, Harrington told him where to go and what to do when they got there, and would be in command if they got into a fight. Geoff's crew were of the opinion this was a fool's errand and the men were doing it because it paid well and was easier than fishing. In any case they, and the Royal Navy sailor boys, were getting what the Admiralty called "hazardous duty pay" and might earn a nice bonus if they did manage to sink a submarine.

Once they cleared Cork Harbour, Geoff rang for full speed and steered north by west. This took them out into a moderate Irish Sea with four-foot waves and a westerly wind of around six knots. At night they slowed to half ahead with Geoff and his first mate Charlie keeping watch: four on, four off. This way they covered 150 miles a day. By dawn of day two they had cleared St George's Channel and turned north and the engine, a three-cylinder triple-expansion engine, chuffed away merrily. The only unhappy people on the boat were the stoker and his mates, who had to keep the boiler fed. There were only three so Geoff gave them an extra hand so they too could do four on and four off as well.

The Isle of Man passed serenely down the starboard side, and they turned north-west to exit the Irish Sea into the Atlantic. The waves got bigger but were spaced further apart, and the wind increased as they left the lee of the Irish coast and rounded Islay. Then, as they turned north again, the sea came in on the beam. The *Taranaki* had a steel hull to withstand the worst the North Sea could throw at her, but she was only 120 feet long and rolled and pitched in a nasty corkscrew motion.

"Are your gunners not used to being at sea?" Geoff asked a rather pale Harington as a gunner threw up over the lee-side gunnel.

"Not in boats that roll like this one."

"They'd better get used to it," Geoff said with a straight face. This was business as usual for the fishermen.

Those fishermen took no notice of the sea, apart from always having one hand for themselves while they moved around. There were no safety lines strung and not one of them wore a life jacket. The gunners were either huddled on the deck or laid out below, wrapped in their kapok-filled life jackets. Most chose the deck, since the hold had a lingering smell of fish that made things worse.

Geoff quietly took pity on them and steered a course to take them behind the islands of Tiree and Coll, giving them an hour or two's respite. They were then behind the islands of the Outer Hebrides in the Sea of the Hebrides, steering due north into the Little Minch. It was cooler in early June than down south, being between fifty and sixty degrees Fahrenheit on land, and at sea five to ten degrees cooler than that. The fresh air and a simple pitching motion as they crossed the much smaller waves was the cure the navy boys needed to start their recovery.

The corkscrewing started again once they cleared the lee of the Isle of Lewis, but once they turned east around Cape Wrath they had the sea on their stern — and the leg to the Orkneys was actually quite pleasant. Harrington regained his colour and the gunners stopped puking. They slowed as they passed Scapa Flow and kept out of the way of the big warships of the Home Fleet as they came and went. Geoff had not seen the Home Fleet in all its glory before and marvelled at the huge battlecruisers and dreadnoughts. Then they were on the final leg to Dundee where they would take on coal before making the rendezvous with their submarine.

Farnborough

* * *

Dundee, famous for shipbuilding, whaling, jute, whisky and marmalade, lies on the Firth of Tay and is dominated by the Law, a 572-feet-tall volcanic hill to the north of the city centre that was once the site of an Iron Age hill fort, and had been used as the central defence of the city throughout the ages. They made their way to the coaling dock and tied up there to be refuelled. All signs that the *Taranaki* was anything other than a trawler were carefully concealed.

The coal — in sacks, each of two hundredweight, on sack trucks — was brought aboard by stevedores via a ramp from the dock before being emptied into the coal bunker. The cost of twelve bob a sack was set by the government, and this was good-quality stuff. Much better than what was passed off to them as good coal down in Cornwall.

Harrington paid in cash and then went to the Admiralty office, where he claimed the money back and messaged Queenstown that they had arrived in Dundee. He was told to rendezvous with submarine *C27* off Peterhead to begin working up the technique on 24 May. Several patrols followed, but it wasn't until 8 June they got their first bite.

"Skipper, U-boat a mile and half to the north."

Harrington and Geoff both grabbed binoculars and found their target. Harrington picked up the telephone to the *C27*.

"*C27*, we have a U-boat approaching from the north."

"Stand by. Yes, I have it in my periscope. Slipping the tow."

The line went dead and the *Taranaki* increased speed as the drag of the submarine was removed. Whether that spooked the commander of the *U-19*, Constantine Kolbe, or he saw the periscope, they never knew, but the U-boat sped up to fifteen knots and headed straight for the *C27*'s periscope.

The *C27* dived to avoid being run down by the *U-19* and never got a shot off. The German sailed away at full speed so that by the time the *C27* was at periscope depth they were long gone.

Back in Aberdeen, Harrington reported to the Admiralty office and handed in his report. He returned with news: they would have time in port as the *C24*, their next tow, was delayed and would not be in until the twentieth June, and today was the seventh.

"Typical bloody navy, have you hurry up then wait," grumbled Charlie, the first mate.

"Look on the bright side," Geoff said with a grin. "You get to sleep in a bed and eat grub without coal dust in it."

Charlie chuckled. "I'll be staying at Ma McPherson's."

Geoff knew of that establishment, which was in the seedier part of town and part seamen's hotel, part knocking shop. It had a reputation for (mostly) clean girls.

"Careful you don't catch anything," Geoff cautioned. Sexually transmitted diseases were common in such places.

"I'll be fine. Got me condoms, ain't I?" These reusable rubbers had been imported from America and were available if you knew where to find them.

Geoff was married. His wife of three years had already given him a son and they had a second child on the way. Sex was a rarity at this time, and the temptation for a bit of hanky-panky without any consequences was appealing. He argued with his conscience and decided it would be alright if he was discreet and didn't let the men know. Their tongues got loose when they'd had a few beers and the last thing he wanted was to hurt his wife. So, he headed into the slightly better part of town and took a room in a reasonable little hotel.

Some discreet enquiries at a local pub pointed him to an address on Willison Street. He knocked at the door and a pretty woman answered it. She was dark-haired and about five feet six inches in her shoes, dressed nicely with just the right amount of make-up.

"Can I help you?" She had a voice like velvet.

"I've come for tea," he replied, as he had been instructed.

"Oh, do come in." Her accent was English and her tone was neutral. She closed the door behind him then led him into a sitting room.

A teapot sat on the table, surrounded by teacups. He bent over, took the lid off the teapot and dropped five bob into it.

"I'm Samantha," she purred, and moved in close.

"Geoff." He took her in his arms.

His money bought him her company until the next morning when, sated, he returned to his hotel. She had been amazing, had provided the condoms and obviously enjoyed her work a lot. She was inventive, and when she wasn't having sex, intelligent and witty. He would try and visit again.

The nineteenth came and the men returned to the boat. They were rested and ready to go. Harrington had their orders.

"The rendezvous will take place around dawn, twenty miles due west of the Tay Estuary. Sunup is at 04:20 and we need to be in position before that, so we will leave at 02:00. The submarine will flash a recognition signal, which I will answer. Then he will come alongside to receive the tow."

They were in position at 04:00. The lookouts were vigilant. False dawn gave the horizon to the east a grey tinge as the stars faded. They waited.

Harrington was nervous — they were too close to the coast for his liking.

"Man the guns."

The men quietly went to their stations.

Sunrise. The horizon lit up with a golden light that spread slowly upwards. The *Taranaki*, however, was still in the earth's shadow as daylight marched towards them.

"Ship off the port quarter," one of the lookouts cried.

"Damn," said Harrington.

Geoff examined her through his binoculars. "Norwegian-flagged cargo ship heading south, doing around eight knots," he said. "Probably heading to the Firth of Forth."

The ship gave them a toot in greeting as she passed a mile off their port beam before disappearing into the distance.

"Periscope dead astern," the aft lookout called, ten minutes after that.

Harrington visibly relaxed.

"I hope that is ours," Geoff said.

"Probably been watching all this time," Harrington said.

The slick grey shape of a conning tower slowly rose out of the water, followed by the hull. Water cascaded down its sides as the submarine rose out of the depths. A figure appeared in the conning tower and used a lamp to send the recognition signal.

"Throw across the messenger line once they are ready to receive," said Harrington.

Men came out of a hatch that opened forward of the sub's conning tower, and indicated that they were ready. The line was expertly thrown by one of the fishermen and the submariners hauled across the tow chain and telephone line by forming a line of bodies that marched along the deck before, one by one, going back to the bow to latch on and haul again.

The telephone crackled into life. "Good morning, *Taranaki*. *C24* here. Can you hear me? Captain Taylor here."

Harrington had the receiver. "Hello, *C24*, receiving you loud and clear."

"Good to hear you. Ready to commence hunting. Start the tow and we will submerge."

"Received and understood," Harrington replied, then said to Geoff, "Please start the tow, bearing 1, 3, 0."

Geoff asked for "ahead dead slow" on the engine telegraph and the engine thumped as the propeller started to turn. They gently took up the slack in the tow and, as the submarine started to move, he increased to half ahead. As soon as the speed settled, a blast of air from *C24*'s ballast tanks warned them she was submerging. After less than a minute they looked, to all outside observers, like any other trawler with her net on a stern tow.

In the *C24*, the sixteen-man crew listened to the steady *thump-thump-thump* of the fishing boat's propeller. They trimmed her to overcome the upward pull of the chain and kept her at a steady thirty feet. Lieutenant Frederick Taylor, the skipper, was relaxed. They were only using the batteries to power the lights and a couple of their instruments, and they had sufficient air to stay down until dark.

"Do you think this will work?" Miles Greyson, his number two, asked.

"It has as good a chance as any," Frederick replied. "We know one of theirs is operating in this area."

"Well, I hope we do. It will do the men's morale the power of good."

Pickings were thin with the Germans blockaded in their ports.

Frederick smiled grimly; this was new territory, and untried. There were a thousand things that could go wrong.

Frederick was right on one thing. The *U-40* had already sunk a trawler and a collier in the last three days and was looking to finish off her cruise with one last kill. The German captain, Gerhardt Fürbringer, had four of his six torpedoes left, having seen off the trawler with his deck gun and used two torpedoes to sink the collier. A third kill would keep up his average and earn him and the crew praise when they returned home.

They were cruising on the surface, thirty nautical miles off the coast of Dunbar, Scotland, when they spotted smoke on the horizon. Fürbringer took the bearing using the bridge pelorus. The vessel was heading south, as far as he could tell.

"Steer 3, 0, 0, ahead full."

As soon as he could identify the target and its course, he would manoeuvre ahead of her, submerge and wait for her to come to him. It was a routine intercept. As they got closer he was able to identify her.

"It's a trawler, looks like she's fishing. Take the boat down to periscope depth. Clear the deck!"

Geoff kept his course and speed constant, as if he was trawling. They were making just three knots.

"So, this is what fishing is like," Harrington said with a smile. "Seems easy to me."

"There's hardly any sea running," Geoff answered. "You should try it in a force-eight gale."

"Skipper," a lookout called, "I saw something on the horizon, but it just disappeared."

"Where?" Geoff called back.

"Dead ahead. I could have sworn it was coming towards us."

Harrington looked at Geoff. "Is he reliable?"

"Best eyes on the boat — he can spot a gull poop at three miles."

Harrington chuckled. "Could be our submarine," he said quietly.

"If it is, then we should get the lookouts down," Geoff answered — equally quietly, as if the sub could hear them.

Harrington agreed and Geoff shouted orders. "Lookouts to the deck, gunners to your stations."

Harrington picked up the phone. "*C24*, please stand by, we may have a nibble."

"Good, we were getting bored," Frederick replied, as the submarine crew in the control room gave a quiet cheer.

Gerhardt looked at his watch; they had been under for twenty minutes. "Up periscope." He reversed his cap to get the brim out of the way and glued his eye to the viewfinder. He checked all around then focused on the trawler ahead of them. She was some 1,500 metres away and trawling.

"Down periscope, prepare to surface, gun action."

He waited another ten minutes.

"Up periscope." He checked the range and relative bearing. "Bring us a point to starboard and surface."

The klaxon rang through the submarine.

In HMS *C24*, Frederick's head jerked up as he heard a noise. He looked at Miles. "Was that a klaxon?"

"I believe it was," Miles said, and grinned.

"Battle stations, ready torpedoes," Hutchings said. "And do it quietly."

Geoff watched as the sleek grey shape of the submarine emerged from the depths slightly to port of their bow and around 800 yards away. Their crew were manning their guns and puffs of smoke showed she had started her diesels.

Harrington had the phone with the *C24* to his ear.

"Submarine on surface, 800 yards, ten degrees off the port bow. Closing at three knots. Signalling for us to stop. Drop the tow."

Geoff yelled, "Panic party away!"

Frederick acknowledged the call and ordered, "Drop the tow." The chain would be discarded to avoid it either entangling the trawler or interfering with the submarine's shot.

A minute later a crewman appeared, looking worried. "The tow won't release, the mechanism's jammed, sir." What they didn't know was that it had twisted, which jammed the shackle in the release mechanism.

Frederick got on the telephone, "*Taranaki*, this is *C24*. We are unable to release the tow. Repeat, we are unable to release the tow. Can you release at your end?"

The submarine lurched as the tow was dropped from the *Taranaki*.

"Damn! Well, we will have to shoot around it." He checked the trim. The hundred fathoms of chain were pulling the bow down. "Put some air into the forward ballast tanks."

Miles knew what his skipper was trying to do and gave the forward tanks a squirt of air. The fore and aft trim was better but not there yet. He gave her another squirt.

"That's done it. The chain is hanging to port, give the port tank one more to bring her level," Hutchings said as he checked the bubbles in the trim indicators. They were as trimmed as they were going to get. "Up periscope. We will fire the starboard tube."

The periscope was raised by hand using a chain, and the one in the conning tower was the captain's. There was a second one for a lookout, set aft of the conning tower.

Gerhardt steered his boat using the controls in the conning tower bridge. She was 100 metres off the trawler's port bow, in an ideal position to sink her with his guns. The crewmen of the trawler were abandoning ship already and making a complete mess of things. He watched scornfully — they were like rats abandoning ship.

"As soon as they are out of the way, open fire."

The lieutenant in charge of the gun saluted him to acknowledge, then barked an order. The gun was trained around until it was aimed at the trawler's waterline.

Frederick viewed the *U-40* through his periscope and calmly called the numbers as he estimated the target's range. "Bearing minus ten degrees relative. Range 300 yards, set depth six feet."

The numbers were relayed to the torpedo room, who replied, "Torpedo ready."

"Shoot."

The submarine kicked as the torpedo left the tube and the air pressure inside increased as the air vented into the submarine's interior.

On the *Taranaki*, Harrington was watching the point at sea where he estimated the *C24* to be, and saw the torpedo track.

"Guns fire, target their gun!"

The disguise was shed and the 3-pound gun swung to her target, firing almost immediately. He didn't expect to do much damage, but wanted the Germans concentrating on his activities so they did not see the torpedo track.

Exactly at the point Gerhardt was about to command his gun to shoot, the trawler sprouted a gun that fired at their deck gun. Machine gun bullets and shells ricocheted off the deck as men fell or dived for cover. Then a lookout screamed, "TORPEDO TRACK!"

He stared in horror at the silver track heading towards him at thirty-five knots. He just had time to yell before it hit right under the conning tower.

The explosion sent a shudder right through the *Taranaki*'s hull. The submarine reared up in the middle, a column of water pushing it upwards. The gaping hole in her side was visible before she split in half. She sank within seconds. Silence fell over the sea, broken only by the sound of bubbles. Then the cheering started.

The *C24* surfaced 200 yards astern, her crew clambering out of hatches onto the dripping deck to see the results of their handiwork. Harrington saluted the figure in her conning tower, who saluted back.

"Search for survivors!" Geoff called to the returning boats.

The *C24* came up alongside and stopped. Frederick called across: "Couldn't give us a hand with the tow, could you? The damn thing's stuck."

The boats searched for survivors, but only Fürbringer and two other men were found, the other twenty-one perished.

Farnborough

A radio message was sent to Queenstown by Frederick immediately:

SUBMARINE U-40 SUNK BY TORPEDO FROM HMS C24 FIFTY NAUTICAL MILES SOUTHEAST OF ABERDEEN. 3 SURVIVORS. NO CASUALTIES OR DAMAGE TO EITHER C24 OR TARANAKI. RETURNING TO PORT.

It was the first kill for the Q-ships and the very first using the towed submarine trap tactic. Harrington Edwards was awarded the DSO (Distinguished Service Order) and Frederick Taylor the DSC (Distinguished Service Cross).

William Penrose Mark-Wardlaw

January 1915 — Bedford, England

Lieutenant William Penrose Mark-Wardlaw was at home with his mother and father, having enjoyed his Christmas leave, when a courier arrived with new orders. His father, a retired merchant captain, looked up from his newspaper.

"Orders?"

"Yes, I have been accepted by special operations. I have to report to Queenstown to join my ship."

His father sensed there was more in the letter than that, but didn't ask for details. Any officer working in special operations was necessarily subject to a high level of secrecy.

His mother came in with a tray of tea and stopped in the doorway as she saw the letter. She recovered herself and placed the tray on the parlour table.

"Our boy has new orders — he's off to Ireland," Mark-Wardlaw's father said, stuffing his pipe with fresh tobacco.

"Do you know who the captain is?" his mother asked.

Will looked up with a grin on his face. "Why, it's me. I'm the captain."

His parents were overjoyed, and his father broke out his precious bottle of Oban whisky to toast the event.

"Will you tell Sandra?" his mother asked. Sandra was his girlfriend of the moment. Will was twenty-eight years old and, so far, a bachelor.

"This afternoon. I will be leaving tomorrow for Bristol, where I can get a ferry across to Cork."

At just 270 long tons displacement and 135 feet in length, HMS *Prince Charles* was small by anybody's standards. But she had been chosen as a Q-ship and that was enough for Will. She was in dock at Queenstown at the end of June 2015 after her refit and he looked her over with a certain amount of pride. He was well satisfied with the transformation he had overseen. She was his first command. He had come from a destroyer, where he had been the first lieutenant. His orders, from Admiral Sir Stanley Colville the Commander-in-Chief Orkney and Shetlands, read as follows:

MOST SECRET

You will set sail from Oban on 20 July and patrol the Outer Hebrides. The object of the cruise is to use the Prince Charles *as a decoy, so that an enemy submarine should attack her with gunfire. It is not considered probable, owing to her small size, that a torpedo would be wasted on her. In view of this I wish to impress upon you to strictly observe the role of decoy. If an enemy submarine is sighted, make every effort to escape. If she closes and fires, immediately stop your engines and with the ship's company — except the gun crews, who should most carefully be kept out of sight behind the bulwarks alongside their guns, and one engineer at the engines — commence to abandon ship. It is very important, if you can do so, to try and place your ship so that the enemy approaches you from the beam. Allow the submarine to come as close as possible, and then open fire by order on whistle, hoisting your colours. It is quite probable that a submarine will be observing you through her periscope unseen by you and therefore on no account should the gun crews on watch be standing about their guns.*

The *Prince Charles* had already been fitted out and crewed with an extra ten naval men on top of the ten merchant marine men who formed her regular crew. A QF 6-pounder and a QF 3-pounder had been added to her deck, concealed behind fake deck cargo that dropped down at the pull of a lever.

It's all very ingenious, Will thought as he inspected his new command. The concept of a decoy ship was new to him, and he pondered the ramifications as he moved through the ship. The cargo hold was empty. If she was holed there, they would sink like a brick. He found the ship's merchant master Stanmore, who had been the captain of the *Prince Charles* before she was requisitioned and now ran the ship day to day.

"Mr Stanmore. You normally carry coal, which won't do at all for our mission. Could we fill the hold with something more buoyant?"

Stanmore bristled; he was royally pissed off at having his ship requisitioned and saw Will as a usurper. "Are you thinking about getting my ship sunk?" he demanded with visible hostility.

Will smiled gently, his upbringing and training showing. "Not at all, old chap. I want to keep her afloat."

Stanmore pulled in his horns a little; maybe this navy boy wasn't so bad after all, despite being an upper-class ninny. He was wrong on both counts. Will was middle class and, far from being a ninny, he had graduated from Brittania towards the top of the class.

"Well, in that case, we could take on a cargo of empty barrels. Might even be able to sell them in Scotland," Stanmore conceded.

"Excellent idea, let's do that," Will agreed.

So barrels were sourced and loaded, then packed tightly and secured to the cargo deck floor by strong nets and capped by a hatch that was welded shut. The *Prince Charles* now swam a little lower in the water due to their weight, which would help with the deception as well.

Sometime later, Will addressed the naval contingent.

"I want all you naval chaps to either dress as merchant navy men or stay out of sight at all times, unless we are attacking. To be absolutely clear, no one is to appear on deck in uniform. The rules of engagement are that we maintain our guise as an innocent merchantman until we are in range of a German submarine on the surface. Then we raise the White Ensign, drop the disguise and pour shot into her as fast as we can. We will have less than a minute, once the first shot is fired, until the enemy submerges. So, before we leave port you are to practise with the guns until you can fire twenty-five rounds a minute. You will not have a chance to practise once we are at sea, so go to it now. The panic party will also practise. I want to see the most lubberly display of lifeboat deployment ever witnessed on the high seas! Remember, the clue is in the name. Panic!"

The gunners took to their stations and soon the clank of empty shell cases hitting the deck and the shouts of the loader and layer told Will they had taken him at his word. The panic party had all sorts of fun. Men ended up in the drink and they supplied endless entertainment to other boat crews.

Will wrote up his log.

15 July 1915 — Ship loaded with empty barrels and hatches sealed. Gunners practising in port with spent cartridges. Target is to reach twenty-five rounds a minute or as close as they can get. Panic party has reached a level of incompetence that only dedicated practice can achieve. Captain Stanmore says we will be ready to sail on the tide in the morning to transfer to Oban.

Will sucked the end of his pen, a habit he had developed in college when he was deep in thought. He continued:

Crew will sleep aboard tonight. High tide is at 05:12.

Will himself slept badly, his mind going over every possible scenario, and when he did sleep, he dreamed of swirling dark waters closing over his head and a huge grey shark coming to gobble him up. He woke at 04:00, pulled on a fisherman's jumper and a pair of sea boots and went to the bridge. Stanmore was already there and handed him a mug of strong tea.

"The boys are getting up steam. We will be ready to sail at half past five or thereabouts."

Will sipped his tea. "Perfect."

Stanmore wasn't sure whether he was referring to the tea or the ship. He decided he didn't care. They stood in silence for a few moments, then: "Do you think we will find one?" Stanmore asked.

Will cocked his head and pursed his lips. "The question is, will they find us? The last report said that there is at least one U-boat active in that area, so I think we have a chance."

Stanmore glanced over at the chart, then traced a finger from Queenstown to Oban. "We should follow the main shipping lane to Oban."

The hour and a half passed slowly then a voice pipe whistled, and Stanmore answered it. "Hello, Bert."

"We have steam, Skipper."

"Thanks. Stand by."

The crew was called, and they made ready to cast off.

"Let go forward. Dead slow ahead, full right rudder," Stanmore called, fully in command.

Under the turning force exerted by the propeller on the rudder the bow inched away from the dock, pivoting around the aft mooring.

"Stop engine. Let go aft."

The ship was freed from all land constraints. The sun rose in the east, making the day feel routine.

"Ahead dead slow, rudder amidships."

They crept out of port and turned around Spike Island to head south and out to sea.

"Half ahead. Steer 1, 7, 0."

"Lookouts aloft," Will ordered as they passed Roches Point and entered the Celtic Sea.

"Full ahead. Steer 0, 9, 0," Stanmore ordered.

They were on their way.

The *Prince Charles* could make nine knots with a following wind and sea; today she could only manage eight. With the outgoing tide, that actually only equated to six knots ground speed as they approached St George's Channel and it would take almost three days to get to Oban, their new home port.

They chugged across the Celtic Sea and turned north when they were five miles west of Moore's Light off the Welsh coast at St Annes Head. Most of the navy boys were dressed in what could pass for merchant marine clothes, and lounged around on deck unless they were on lookout duty. They had one man on the monkey island (the roof of the bridge), one in the bows and one in the stern. This was not unusual for commercial ships in busy inshore waters, where ships or fishing boats could come from any direction.

Then the tide turned and their speed picked up — but she was still slow and, frustratingly, Will could see other ships, both large and small, overtaking them. The only good thing was they didn't have to slow down at night.

They arrived in Oban around midday on 19 July and coaled. Will wanted the bunker full now, to keep them low in the water. They slept on board and set sail for the Hebrides at 06:00 the next morning. They entered the Sound of Mull and made their way through it to pass the Tobermory Light. From there they would head north, up into the northern sea lane.

They passed the Isle of Skye then up past Lewis and Cape Wrath on the most north-western tip of Scotland, heading towards North Rona island to turn east to the Orkney Islands.

"Skipper, there's a ship to the north, looks like she's stopped in the water," a lookout called.

"Can you identify her?" Will asked.

Farnborough

"Coaster, looks like Danish markings."

"Action stations! Skipper, if you would steer directly for her, please."

Will smiled a little wolfishly. He had been waiting for this, but never expected it to happen so soon.

On the *U-36*, Kapitänleutnant Ernst Graeff was watching his men throw the cargo of the Danish vessel overboard. He wouldn't sink her, but he would not permit her to carry cargo to Britain.

The lookout called down, "Ship to the south, looks like a British collier."

Ernst took his binoculars and scanned the sea. Sure enough, there was a tramp steamer chugging its way towards them — probably to aid the Dane. The incomer was too small to waste a torpedo on, so he called his men back aboard and watched her carefully.

"Reduce to half ahead," Will ordered, now fully in command. "You in the bow, wave at the Dane. Panic party get ready."

They were 1,200 yards from the ship when the dark shape of the submarine appeared from behind the coaster. Will pretended not to notice until the conning tower could be seen.

A puff of smoke came from forward of the conning tower and a shell exploded just off their starboard bow. Will blew the horn three times and yelled, "Panic party away! Guns stand by. Rudder hard to port, engines stop."

Ernst smiled as the ship chugged towards him. They were handing him a prize on a plate.

"We will fire a warning shot then let them abandon ship before we sink them with the gun. Ahead slow."

As soon as the gun fired, the British ship blew her whistle three times and men started lowering boats. It looked as though the wheel had been inadvertently left hard over to port, as she was slowly turning broadside on to them.

"They are incompetent, look at the mess they are making of the falls!" Ernst said.

A crewman laughed and swung his machine gun to follow them; but Ernst would not allow him to fire. They were there to sink ships and cargo, not kill the crews.

They closed, and when they were 600 metres away, he ordered, "Turn us broadside on, we can use her for target practice."

Will watched and waited. The submarine was bow on to them and presenting a very small target. Not only that, they were looking down the barrel of her torpedo tubes. The boats were away, and the panic party rowed furiously out from between the submarine and the *Prince Charles*. They only caught the occasional crab with the oars, and shouted insults at the submarine.

"She's turning," Stanmore said — surprising Will, who thought he had gone with the boats.

She was, and Will almost yelled in joy ... but managed to contain himself.

"Why are you still here?" he asked Stanmore.

"It's my ship."

Will nodded; he could understand that. The submarine had almost completed her turn. The arrogant bastard wanted both his deck guns to bear. His hand was now on the release lever and when he could clearly see the number on her bow, he pulled it and blew a whistle.

Farnborough

"FIRE AT WILL."

The concealing panels and fake boxes collapsed to the deck and the guns turned towards the enemy. The 3-pounder fired first by a few seconds, followed by the 6-pounder. They both missed.

"Shit, it is a trap! Clear the bridge. DIVE, DIVE, DIVE!" Ernst yelled as the guns appeared out of nowhere and started shooting at them. But it took time for the men to get below and the hatches to be shut. In fact, it took about a minute. A minute too long — navy guns fired very fast.

The navy gunners were cool, and adjusted their aim for the second salvo to score hits on the hull some twenty feet behind the conning tower. More shots slammed home, hitting vital places in the aft section of the U-boat.

"We've got him, he's caught between his diesels and his electric motors!" Will cried, and punched the air.

The gun crews were firing a volley every three seconds, the loaders sweating profusely. Hits left gaping holes in the *U-36*'s hull and men started to jump off the side. Her stern was visibly sinking.

They were drifting away from each other.

"Full speed ahead!" Will shouted, and Stanmore cranked the telegraph. Will took the helm and steered to bring them alongside the almost-stationary submarine.

Suddenly, without warning, the bow of the *U-36* rose out of the water and the submarine looked like it was standing on its tail. Then, in a hissing, burbling cloud of escaping air, she slid out of sight to the bottom of the ocean. A bubble of oil came to the surface, along with some pieces of her deck timbers

The guns ceased fire and only the cries of men in the water could be heard.

"Stop engine."

Will looked at Stanmore, who yelled, "Yippee!" and shook his hand vigorously.

"Recall the boats and pick up survivors," Will said, then laughed. But then he looked aft and saw what he had forgotten to do. The Red Ensign was still flying.

"Oops," he said — but it was too late now.

They picked up fifteen survivors, including the captain — who had something to say about the flag.

"You have broken international law. You are a pirate and should be tried as such," he told Will in English as he sat huddled in a blanket on the deck. Even in July, the Atlantic was terribly cold this far north.

Will shrugged. He wasn't the first or the last who would forget to change their colours. Anyway, the Germans shot first, so the British were only defending themselves. However, all that really mattered was that they had won and sunk a U-boat, saving a friendly ship in the process.

He sent the message he knew his admiral wanted to hear.

Q-02 HAS SUNK U-36 OFF NORTH RONA. 15 SURVIVORS. Q-02 AND CREW UNHURT. RETURNING TO BASE.

They returned to Oban, where they handed over their prisoners to the British Army for internment. No complaint was made by Ernst

Graeff, so no charges were brought for the flag incident. The admiral was very happy and told Will to "keep up the good work". The *U-36* had been a thorn in his side. He made several recommendations to the Admiralty, who listened and acted.

Will was on leave when he learned he had been awarded the DSC for the action and the merchant crew had been awarded a £1,000 bounty to be shared between them. His DSC would be upgraded later, upon review after the war, to a DSO.

Ernest Martin Jehan

Based in the port of Lowestoft, the *Inverlyon* was a fishing smack. She was a sailing boat of just fifty-nine tons burthen, with a flush deck, no engine and two masts. Being one of the bigger boats in the fishing fleet, she was ketch-rigged with a long bowsprit. Her hull was made of wood. She was brought in to navy service on 2 August 1915 and converted to a Q-ship, her crew and skipper being retained.

The navy gave overall command to Ernest Martin Jehan, a career warrant officer gunner from the Channel Islands who had joined the navy as a boy in 1894. He made ordinary seaman when he turned eighteen. By 1896, when he started specialist gunnery training, he had already served on HMS *Boscawen*, HMS *Victory*, and HMS *Fox*. He served on HMS *Duke of Wellington* in 1899, where he was rated leading seaman, then attended HMS *Excellent* on Whale Island, which was the naval gunnery school. He made petty officer then petty officer first class in 1904 and acting gunner (a warrant officer rank) in 1905. He got more sea time on the Canadian ship HMCS *Rainbow* until April 1914, when he was posted to HMS *Dryad*, a torpedo boat turned minesweeper.

Ernest took command of the *Inverlyon* after she had been converted. He came aboard on 2 August 1915 along with three gunners from the *Dryad*: PO Toby Granger, Leading Seaman Fredrick Outfield and Seaman First Class Archibald Smith. His gun, a single QF 6-pounder, was mounted on the deck between the foremast and mizzen. The only other weapons aboard were some rifles for the crew. They had no radio set, just a basket of pigeons to send messages to shore.

The ship's skipper was Ray Phillips, a lifelong fisherman. His six crewmen were all experienced fishermen and sailors. Ernest would leave the sailing to him. As part of the fishing fleet based in Lowestoft on the Suffolk coast, they would be the livestock-guardian dog among a flock of sheep, protecting them from wolves.

As soon as all were aboard, they set sail with the rest of the fishing fleet. Everyone was nervous, as U-boats had sunk a large number of fishing boats in the previous months. Red-ochre sails set, the fleet made its way out of port and headed towards their fishing grounds. The sails in the morning sun provided a picturesque sight for anyone looking on from shore.

Ernest checked the gun and made sure the fake deck housing that concealed it would drop at the pull of the release. He was tempted to load it with one of their steel shell rounds in readiness, but dismissed the idea as dangerous. The steel shells were of a fixed construction, meaning that the cartridge and the shell were fixed together, while the cordite cartridge gave the gun a muzzle velocity of 1,880 feet per second and a range of 4,000 yards. The shell was full of fine-grain gunpowder and would penetrate the hull of a submarine before exploding.

* * *

"Lovely day for sailing," Phillips said as he stood at the wheel.

Ernest looked at the fleet, spread out to leeward. "Why are we staying over here?" he asked. "Won't the U-boat come up on the seaward side?"

"You think like a steamer man," Phillips said, and smiled. "We are a sailing boat, we have to behave more like the old three-masters and stay to windward." He saw that Ernest didn't have a clue what he was talking about. "Look, if we need to help a ship that is being attacked, we are better upwind of it so we can get to it fast. That is called, in sailing terms, *having the wind gauge*. So we stay over here on the windward side of the fleet at the back."

"Oh, I see," Ernest said, and scratched his beard. He could see the sense in that. "If you were just fishing, where would you be?"

Phillips grinned. "At the front, so I could take my pick of the grounds."

Shortly afterwards, they met a smack returning to port, whose captain told them that the smack *Bona Fide* had been sunk forty miles north by north-east of Lowestoft by a submarine believed to be the *UB-4*. The returning smack had the survivors aboard.

"We will be in that area tomorrow," Phillips said.

On the *UB-4*, Oberleutnant zur See Karl Gross knew that his sinking of the *Bona Fide* would have been reported by now, as there were other fishing boats in the area. So he slunk away on the surface to overnight and recharge his batteries.

The next morning, he returned to the fishing grounds intent on sinking more fishing boats. They were easy targets and he didn't have to work hard: a medium-sized explosive charge was enough to blow out their bottoms and sink them.

"That's perfect," he said as they spotted the fleet of smacks that included the *Inverlyon*.

He pressed the dive alarm and gave orders: "Clear the deck. Dive, dive, dive."

Along with the rest of the fleet, Phillips cast his nets to maintain the illusion of harmlessness. They would probably catch some herring, which would make them a bit of extra cash when they sold them. The lookouts were keeping an eye on the other boats and the sea in general to avoid getting tangled. No one spotted the periscope that came up 1,000 yards astern.

It was getting late in the day, and Ernest was starting to think they would finish fishing before seeing any action, when a crewman spotted the periscope about 300 yards off their port quarter. A few minutes later, the U-boat surfaced. A machine gun was mounted and manned on her conning tower.

"Stoppe dein schiff. Bereiten sie sich darauf vor, geentert zu werden!" a man in the conning tower shouted.

Phillips shouted back, "Sorry, I don't understand."

Ernest and his men were already at the gun by then, and without hesitating Ernest released the disguise. The gun was spun around and a round rammed home in the breach. Ernest had the conning tower in his sights and pulled the trigger. The gun was reloaded … he fired again … and one more time … before the U-boat moved out of his arc.

A body had been blown out of the bridge and into the water.

Now missing a captain, and with her bridge and steering shot away, the *UB-4* was drifting behind the *Inverlyon*, whose crew had now taken up their rifles and lined the side, peppering the submarine. When she drifted clear of the mizzen mast, Ernest commenced fire again and put another six shots into her hull at point-blank range.

The *UB-4* started sinking by the bow; the sound of air escaping from ruptured tanks told all on the *Inverlyon* that the crewmen were fighting to keep her afloat. Then her stern lifted out of the water, the propeller turning slowly. Air gushed out of the holes in her hull, and she was almost vertical when she slipped below the waves. One of her crew made it into the water but was foundering as the suction formed by the sinking U-boat took hold of him. Phillips threw off his coat and boots and dived into the water to try and save him, but it was to no avail. The man sank out of sight before he could reach him.

The *Inverlyon* jerked to a stop, which helped Phillips get back aboard but presented a novel problem. The submarine was tangled in her nets.

"What do we do now?" Phillips asked. "Does the navy want to salvage her?"

"Buggered if I know," Ernest said. That level of understanding was way above his pay grade. And so they hailed a smack that was returning home and asked her to carry a message, requesting orders back to the Admiralty as to what to do with the *UB-4*. They also put that message on a couple of their pigeons and sent them off.

The reply — when it arrived, on a launch — rejected the idea of salvage, so they cut their nets and let her sink to the bottom. The wreck of the *UB-4* still lies at 52°43'N 2°18'E.

Three weeks later, they had another chance to sink a U-boat that popped up close to another smack. But they only succeeded in chasing it off with a damaged hull.

On 19 November 1915, Ernest Jehan was awarded the DSC for the sinking of *UB-4* and promoted to lieutenant in 1916. The crew split the £1,000 bounty between them with Ernest getting fifty shares. The *Inverlyon* was returned to service as a humble fishing boat in early 1916. She was shelled and sunk by the *U-55* — fifteen miles off Trevose Head and with no casualties — on 1 February 1917.

The Baralong Scandal

The newspapers of May 1915 were full of the sinking of the RMS *Lusitania*. The headlines screamed how the perfidy of the Germans was revealed in their attacking an unarmed liner, killing 1,197 passengers and crew (newspaper accounts varied but the official death toll was found to be 1,197 of 1,962 passengers and crew, including stowaways), and the German embassy in America had the audacity to place fifty newspaper advertisements warning people they were going to do it.

NOTICE!

TRAVELLERS intending to embark on the Atlantic voyage are reminded that a state of war exists between Germany and her allies and Great Britain and her allies; that the zone of war includes the waters adjacent to the British Isles; that, in accordance with formal notice given by the Imperial German Government, vessels flying the flag of Great Britain or her allies are liable to destruction in those waters and that travellers sailing in the war zone on ships of Great Britain or her allies do so at their own risk.

IMPERIAL GERMAN EMBASSY
WASHINGTON, DC, APRIL 1915

No one believed that the Germans would attack an American ship, especially one carrying as many illustrious passengers as the *Lusitania*. It would turn out to be another flawed decision by the Germans — and the one which drew the Americans into the conflict in 1917. Prior to this they only supplied war goods and did not take an active role.

Like many others, Godfrey Herbert Lieutenant RN read the article in the *Guardian* newspaper dated 10 May 1915 and fumed.

The Lusitania *Disaster*

Over fourteen hundred persons lose their lives / Worldwide condemnation / German crime received with horror by all neutrals

Monday 10 May 1915: *The death toll in the* Lusitania *disaster is still not certainly known. About 750 persons were rescued, but of these some fifty have died since they were landed. Over 2,150 men, women and children were on the liner when she left New York, and since the living do not number more than 710, the dead cannot be fewer than 1,450.*

What the American people think of the crime is plain. Their newspapers are violent in denunciation; the public, except for the German-Americans, who have celebrated the event as a great and typical victory for their native country, are enraged. How President Woodrow Wilson regards the affair no one knows. A semi-official statement issued from the White House says he knows the nation expects him to act with deliberation as well as firmness.

It should be remembered that the United States have many and peculiar difficulties of their own, and that Dr Wilson personally will go to almost any length before he consents to a breach with Germany. His fixed aim is to preserve the world's respect by abstaining from any course of action likely to awaken the hostility of either side in the war, and so to keep the United States free to undertake the part of peacemaker.

Throughout the world the news has been heard with horror. In Norway, Sweden, Holland, Spain and Italy, as well as in the territories of the Allied Powers, the newspapers express an unhesitating condemnation. Even journals who regard Germany as a friend have no excuse to offer. In several quarters the British navy is sharply criticised. Why, it is asked, were not the submarines known to be off the Irish coast hunted down? Why was the liner not escorted into safety? These questions, which are to be found here and there in the neutral press, have been put also by many among the survivors. Possibly an official answer will be made in due course.

Godfrey Herbert was a former submariner and survivor of the sinking of HMS *A4*, who was mentioned in despatches when his commander Eric Nasmith won a Victoria Cross in the Gallipoli campaign. *The Times* had commented:

Nothing but the admirable steadiness of the men and the splendid presence of mind of Lieutenant Nasmith and Sub Lieutenant Herbert could have saved the country from another appalling submarine disaster.

Godfrey had been promoted to lieutenant in December 1905 and commanded Submarine *C36* in 1911. After that, he took command of Submarine *C39*. He was in command of Submarine *D5* when he got his orders to transfer to Q-ships in August of 1914. His first Q-Ship was RMS *Antwerp*, a converted steam packet. It was not a good choice or a lucky ship, and he was transferred to command HMS *Baralong* in April. He was looking forward to his first cruise in her when the *Lusitania* was sunk.

The *Baralong* was a converted cargo liner that had been requisitioned in September 1914 to act as a supply ship. In March 1915 she was sent to Barry Docks to be converted to a special service vessel. She was given three QF 12-pound naval guns and devices to simulate damage such as smoke generators and fire pots, as well as the usual Royal Navy equipment, before being moved to Queenstown for commissioning.

Now she was his, he intended to teach the German submariners the error of their ways. He had a good crew of volunteers whom he was training to be a crack crew. Many were Irish and some even knew people who had been on the *Lusitania*. In England and Ireland, German businesses were being attacked and burned, and anyone with a German name had to be very careful if they walked out alone. Feelings would be running high on this cruise.

Godfrey had arranged for the ship to be equipped with enough rifles and handguns for the entire crew to be armed. He also had ten marines aboard. All in all, he felt well prepared

Godfrey was getting ready to sail in early April 1915 when two officers visited his ship in Queenstown. They introduced themselves as members of the Admiralty's secret service branch. They declined to give their names but told him, "This *Lusitania* business is shocking.

Look, unofficially, we are telling you this: take no prisoners from U-boats."

"What? None at all?"

"None."

The fact that they were acting unofficially told him that the navy didn't want this information to be public or to be held accountable. He set sail with this in mind.

Godfrey gave his cover story a lot of thought. He was a poacher-turned-gamekeeper, being an ex-submariner, and wanted his ship to be believable. He firmly believed that the enemy had eyes everywhere. Consequently, he ran his ship like a merchantman, with a complete lack of navy discipline. Even the marines under the command of Corporal Collins had to put aside their uniforms and dress in civvies. He instructed the crew to call him Captain William McBride — his civilian pseudonym — and let them go ashore with no restrictions on their behaviour. They dressed however they wanted to. Godfrey was addressed as Skipper rather than Captain, and no one saluted.

After they sailed later in April, they called in at Dartmouth and a number of his crew got into a fight with regular navy men at a local pub. That there was a fight wasn't unusual, but the fact that the pub was, to all intents and purposes, destroyed in the mayhem was. Godfrey had to compensate the landlord and pay the crew's bail before they could leave port with everyone aboard.

Their routine patrols in the Irish Sea over the summer of 1915 didn't come to anything. They did not see a single submarine, but the sinkings continued. "We have just not been in the right place at the right time," Godfrey told his crew.

Then, on 19 August, the White Star Liner SS *Arabic* was sunk by the *U-24* — an incident that killed forty-four passengers and crew members, three of whom were American. This not only caused a diplomatic incident with the USA, but further infuriated Godfrey's men — as the *Baralong* was only twenty nautical miles away when they received the mayday call from the *Arabic*. They rushed to the scene, but were unable to find any survivors. All they could do was recover the dead from the sea. To make matters worse, there were children among them.

Godfrey sensed the heated emotions of his crew and called them together.

"We didn't get here on time and I know you are angry, but remember your training because cold efficiency will get our revenge, not hot anger."

They had barely finished dealing with this when the radioman called out, "Skipper, another mayday, the *Nicosian* is under attack by a U-boat. They have been commanded to abandon ship." The radioman also gave the location.

"Tell them to take their time," Godfrey said. "We can be there in less than an hour." He checked the chart and ordered, "Full ahead. Course 1, 6, 5."

Just thirty minutes later, he raised the American flag, it being officially neutral at the time, and sent the crew to action stations.

Captain Manning of the *Nicosian* got the message and told his crew to abandon ship, but slowly. Frustrated by their tardiness, Captain Bernd Wegener of the *U-27* sent a boarding party across to start searching the ship. Meanwhile, the crew of the *Nicosian* filled their eight lifeboats and started to move away from the area between their ship and the submarine. In the distance, they could see the *Baralong* approaching.

The boarding party reported back to Wegener that the ship was carrying mules and munitions for the British Army in France. He had everything he needed to justify sinking the ship.

"Deck gun, commence firing."

The *Baralong* was closing fast and was sure they had been spotted.

"Run up a signal that we will rescue the crew," Godfrey ordered. He watched the submarine intently as she fired on the ship. "Issue all crew with small arms."

Rifles were brought up from the armoury with bandoliers of ammunition. Meanwhile, he steered the *Baralong* to pass down the starboard side of the *Nicosian*, to get between her and the lifeboats. The *U-27* acknowledged their signal, ceased fire and started to move along the *Nicosian*'s port side to intercept them.

Timing will be everything, Godfrey thought. He waited, and just before the submarine came around the *Nicosian*'s bow he gave orders to "Raise the White Ensign. Guns engage!"

The disguise panels dropped and the three 12-pounders opened up. Thirty-four shots — at almost point-blank range. In less than a minute the submarine, which only got one shot off in reply, was decimated. She started to capsize, men clambering out of the hatches, ripping their clothes off so they could swim away. Then, with a mighty roar of escaping compressed air, she sank — leaving a maelstrom of giant bubbles behind her. The entire action had taken just under a minute.

The massacre started when one man on the *Baralong* raised his rifle and shot a German survivor, then the rest of the crew joined in. Even the gunners left their deck guns and grabbed a weapon to rain unholy revenge on the German sailors for the sinking of the *Lusitania* and *Arabic*. Many shouted curses as they fired.

In the lifeboats, men were cheering. Captain Manning yelled, "If any of those bastard Huns come up, lads, hit 'em with an oar!"

Most of the survivors swam for the *Nicosian*. Godfrey called the corporal in charge of his marines to him.

"Take your men and board that ship. Find any Germans and kill them before they can scuttle her."

Corporal Collins grinned and saluted. "Aye-aye, sir."

A boat was lowered and the men rowed across. As they came around to the port side of the *Nicosian*, they saw German sailors trying to climb the hanging lifeboat falls.

"Smith, Johnson, pick them off," Collins told the marines in the bow.

They started shooting and men began to fall; the fact they were unarmed made not a jot of difference.

The marines boarded and swept through the ship. A brief firefight started when they trapped the boarding party in the engine room — the sailors did not stand a chance and were shot on sight. Wegener, who had managed to get aboard, ran to a cabin on the upper deck and began to escape by squeezing through a scuttle into the water. Collins saw him, took aim carefully and shot him through the head.

It was over. The sea was strewn with bodies, which were added to when the marines threw their victims overboard after making sure they were all dead. However, not a soul cared. As far as the crew of the *Baralong* — and the crew and passengers of the *Nicosian* — were concerned, revenge tasted sweet.

The *Baralong* waited until the lifeboats had returned to the *Nicosian* and she was underway before departing the scene. However, that was not the end of it. In his report, Godfrey stated he had feared the U-boat's men would scuttle the freighter, so he ordered the marines to shoot the survivors because, if they had succeeded, it would have been considered negligence on his part. The Admiralty immediately suppressed the report and imposed strict censorship on the whole incident. However, the German government found out about it through statements made by some of the US citizens on board the *Nicosian*, and demanded that the captain and crew be charged with murder. Sir Edward Grey, a prominent politician and the man behind British Foreign policy at the time, replied through the American Ambassador:

> *The incident can be grouped together with the Germans' sinking of SS* Arabic, *their attack on a stranded British submarine on the neutral Danish coast, and their attack on the steamship* Ruel, *and we suggest that they be placed before a tribunal composed of US Navy officers.*

The Germans let it drop, but added Captain William McBride to their list of Englishmen who had committed war crimes. Godfrey heard about that and was quietly proud. *Baralong*'s crew were awarded £185 for sinking the *U-27*, to be shared among them. The *Nicosian* was renamed *Nevisian* and the crewmen were issued with new discharge books with the relevant voyage omitted, to avoid reprisals.

The *Baralong* got a new master, Lieutenant Commander Andrew Wilmot-Smith, and was relocated to Falmouth at the beginning of September 1915. Smith didn't have the submarine experience that Godfrey Herbert had, but was a keen officer with good prospects. They also got a new engineering officer, Lieutenant James Dowie, and a new gunnery officer, Lionel Everton. The rest of the crew remained.

They left Falmouth at dawn on 23 September and steamed south for a day. The sky was unusually clear and the sea calm. Andrew was enjoying the sailing when his gunnery officer came onto the bridge.

"Skipper, did you know that the armoury is full of rifles and ammunition?"

Andrew replied, "You didn't?"

"No one told me we had an armoury, and it's not marked on the door."

"Are the guns in good condition?"

"They are, I checked them."

"Talk to Corporal Collins, he knows all about them. If we get into a fight, issue the men with the guns."

It was two hours after dawn on the second day when they heard gunfire and saw smoke on the horizon.

"Full ahead, action stations!" Andrew ordered. He grinned at his number two. "Looks like we get to practise for real today."

"What colours should we fly?" Lieutenant Tim Harding asked.

"American — they are wary of shooting at them and let them pick up survivors. We will raise the White Ensign immediately before attacking."

As the *Baralong* closed on the action, the crew could see that a submarine was in the process of sinking a coaster — the SS *Urbino* — with gunfire. The crew of the coaster were watching from a safe distance in their lifeboats. When they got to within a mile, the U-boat signalled for them to stop and not to pick up survivors. Andrew acknowledged that and signalled for the engines to go to dead slow. Then the *Baralong* drifted in a long slow arc that brought her broadside to bear and to within 700 yards.

"She is the *U-41*. Issue the rifles."

"Run up our colours." The American flag fell to the deck and the White Ensign ran proudly up the mast.

"Open fire!"

The 12-pounders swung into action, aided and abetted by the marines who lined the side, rifles in hand. The first volley struck the conning tower, killing Captain Klaus Hansen and six of the crew. The gunners dived for cover as the marines targeted them at extreme range.

"Slow ahead, close the target," Andrew ordered. The crewmen were joining the marines now.

More shots hit the *U-41*'s hull and she started to list ... then dived. The guns fell silent, and they waited. Andrew realised he was holding his breath. Suddenly, the submarine came back up and the *Baralong*'s guns went back to work. Two men came out of a hatch and jumped overboard before the *U-41* sank for the last time.

"Cease fire, pick up survivors."

Cargo nets were hung over the side and crew of the *Urbino* were brought aboard, along with the two Germans they had picked up. The wounded officer was Oberleutnant sur See Iwan Crompton, a renegade Welshman with German citizenship. He confronted Andrew when he discovered it was the *Baralong* he was aboard.

"You fired at us under the American flag."

Andrew pointed to the White Ensign. "No, we didn't. Were you on the bridge?"

Crompton didn't answer. Andrew looked at him in distaste. "I ought to have you shot as a traitor."

"Fuck you and all Englishmen," Crompton replied as he limped away.

After the war, Crompton returned to Germany and wrote an account of the action where he falsely accused the *Baralong* of running down his lifeboat.

The *Urbino* was doomed and sank, so the *Baralong* returned to Falmouth. The survivors were put ashore and the prisoners interned. Andrew was awarded the DSO and Dowie, the engineer, got the DSC. The crew got a £1,000 bounty and later Andrew received an individual award of £170 from the Prize Court.

It was decided that the *Baralong* had done her duty, and so she was renamed HMS *Wyandra* and transferred to the Mediterranean, her name deleted from Lloyd's Register. The crewmen were transferred to other ships in the navy, to protect them from reprisals.

Harold Auten

Lieutenant Harold Auten, RNR, was no stranger to the sea, or Q-ships. He was born in 1891, in leafy Leatherhead in the county of Surrey. His father, William, was ex-navy, having served as a paymaster, so it was somewhat expected that Harold would go to sea. What surprised his family was that, after attending Wilson's Grammar School in Camberwell, he joined P&O as a cadet just after his seventeenth birthday. He spent two years at sea, then in 1910 he joined the Royal Navy Reserve as a midshipman. In May 1914 he was promoted to sub lieutenant.

He was a bit of a loner and didn't stay in touch with any of his schoolmates, and apart from the odd dalliance was not interested in a long-term relationship at that time. In the summer of 1915, he was placed on the staff of the captain of Devonport Dockyard, as junior assistant to the commander in charge of fitting out trawlers for patrol work.

Harold was pleasantly surprised when, in September 1915, he received new orders. He was to report to HMS *Zylpha* in Queenstown, Ireland. What he didn't know at the time was he was one of six chosen officers (including Gordon Campbell, of whom we shall learn more later) who had shown the qualities Admiral Bayly was looking for.

Harold reported to the admiral. "He will be available soon," June, his secretary, said.

She's a pretty girl, Harold thought. She sensed him looking at her and smiled at him. "The *Zylpha* is Q-6." She pointed to a large chalk board and he started to study it. *Farnborough* was Q-5, under a Commander Gordon. Just then, the door to the admiral's office opened and he stuck his head out.

"Lieutenant Auten? Come in. June, some fresh tea, please."

The admiral shook his hand and asked him to sit down. "Do you have any idea why you are here?"

"Not a clue, sir," Harold replied.

"This is a special service unit of decoy ships known as Q-ships. Our job is to tempt German submarines to the surface by pretending to be innocent merchant ships — then blow the buggers out of the water with hidden cannon."

Harold's heart started to beat faster. "I'm getting my own ship?"

"Yes, the *Zylpha*, a tramp steamer that has been hauling coal around the coast of England. You have a navy crew — we have found that works best — who are already aboard. She is waiting for you at the docks."

"What will be my patrol area?"

"South-west Ireland, otherwise known as Area G."

Harold found his ship. She was, in his own words, "a dirty old tramp". Fitted out with a single QF 12-pound cannon — hidden by a lifeboat that had been cut in two and hinged to drop down out of the way — and two QF 3-pound guns concealed inside false deck housings, she packed a punch. He had the idea of making her look more damaged than she was by the addition of a tub of dried seaweed, which could be set alight to simulate a hit. Other than that, the *Zylpha* was just like any other Q-ship: scruffy, and nothing out of the ordinary.

However, Harold's initial zeal was tested after many fruitless patrols off the coast of Ireland, during which they didn't see so much as a patch of oil. Then, in early 1916, he received new orders — he was to take her to the West Indies station for a three-month patrol.

It was while they were cruising in the sun, west of Jamaica, that he received a message from the CinC (Commander-in-Chief) West Indian Station:

SUBMARINE SIGHTED SOUTH OF MONTSERRAT. PROCEED TO AREA AND ENGAGE.

This was the best lead they had ever had and Harold was quick to respond. "Plot a course for Montserrat, full ahead."

"Which side of the island do we aim for?" asked the navigator, a quiet, bookish man from Newhaven.

"The south side," Harold said. "Steer 0, 9, 0 until the pilot works out a course."

"Aye-aye, sir."

Harold exulted internally. *At last, a chance to get to grips with the enemy!* He knew that it was becoming increasingly hard for the Q-ships to get a submarine to engage. The U-boat captains were wary of approaching any merchant ships and now preferred to stand off and torpedo them from a safe distance.

Farnborough

As it was, they steamed 850 miles from their patrol area west of Jamaica to the island of Montserrat. After talking to some local fishermen — who seemed somewhat amused by their interest — they spotted the submarine the day after they arrived in the area. It was cruising beside a cargo steamer and several small boats.

"Action stations," Harold ordered, and the gun crews went to their posts. Ammunition was brought up and the guns loaded. "Steer to pass within 300 yards, fly the American Ensign."

He watched the ships as they approached; there was something odd about their behaviour. "Tim, what do you make of it?" he asked his number one.

"I don't know, the steamer doesn't look in distress and what are all those launches doing?"

Harold decided to approach directly; the sub was on the surface and not taking any notice of them. "When we get to 400 yards, drop the disguise."

"You want a shot across their bows?"

"Yes, but fire high — we don't want to hit any of those launches, and make sure to show our colours first."

At 400 yards the White Ensign was run up and the shot rang out, which got the attention of the submarine, steamer and the launches. A launch sped towards them; a 3-pound gun tracked it as it came alongside. Harold looked down at it and saw a man dressed in checked wide-leg trousers and an open-necked shirt with a red neckerchief. He was holding a speaking trumpet and seemed upset.

"What in the name of all that is holy are you doing?" he shouted, with a pronounced American accent.

"This is His Majesty's Ship *Zylpha* — we are hunting submarines. What are *you* doing?"

"I am Leonard B. Goldsmith, film director. We are making a film about submarine attacks on merchant ships."

Harold looked at Tim, who shrugged. "Get him aboard," Harold growled.

Goldsmith explained: "The audiences in America are crying out for films that show what our brave sailors are suffering, and the government wants us to show them how perfidious the Germans are, given the sinking of the *Lusitania*. Hollywood is behind the war effort, we want to show what you boys in Europe are doing."

Harold sipped the tea that had been served. "So, you're using a real submarine and a real steamer to make this film?"

"Yes, we want it to be as realistic as possible."

"Secure from action stations," Harold said, and a grinning Tim bellowed the orders. Harold sent a despatch:

SUBMARINE LOCATED. OWNED BY AN AMERICAN FILM COMPANY MAKING A FILM, CREWED BY AMERICANS. MOSTLY HARMLESS.

The CinC replied:

KINDLY REQUEST THEM TO SEND THEIR SCHEDULE. WOULD HATE TO RUIN A GOOD FILM BY SINKING THE STAR.

The *Zylpha* was on her way home and was only seventy miles off the Irish coast in April 1917 when a lookout shouted, "Torpedo track port twenty!"

"Hard to port," Harold shouted, and the ship turned towards the oncoming silver trail. It was a close call. They managed to turn just enough for the torpedo to run down their starboard side.

They followed the track.

"Submarine surfacing 2,000 yards astern and closing!"

"Get ready to light the tub! Action stations."

The tub was not needed. The submarine's deck gun crew were experts. Shots started to hit the *Zylpha* and were coming in at an astonishing rate. Harold needed to bring his guns to bear.

"Hard to starboard, get that 12-pounder firing as soon as she bears."

They were taking an absolute pounding, but the gun crew kept their cool and started firing back. Harold made them as small a target as he could, while still giving the 12-pounder something to shoot at.

"A hit!" a crewman yelled, and sure enough, smoke was coming from the submarine's conning tower. Harold could not tell if the hit was on the conning tower or the hull.

"She's turning away, they're making a run for it."

They tried to pursue her, but the submarine made its escape. Tim told Harold, "She fired fifty-three times to our ten. We took thirty hits."

However, the *Zylpha* was still afloat and under power. The radio antenna was destroyed, and the afterdeck a mess. She limped back into Queenstown for repairs.

In April 1917, Harold was reassigned to the Q-sloop *Heather* (Q-16), an Aubrieta (Flower)-class sloop. Her former captain, Lt-Cdr Hallwright, had been killed in an action against a U-boat. Harold was never convinced about using the Flower-class Aubrieta sloops as Q-ships. They didn't look like merchant ships from ahead or either quarter, and with a ninety-two-man crew it was hard to pull off a convincing panic routine. But one good thing about *Heather* was the fact she had depth charge throwers.

But orders are orders, and he was given the Irish Sea as his patrol area — which should have given him a chance. The *Heather* sailed up and down the coasts of Ireland and Western England without so much as a sniff of a U-boat for the rest of the year.

At the end of 1917, Admiral Bayly took pity on the frustrated officer and gave him permission to find his own Q-ship. By then, Harold had been awarded a DSC "for services in vessels of the Royal Navy employed on patrol and escort duty". Harold spoke to Commander Gordon, who had already chosen a ship for himself, and went on the hunt. He found a small coastal steamer of just 732 tons, which was ideal.

In January 1918, she was procured by the Royal Navy's Q-ships division. Less than a year old, the steamer had been built by the Dundee Shipbuilding Co. Ltd for W.S. Kennaugh & Co. of Liverpool. She was propelled by a three-cylinder triple-expansion engine driving a single screw.

The shipyard at Haulbowline Island was tasked with fitting her out, including a few little extras to give her some teeth and to make her harder to sink. Her steel hull made her strong, and new reinforced bulkheads and watertight doors would make her hard to sink. On deck they were busy adding two 4-inch, one 12-pounder, one 3-pounder guns and two 14-inch torpedo tubes. Collapsable screens resembling deck housings would disguise them.

The work took a couple of months, and she was named HMS *Stock Force*. Harold was present every day of her refit and made sure he knew his new ship inside and out. He hand-picked his crew, choosing men he had sailed with first, and experienced Q-ship men he didn't know second. After that he went into Queenstown to a second-hand shop and spent £60 on a job lot of eighty men's suits, a scruffy working one and a smarter shore-going one for each crew member, and handed them out to the crew.

"Put your uniforms away. You will wear these at all times, whether afloat or ashore."

The reinforced bulkheads effectively divided the ship into three parts. Any one of the compartments could be flooded and the ship would stay afloat. Any space not used for berths or storage was packed with cork.

Harold decided they had too many deck housings and replaced the 12-pounder's concealment with a split lifeboat that hinged along its length at the flick of a lever. A fake 4-pound deck gun was mounted on the stern to complete the illusion of this being just another cargo ship.

The next thing was to instil the correct discipline in the crew. No saluting, no standing to attention, no calling officers *sir*. The officers were Harold, the skipper; First Mate E. J. (Ed) Grey; Second Mate L. E. (Len) Workman; Third Mate Miles O'Brian; and Surgeon Probationer Dr G. E. (Doc) Strahan.

They were to behave like merchant seamen even when ashore. Harold instilled in his men a belief that their sole purpose in life was to destroy an enemy submarine, whatever the cost. They were fanatics, out to teach the Hun a lesson for preying on their ships.

Panic party drills polished their performance of mock abandon ships. Tactics to lure the enemy in close were discussed openly, so that every man understood what was going on. Suggestions were taken from anyone who came up with an idea, and those ideas were examined for their viability. Usually, if they decided to adopt an innovation, the man who suggested it was put in charge of implementing it.

By the end of March, they were at sea patrolling the south-west coast of England from Land's End to the Isle of Wight. On 10 April they spotted smoke — a *lot* of smoke — and Harold ordered them to change course towards it. They soon spotted a burning tanker about fifty miles south of Bridport. They closed, expecting a submarine to be close by. The crew was at action stations, lookouts straining their eyes as they scanned the sea.

There were men in the water — which was covered in oil, some of it burning — and men in boats. None looked to be in good shape.

"Get two boats over the side and help them," Harold said.

The *Stock Force* came to a stop. She was a sitting target. Nerves on edge, the men set about the rescue of the stricken crew. Many were suffering from terrible burns or the effects of ingesting oil. They had to tow one of the boats to the *Stock Force*, as their oars had burned when they tried to get to some of the men in the water.

Ed came up onto the bridge with tears in his eyes. "They were torpedoed twice. The first hit their engine room, the second split the ship in half. They were carrying light crude oil."

Harold understood; light crude was like petrol, it burned easily and with great heat. "How is Doc coping?"

Ed puffed out his cheeks. "He's got his hands full. Miles is helping him."

Harold knew that his best course of action was to get the wounded to the hospital in Plymouth as soon as he could. "Steer course 3, 0, 0, ahead full." It was 62 miles to Plymouth and the Royal Naval Hospital, and if he pushed his ship to the limit he could get there in six hours.

In fact, they did it in slightly less — which was just as well, as Doc was all out of morphine by the time they got there. A signal ahead had the dock lined with ambulances, doctors and nurses when they pulled alongside. The wounded were offloaded as gently as they could be. One young seaman was traumatised when he tried to help a man up, and the skin of his hand came off like a glove. The boy was understandably upset and made his mate promise to shoot him if they ever got into that situation and he was burned.

The hospital gave them some supplies to replenish what they had used. They were mainly short of morphine, so Doc went scavenging. He managed to get one more small bottle before they cast off.

Their next patrol started towards the end of June 1918, and they wandered between the Channel Islands and the south coast of England. The days were long and the weather generally good — which should be perfect conditions for submarines. They didn't dawdle as much as stroll across the sea, making a steady five knots, which Harold thought was a respectable speed for a merchantman.

They had kept that up for a month when they were approached by two French seaplanes, who signalled them that there was a submarine operating in the area and to stay away from danger. They, of course, did not know the *Stock Force* was a Q-ship and about to do the exact opposite. The French were quite insistent and kept up the warnings until they had to return to base to refuel. The *Stock Force* maintained her course and speed.

Then came the shout, "Torpedo track, starboard side!" Harold was in his day room and leapt into action immediately. He was on the bridge before anyone else had reacted.

"Hold our course!"

"What?" Ed said.

"Maintain our course, we haven't seen it."

Ed rolled his eyes and blew out his cheeks.

"Brace for impact!" Harold bellowed. "Action stations!"

On the *UB-80*, Kapitänleutnant Max Viebeg watched the torpedo run through his periscope. It was, in his view, a thing of beauty as it carved through the sea, leaving its silvery track behind it. He had sunk fifty-one ships — that was 80,000 tons of shipping — and he was one of the most successful captains of the war. The set-up and shot had been easy, the foolish merchantman hadn't even tried to zigzag. Now his fish was about to bite him — just aft of his bow.

The *Stock Force* shuddered and reared as the torpedo hit just below the number one hatch, causing massive damage and destroying their forward gun. Unexploded shells and debris flew into the air, only to crash down onto the deck as gravity took its toll, wounding more men. Ed and Len were both wounded, along with four others, one of whom was pinned under the wreckage of the forward gun.

It was exactly 17:00. "Len, can you command the panic party?" Harold asked. "Ed's taken a hit to the head."

"Aye, Skipper, I've only got a flesh wound." He had more than that, but he had his arm bound and in a sling. Not until they got him to hospital would they find out just how serious it was.

"Get the wounded below with Doc, then get the boats away."

It took a moment or three, but soon the *Stock Force* looked abandoned as three boats rowed away from her. Harold crouched behind the bridge wall, peering through a newly acquired hole, and the remaining gunners were in position behind their screens. Doc was below, up to his knees in water but still tending the wounded, while a two-man crew manned the engine.

Max watched the boats leave the ship — which was settling by the bow — through his periscope. He was in no hurry. She looked deserted but he had not been so successful by not being cautious. He asked his executive officer what he thought.

"She looks dead in the water. I can't see any movement."

Max took another long look.

He made up his mind. "Battle surface. Gun action!"

The gun crews crowded the ladder to the hatch as the submarine came to the surface in a rush and were quickly to their station. They were 900 metres away from the steamer, engines stopped.

Max leaned on the conning tower rim, binoculars to his eyes. The minutes ticked by.

After fifteen minutes he had seen no movement.

"The boats are returning to their ship!" a lookout called.

Max could not allow that.

"Ahead, dead slow, both. Signal those boats to get clear."

He would close slowly, his gun crews ready.

Harold stayed still. It had been almost thirty-five minutes since the torpedo struck. He could see the *UB-80* approaching and he hoped his gunners would maintain discipline, as he couldn't talk to them. On the foredeck he could see the trapped sailor, who appeared to be quite comfortable and was even chatting to the gunners. He was sheltered by what remained of the bulwark, his lower body stuck under the wreckage of his gun.

The *UB-80* got to 300 yards off the starboard bow, her skipper yelling at the boats to stay away in broken English. Still Harold waited. He had two guns left and wanted both to be able to fire.

The submarine's gun swung back and forth, covered the length of the ship and finally settled on pointing directly at him. He ignored it. He watched as the submarine stopped its engines and drifted alongside them. They were in the perfect position. He leapt to his feet.

"NOW! LET THEM HAVE IT!"

It was 17:40.

The last thing Max saw was the young British officer on the bridge of his stricken ship waving a fist in the air.

The screens crashed down and the guns started firing. The first shot destroyed one of the periscopes, the second hit the bridge in the conning tower and blew Max into the air, killing him instantly. The third shot hit the waterline, blowing a massive hole in the side which the sea greedily rushed into. Further shots hit her waterline, accelerating the intake of water. Her gun crew was shredded by a shot that hit the breach, and machine gun fire. The bow rose and still the shells kept pounding her hull. The gun loaders were performing Herculean feats as they fed the roaring beasts.

Then, finally, the *UB-80* sank by the stern.

Harold helped the gun crew to free the gunner trapped under the forward gun. They were not a moment too soon, as he was close to drowning.

"I thought you would never give the order. I was getting worried!" he said with a grin, as Harold helped him to the side.

The boats returned and the wounded were brought up from below. Then they went to work to keep her afloat.

"Send another mayday message. Give our position and send a message to Queenstown."

UB-80 *SUNK, ALL HANDS LOST.* STOCK FORCE *BADLY DAMAGED, WOUNDED ABOARD. SINKING.*

A reply came ten minutes later.

CONGRATULATIONS. HELP IS ON ITS WAY.

They knew they were fighting a losing battle, but they fought anyway. She was their ship, and they wouldn't let her die without a fight. An hour passed — although it seemed like a week — and still they fought. Then a lookout called, "MTBs approaching!"

The motor torpedo boats approached with bows high as they planed over the water, and all could hear the roar of their powerful engines. They were followed by a trawler and between the three of them, they got the crew off the *Stock Force*. Harold stood on the bridge of one of the MTBs and watched as his ship finally succumbed and her stern slipped below the waves.

On his return to Queenstown, Lieutenant Harold Auten was awarded the Victoria Cross, which was later presented to him by the king. The citation did not say much, and very little detail was given of the action involved.

Gordon Campbell

Gordon Campbell, the ninth son and thirteenth child of sixteen, whose father Frederick had served in the New Zealand War of 1865 as a junior artillery officer, grew up in genteel poverty in Croydon. His father joined the Army volunteers (the Regular Reserve) when war broke out and would eventually make lieutenant colonel. However, no matter how much money his father earned it would never be enough until all his children flew the nest. By the time he was at school, one of Gordon's older brothers was a politician and married with a son and daughter.

In 1898, at the age of fourteen, Gordon left Dulwich Preparatory School for Dulwich College, following in the footsteps of another of his older brothers. Here he gained the academic and athletic foundations he would need to go on to the Royal Naval College (Britannia) at Dartmouth. At Dulwich he rowed, played rugby and joined the Combined Cadet Force, where he was a member of the Royal Navy section. He was a good, albeit not exceptionally brilliant, student and graduated towards the top of his class.

In 1900, after two years at Dulwich, he was granted a place at

Britannia. To his surprise, the college was not on shore but in an old 121-gun, three-decked line-of-battle ship dating from 1860, originally named *Prince of Wales*. The hulk had no engines and only stub masts, and the boys lived on her during term time. Here Gordon learned how to *be navy*; to march, to navigate, the principles of weaponry and ballistics, engineering basics, the history of the Royal Navy and the various other disciplines and bodies of knowledge deemed essential for officers of the future.

He qualified as a midshipman after two years and joined HMS *Prince George*, a seven-year-old Majestic-class battleship. The *George* was part of the Channel fleet and was, to say the least, old school. She had many *sprogs* (new recruits and trainees), who were ruled with an iron hand by a senior midshipman and sub lieutenant.

Gordon was not a bad lad, but many of the officers believed that midshipmen were improved by regular caning for even the slightest misdemeanours, let alone crimes, and they were often bent over a cannon and given twelve of the best. In fact, Gordon recounted that barely a week could pass without him being found guilty of *something*. As a student of history and a reader of books, he blamed his harsh treatment on the Spartans.

For Gordon, the next trip was to the Mediterranean on HMS *Irresistible*, but this proved Gordon's undoing as he managed to aggravate an old rugby injury to his knee and had to be shipped home for surgery.

"We are going to have to remove the cartilage," Doctor Quinton Netherton told him at the naval hospital Haslar.

Gordon looked at him in terror. "Will I still be able to walk?"

The good doctor squinted at him. "Certainly, and you will have some fine scars — six months will see you as right as rain."

Six months?

Gordon decided to use the time wisely. He studied and applied to take the examination for lieutenants. He passed and was made sub lieutenant in 1906. He went home before he was deployed, marching proudly down the road in his new uniform.

"Oh my Lord! You are so handsome," his mother cried when she answered his knock on the door. His father, in his army uniform, met him later that day in the parlour.

"You are doing well, my boy. Proud of you."

That was the first time his father had ever praised him, and the compliment made him grow an extra inch. His brothers, many of whom were not in uniform at this time, patted him on the back and congratulated him.

"Where are they sending you?" his mother asked.

"HMS *Arun*. She's a Laird-type River-class destroyer. She's in Harwich after being refitted with bigger guns."

What he didn't tell them was that the *Arun* had been in a collision with HMS *Decoy*, another destroyer, off the Scilly Isles. The *Decoy* had sunk, and the *Arun* had to be towed to Harwich for repairs to her bow. Her captain became the subject of a court martial and was replaced.

In contrast, the *Arun* was a lucky ship for Gordon, as he was made a lieutenant in October 1907. The new captain liked him and appreciated the young officer's quick mind and courage. He encouraged him to pursue promotion even if that meant he would be transferred to another ship. Gordon did exactly that, and his other ship turned out to be HMS *King Alfred*, the flagship of the China station.

HMS *King Alfred* was an armoured cruiser of the Drake class, built in 1900. Gordon had to learn her vital statistics and had to prove by verbal examination that he had. He reported: "The *King Alfred* is of 14,150 tons displacement, 533 feet long and seventy-one feet at the beam. She has forty-three boilers powering two triple-expansion engines producing 30,000 indicated horsepower, giving her a top speed of twenty-three knots."

"What armaments do we have?" Lieutenant Keith Chelmsford asked.

Gordon squinted as he searched his memory. "Two 9.2-inch, sixteen 6-inch, twelve QF 12-pounders, three QF 3-pounders and two 18-inch torpedoes."

"Good — and armour?"

Gordon looked at him as if he was kidding. "Good Lord, that an' all?"

Keith nodded.

"All right ... 2 to 6 inches in the belt, 2.5 inches on the deck, barbettes and turrets 6 inches and conning tower 12 inches."

"Bulkheads?"

"Oh bother ... umm, 5 inches."

"How many men?"

"Including officers?"

"Yes."

"Nine hundred."

"Well done! You passed," Keith said, and laughed.

The wardroom (the officers' mess) on the *Alfred* was run by the executive officer Commander Ernest Wise, who encouraged his officers to know their ship from stem to stern. "After all," he would say, "you never know where you will end up in action." He also rotated his lieutenants every two years, so that they would learn new skills. Gordon started on the 6-inch guns and had the forward starboard four that were mounted in turrets on the side of the hull. Keith ran the aft eight. The four on the main deck could only be used in calm waters, as waves of any height would swamp them.

The China station was fairly relaxed, as Britain was not at war with anybody in particular at the time. The Chinese were modernising their army and navy but could not challenge the European superpowers in any way.

After two years on the 6-inch guns, Gordon was moved to torpedoes under the torpedo officer Lieutenant Mitch Milford.

"Torpedoes provide a punch much larger than the 9-inch guns and have a maximum range of … ?"

Gordon was not caught out by the sudden question.

"The Mk VII has a range of 7,000 yards at twenty-nine knots or 5,000 yards at thirty-five knots."

"Good. Warhead?"

"320 pounds of TNT."

It was at this time he learned how to calculate the sight angle when firing at a target:

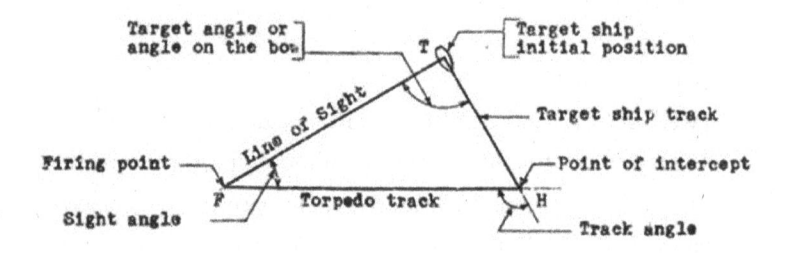

[Diagram: Triangle showing torpedo firing geometry with labels — Target angle or angle on the bow, Target ship initial position, Line of Sight, Target ship track, Firing point, Point of intercept, Sight angle (at P), Torpedo track, Track angle (at H)]

The solution was calculated using a slide rule, of which the ship had many — slide rules being the calculators of the time.

Farnborough

* * *

Gordon was recalled to Britain in 1910 and ended up back in hospital for a short time, having caught influenza after he arrived home. The virus knocked him completely for six and caused him to have trouble breathing, severe joint pain and dizziness. Luckily, he was staying in the wardroom in Portsmouth when these symptoms became apparent, and was rapidly hospitalised.

He reported to HMS *Impregnable*, the training ship for boy ratings, as an instructor. It was run under the old rules with a regime of beatings — which he did not support — but it did not quench his spirit. At this point, he decided to get married. Unfortunately, his senior officer did not approve, and under navy regulations any officer under twenty-five years of age had to have permission from his senior officer to marry. Even if permission was granted, it was not viewed as a sensible career move for a junior officer. However, he was determined — and eight days after his twenty-fifth birthday, Gordon married Mary. His view was that the Royal Navy had no claim on his private life, as long as he performed his duty. "She [Mary] holds my heart and my soul," he said at the time

His commander's reaction to this act of rebellion was predictable — he asked for Gordon to be removed. Luckily, the intransigent old fart was retired and made a rear admiral before the request could be actioned.

Gordon finally received a command two years later, and it reflected the navy's disapproval of his marriage. He was posted to HMS *Ranger*, an Opossum-class destroyer of Victorian vintage. She was part of the Devonport Local Defence Flotilla, which was made up of old ships commanded mainly by *no hope* officers. She was a torpedo-boat destroyer and could do a respectable twenty-seven knots. However, Gordon was only on her for six months until he was given HMS *Bittern*, a Vickers three-funnel, thirty-knot destroyer. She, like the *Ranger*, was old — but at least she was a fighting ship and indicated that the navy might be forgiving him.

He and Mary rented a house in Saltash, just across the river from Devonport, and he lived there when his ship was in port. He was at home when war was declared on 28 July 1914. When they heard the announcement on the radio, Mary cried, then squared her shoulders. It was the last time she would cry in front of him.

Bittern patrolled home waters, diligently ensuring that any convoys that came around the south coast to Portsmouth or London were safe. In 1915, the German naval command unleashed the U-boats, removing any and all restrictions on their campaign. British merchant losses went up dramatically and threatened the very existence of Great Britain. Gordon knew something had to be done, and fast, because even if he could find a U-boat it would dive and hide underwater as soon as it saw him.

Gordon knew the theory of decoys. It was simple and based on an existing tactic that has been employed for as long as there have been ships at sea. Sail a ship that looks like a merchantman — and acts like a merchantman — under false colours to lure the enemy in close enough for the hidden guns to destroy it quickly. The *Kingfisher* in the seventeenth century and the *Warley* in the nineteenth were two examples of the successful use of this approach, and Churchill, as First Lord of the Admiralty, was strongly in favour of it. The idea of luring a submarine to the surface with a juicy target then sinking it with his deck gun was irresistible.

Farnborough

Gordon heard that the Admiralty was looking for volunteers for special duty and started looking into it. At first, he could not find where or to whom he should volunteer. "It's most frustrating," he told Mary. "I want to volunteer but I'm damned if I can find where to go."

Mary kept her peace; she knew her husband craved action and that the mundane patrolling of home waters was not satisfying for him. At the same time, she liked that he was relatively safe.

In the end, in early 1915, the relevant people found him. His questions and visits to the Admiralty put his name in the ears of the admiral in charge, and he received an order to report to an office in the Admiralty building in Portsmouth the next time he was in port.

In due course, Gordon entered the building. A guard asked him what his business was, and Gordon showed him his orders. The guard frowned as he read them and directed him towards an office on the ground floor, just off the lobby. Inside was a clerk, who also read the order and frowned.

"Please wait for a moment," he said, and went through a door at the back of his office. He returned several minutes later and, with a completely blank expression, told Gordon, "Go to the top floor. At the end of the corridor is a doorway. Go through it, and you will find a set of stairs before you. The office you need is at the top of those stairs."

Gordon thanked him and started to climb the six flights to the top floor. The building was busy, and messengers hurried up and down the stairs from the first two floors. The third floor was quieter, and the corridor carpeted. He suspected this was the *golden mile* — and indeed that was confirmed as he read the names on the doors. They were all admirals.

The door at the end of the corridor was plain, without markings, and had the look of a storeroom. He turned the knob, and the door swung open on well-oiled hinges. Bare lightbulbs illuminated a flight of wooden stairs which he climbed to a door at the top. *This is the attic,* he thought, and knocked.

A voice called, "Come in," and he opened the door.

What greeted him when the door swung open surprised him. It was indeed an attic space. Illuminated by skylights and a pair of shaded lights hanging from the beams was a sitting room, and in that sitting room sat an admiral and a secretary. The admiral spoke.

"Lieutenant Campbell, please come in and take a seat. I am Admiral Bayly."

Gordon sat in a comfortable chair, the admiral sat opposite him and the girl sat on a sofa with a notebook and pencil in her hands. The admiral crossed his legs and sat back, his fingers steepled in front of his mouth.

"You are looking for some excitement, I hear," Bayly said.

"Sir?" Gordon said, now thoroughly confused.

"You have been looking for a place where you can volunteer for special duty."

"Oh, that! Yes, sir."

Bayly smiled. "Well, you have found it. Tell me why you should be considered."

"I want to take an active role in the war. My present command is just patrolling up and down in home waters while all the action is in the Western Approaches and the North Sea."

"What do you see as the biggest threat?"

"At sea?"

The admiral nodded.

"The German submarines. They sink more tonnage of commercial shipping than anything else."

"How do you stop them?"

"Well, I suppose at the moment we have to catch them on the surface. We have no means of detecting them underwater."

"Then here is a problem for you. Submarine captains are wily devils and as soon as they see a warship, they dive. They can't go far underwater but it's far enough to get away to a safe distance to surface and run. How do you get close enough to kill them?"

Gordon pondered and realised that the challenge was like luring a fox into range of a shotgun.

"Bait. You would have to deploy a bait they cannot resist."

The admiral nodded. "What I am about to tell you is top secret and you can tell no one outside of this room."

"Aye-aye, sir."

"I am in charge of a force of ships, based at Queenstown in Cork Harbour, that look like merchant vessels but are, in fact, heavily armed submarine killers."

Gordon appeared calm on the outside, but his heart started to race.

Bayly continued: "These Q-ships are modified cargo ships, schooners, trawlers and the like, a far cry from the destroyer you currently command. They are tatty, and the crews a mix of navy and civilians. For security reasons you will never be credited directly, and any citation you receive will be shrouded in mystery."

"I would still like to volunteer."

The admiral could see the enthusiasm in his face, the youthful zeal, the steady eye. He liked him.

"Return to your ship, orders will follow."

A letter from the Admiralty did appear, but it was not what Gordon expected. He was promoted to commander, effective immediately. It was not until he returned from his next patrol that another missive landed on his desk, this time in the form of a telegram.

COMMANDER G CAMPBELL TO REPORT TO HMDY DEVONPORT TO TAKE COMMAND OF HMS FARNBOROUGH *ON SEPTEMBER 5.*

The telegram was from the office of the First Lord of the Admiralty.

Soon after, he received orders to hand over his current command to a Lieutenant March, who would arrive on 22 August 1915. He had two weeks' leave until then. In its way, the leave was frustrating. He couldn't tell Mary anything — not because he didn't trust her, the truth was quite the opposite, he just felt it was his duty. As Devonport was so close, she would normally have accompanied him to the dock when he joined his ship. However, as Mary was pregnant with their first child, due in November, she stayed at home, relieving him of the problem.

Devonport

HMS *Farnborough*, newly bought into the Royal Navy, entered HMNB Devonport being fussed around by a pair of tugs. She only had a skeleton crew, which had been assigned to get her from Newcastle to Queenstown with orders to deliver her to the shipyard for a refit. The tugs guided her into the river off Monkstown then around to face the gates of the dry dock. The skipper of the lead tug gave two toots on his whistle and the gates slowly opened.

Gordon Campbell watched all of this from a vantage point on the shore. Commander Campbell was the designated skipper of this new old ship. Originally launched in 1903 as a collier that sailed under the name *Loderer*, she was a tramp steamer with no fixed port and had been requisitioned in mid-1915. It was now a beautiful late-summer morning in September, and the ship was going to change radically.

She wasn't what Gordon had dreamed of when he saw the dashing destroyers that surrounded the *Irresistible*, but by the time the dockyard had finished with her, she would be something quite formidable.

Gordon would live on at home during this time, but spend his days on the ship. Mary would never ask to go with him, as morning sickness effectively made her housebound for part of the day and even as she started to get over it, she realised that her husband was involved with something special.

The tugs fussed and prodded the *Farnborough* into the dry dock and the dockyard workers carefully positioned her over the wooden stocks before closing the gates and pumping out the water. Her boilers were doused, and the ship became a cold, dead entity. A team of inspectors came aboard and surveyed her from bow to stern, keel to bridge. A cleaning team went into the holds to try and get rid of the coal dust. In fact, there was coal dust everywhere and she had to be swept out before any work could start, due to the risk of fire.

Gordon walked up the gangplank and watched the dockyard workers starting to cut her up. They were creating new compartments and moveable bulkheads which would conceal her guns. She would have new magazines installed below the waterline, protected by armour. He had seen the specification and plans. She would get five QF 12-pounder (3-inch) guns, two QF 6-pounder (57-mm) Nordenfelt guns, and a single Maxim machine gun.

Gordon was particularly interested in the positioning of the five 12-pounders. One would be mounted on each side of the foredeck, concealed behind flaps that could drop down on either side. The third would be in a dummy compartment forward of the bridge, able to fire on both sides, and the last two would be mounted on the aft deck behind drop-down panels. The 6-pounders would be mounted on either side of the bridge, concealed in fake compartments. A central mount would be provided for a .50-inch Maxim and mounts were fitted for a pair of Lewis guns on the bridge. The Farnborough's engines, oil-fired steam turbines, were in good shape and she was said to be able to make eleven knots at full speed. Nothing the navy would do could change that.

"Morning, Commander," Captain Jacob Shilling, the architect of the conversion said as he found Gordon on the bridge.

"Good morning, sir."

"Looks like we are making a fine mess of her, doesn't it?"

"It does, but it's all in a good cause," Gordon said philosophically.

"Once we have the gun mount bases and ammunition feed prepared, we will start on the compartments," Shilling said.

Gordon took out a pipe, filled it from a pouch and tamped the aromatic tobacco down ready to be lit. "I have a question about the ammunition feed."

"What's that?"

Gordon applied a match to the bowl and puffed the pipe to life. "The guns are spread out along the deck, and can fire, what, nine rounds a minute? I think an engagement will last, probably, three minutes. How do we get thirty rounds of ammunition to a gun during the action?"

"Good question — and we have thought of that. Each gun has an ammunition store of eight rounds. A crate contains eight rounds, and they are stored in the magazine."

Gordon interrupted him with a gesture of his pipe. "That's what I mean. The magazine is in the forward hold and there's no way the crew will have time to get a resupply of ammunition to any but the forward guns before they run out."

The light dawned in Shilling's eyes as his brain finally did the maths. "Oh, I see what you mean."

"Can you increase the size of the ammunition store at each gun?"

Shilling gazed into space, took out a tin of Player's Navy Cut cigarettes, extracted one and tapped it on his thumb nail before lighting it with a silver cigarette lighter.

"How long will it be from first sighting a submarine to opening fire?"

Now it was Gordon's turn to think.

"I see what you're getting at. You think the crew would supply two extra crates of ammunition to each gun during the initial engagement. That's all right for the forward guns, the magazine is close to them, but the aft guns are a fair way away and most of the crew will be manning the guns, not carrying ammunition."

Shilling's brow furrowed as he thought.

"You need a magazine aft in the rear cargo bay."

"That would certainly solve the problem. Do we have room?"

Shilling pulled some drawings from his document case and sat at the chart table with a pencil and ruler.

"We can fit in an ammunition locker that will hold four crates of ammunition away from the accommodation cabins."

Gordon looked at the drawing and pointed. "There?"

Shilling sat back. "Yes — will it work?"

"Show me on the deck"

They walked aft, past men hammering home hot rivets, until they got to the aft deck. They took a stair down one deck.

"It will go there. The forward of the two guns is up there."

"It will do," Gordon said.

* * *

A week of cutting and welding saw gun mounts fitted to the deck and new wings fitted to the bridge that would carry mounts for the 6-pounders. His executive officer arrived halfway through the refit and found Gordon on the ship. He was lieutenant Rodney Fisher, twenty years old and also straight out of a battle cruiser.

"Lieutenant Rodney Fisher, reporting for duty, sir." He was a scholarly man and rather shy.

"Welcome aboard. She's a bit of a mess but you can see where they're going."

"Absolutely — I visited the armoury and saw the guns on the way here."

"Let me show you around and then we can sit in my cabin, which is one of the few places they haven't torn apart."

The tour didn't take long.

The two men sat in the captain's tiny day cabin, the noise of riveting constantly in the background. Gordon had a pile of dockets on his desk that were the crew records.

"We should be seeing the crew arrive over the next three weeks," Fisher said. "I checked with the deployment office on the way here, and most are coming from Portsmouth when the old *Talbot* decommissions next week. They get a fortnight's leave, then have to report here."

"We are due a sub and a mid as well," Gordon said.

"Yes, the sub has been on a minesweeper and the mid is coming straight from shore duty after qualifying from Britannia. Both should arrive next week."

"We have an engineering officer, Lieutenant Leonard Loveless, and an engineering chief who has been around since they invented the steam engine," Gordon quipped, and passed him the men's dockets.

"The chief certainly has been around. A Scot, Angus Boyd. Served in everything from coasters to battle cruisers over the last thirty years."

Gordon nodded. "If anyone can keep this ship running, he can." He passed over another docket. "Gunner, CPO Jack Salisbury."

Fisher looked at it, flipping to the man's disciplinary record. "Another old hand. Oh, hello. He's got a reputation as a brawler. Broken twice for drunkenness and fighting."

"We will have to watch him," Gordon said.

They worked their way through the pile and soon had them all in the ship's book.

"We will operate a three-watch system unless we are at action stations," said Gordon.

"Hmm, the engineers will like that. We have six in total. The chief, two POs and three mates," Fisher said. "I will make a watch list this afternoon." He was looking down the crew list when he frowned. "Don't we get a navigator?"

Gordon cracked a smile. "No, we will be operating in mainly coastal waters, so apparently do not need one."

"I see, we point the sharp end either up or down the coast and off we go!"

They both laughed, but then noticed that the ship suddenly went quiet. The silence was profound after the constant riveting. Gordon stood up, causing Fisher to leap to his feet.

"Lunchtime. Come on, we will eat ashore in the wardroom."

The sub, Norman Milford, and mid, Hardy Radcliffe, reported on time. Aged nineteen and sixteen respectively, they were relatively inexperienced. But Milford had a passion for guns, had made himself the gunner on his last ship, and would be an excellent foil for CPO

Salisbury. The mid had scored highly in navigation at college, so would be the de facto navigator once he proved himself. Neither had a clue as to why they had been chosen for special duty, and nor did Gordon, who suspected they were either recommended by their previous superiors or just chosen at random.

The crew arrived as the final licks of paint were being applied, and they were informed of surprise additions that were to be added to the stern. The installation was a pair of depth charge racks, along with the half a dozen 120-pound charges in each, concealed under what could only be described as a shed, which looked so out of place that Gordon ordered it removed — "Bloody thing shouts *something is hidden here.* Get it off my deck!" — and for the racks to be covered by a tarpaulin.

In November, the crew came aboard after the ship was refloated and tied up at the dock. Their first job was to provision, which, due to the sheer quantity they needed, entailed forming chain gangs to pass crates and sacks of supplies up the gangways and into the store. They carried around the same amount as a minesweeper for their shakedown and first cruise, which would take them up to Queenstown in Ireland as that was closer to their proposed patrol area. Ammunition followed, with a crate of Lee–Enfield rifles and two boxes of bullets.

Gordon called the crew together on deck before they left.

"Welcome aboard the *Farnborough*, the latest of His Majesty's warships," he began. That got a laugh and relaxed the men somewhat. "Our job is to find and kill enemy submarines and, if we catch an unwary enemy merchant, to sink them. To do that, we are disguised as a collier."

An anonymous voice said, "Nothing changed there, then."

Gordon smiled at the quip, then continued: "Quite, only this collier has teeth and we will be using them. Every U-boat sunk guarantees the people of Great Britain food on their plates and the army oil for their machines. Oh, I nearly forgot — and you get a bonus!"

He paused while the men gave a short cheer.

"You are all to dress as merchant marine men. You get an allowance for that, and I suggest you spend it in the second-hand shops to make it go as far as possible. Now, it's no good us looking like a merchant ship if you do not behave like merchant sailors. So, we have new rules. No saluting or standing at attention, no calling officers *sir*. I am the skipper, and my executive officer is the first mate. The rest of the officers are second, third and fourth mates. However, we may each look like a civilian and we will dress like civilians from now on, but discipline will be one hundred per cent navy! I want a happy, efficient ship that is ready to go into action at any time. Gunnery practice will commence as soon as we are at sea."

The *Farnborough* got up steam, then tugs worked them out from the dock. They had to wait for the Torpoint to Dartmouth chain ferry to cross the Hamoaze, the stretch of water where the rivers Tamar and Lynher meet in the Tamar Estuary. Then: "Ahead slow," Gordon ordered.

They picked up speed to two and a half knots and steamed down the estuary, passing between Mount Edgcumbe and Devil's Point into Firestone Bay. Drake's Island, with its fortifications, passed down the port side and the 100-year-old breakwater that protected Plymouth Sound from storms was just a mile ahead. On the other side of that was the English Channel.

There was a sudden burst of steam from aft, and the engine stopped. The speaking pipe from the engine room whistled and Gordon answered it.

"Captain."

"She's blown the main seal to the turbine, Captain," the gravelly Scottish tones of Chief Boyd told him.

"Can you fix it, Chief?"

"Aye, but it will take at least four hours."

Gordon sighed, then muttered, "These things are sent to try us," before going to the horn pull and giving five short blasts. A tug was in attendance in minutes, and they were taken under tow back into Devonport.

It was mid-afternoon by the time the seal had been replaced and Chief Boyd reported to the bridge, wiping his oily hands on an equally oily rag.

"The old seal had a minute crack and when the engines were off for the refit, the crack opened up. It happens when an engine gets cold sometimes, Skipper."

"Are we up to pressure?" Gordon asked.

"Aye, we are."

"Good job, Chief. I'll get us underway."

A couple of toots called the tugs in, and they went through the whole process again, only this time they sailed majestically past the breakwater.

Gordon decided to test his ship to make sure that nothing else was wrong.

"The Lord only knows how well she was looked after before the Andrew got her," he said to Fisher.

They passed Rame Head and entered the Channel.

"Course 0, 9, 0, full ahead."

The telegraph rang as the command was passed to the engine room. There was a slight pause, and the bell rang again in confirmation. The slight vibration through the deck from the turbine and propeller increased in frequency and amplitude. The *Farnborough* picked up speed and was soon producing a fine bow wave. Their speed was roughly proportional to the speed of rotation of the propeller, but Gordon didn't try to calculate it; instead, he asked Midshipman Radcliffe to do so. It was a good test for the boy.

Radcliffe whistled up the engine room and asked what revolutions they were making. Then he got out the ship's books and checked the pitch of the propeller and the makers' estimation of their top speed. A slide rule was produced, and feverish calculations made. Then Radcliffe presented himself to the captain, stood at attention and saluted. As soon as he did that, the look on his skipper's face reminded him of the new rules. He relaxed and held out his pad.

"Yes, Mr Radcliffe?"

"We are doing ten and three quarter knots, sir — I mean Skipper."

"Thank you, please take a sighting at noon."

That wasn't too bad. The manufacturer's top speed was eleven knots, so she was holding up quite well. They carried out a series of course changes to see how she handled. Her rate of turn at speed was slow.

"Bring her down to half ahead."

Their speed rapidly reduced to five and a half knots and the rudder had more effect. All in all, she wasn't a bad ship.

As soon as their skipper finished *playing*, as the crew put it, they started gunnery practice. Between CPO Salisbury and Sub Lieutenant

Millard, who commanded the fore and aft crews respectively, the crews came together over the two days it took them to sail to Queenstown in Ireland, and by the second day they were firing practice rounds. That got them used to the sound of the guns. Later, they would fire live rounds against a target.

Queenstown

"Slow ahead. Steer due north," Midshipman Radcliffe ordered.

Gordon had given him the bridge — under his own watchful eye, of course. He was testing him.

"What is that to port?" Gordon asked.

"Those lights are from Crosshaven, Skipper."

Gordon cast his eyes forward. "And that?"

"Spike Island, Skipper. Queenstown lies behind it and Haulbowline Island, where the dockyards are."

The helmsman grinned; the boy had done his homework.

A pilot boat rushed out to meet them and the pilot came aboard, climbing the rope side-ladder with ease despite the chop.

"Top of the evening, gentlemen. You're bound for the navy base?" His accent was Cork through and through.

"We are. I am Captain Campbell."

"Toby O'Hanlan, pilot. Pleased to meet you. Keep her steady as she goes, you're set up perfectly."

Gordon smiled at the mid, who looked positively chuffed with himself. "Our navigator is responsible for that."

Farnborough

The pilot did a double-take, then rolled his eyes. "Jesus, but they get younger every day."

They docked, and Gordon immediately went ashore to the Admiralty building, which he had been told was the operations centre. He was directed to an office on the first floor and knocked on the door. It was opened by the same girl he had met with the admiral in Portsmouth. He was struck by her blue eyes and the dark hair that framed a pretty face.

"Yes?" she said.

"Aah ... Commander Gordon, the *Farnborough*?" he said, realising that, being distracted, he hadn't replied promptly.

She smiled. "We've been expecting you. Come in, the admiral will be free soon. Can I get you a cup of tea? My name is June, by the way." Her voice had a soft Irish lilt to it.

He sat and looked around the room. Behind one desk, a chalkboard had a list of ships, each numbered Q something or other, and he spotted the *Farnborough* with the designation Q-05.

"Is that our pennant number?"

"Q-05? Yes. By the way, did Devonport fit a radio?"

"Aah, no they didn't." Why was he tongue-tied?

"The yard at Haulbowline will fit you out with a Marconi set. I will arrange that for you."

The door to a connecting office opened and a man dressed in fisherman's gear came out and threw him a jaunty salute before shaking his hand.

"Ernest Jehan, the *Inverlyon*," he said with a Channel Islands accent.

Admiral Bayly stepped out behind him and saw Gordon. "Commander Gordon Campbell, welcome," he said. As he led Gordon into his office, he continued, "June will organise shore berths for your crew as you will be staying here between missions."

They sat down in the office, which was comfortable and had a large map of the Western Approaches alongside another of the waters around the United Kingdom and Ireland. Patrol areas were marked.

"You have an all-navy crew of what, forty-five?" asked the admiral.

"Yes, that's right."

"Good, you are one of the first ships with a fully enlisted crew. Gunner Jehan is one of only four navy men on the *Inverlyon*. He commands the ship, the rest look after the guns."

"I didn't realise."

The admiral got up and walked over to the maps. "You are our heaviest armed ship to date and one of the fastest. So, you are getting the most dangerous patrol area — the Irish Sea and Western Approaches. The Germans like to loiter in this area, to try and ambush the convoys that are heading to Bristol and Liverpool."

Gordon nodded in acknowledgement. "Close to home base for resupply, that's an advantage," he said. But he didn't say that the disadvantage was no enemy shipping to capture.

"Yes, *Inverlyon* has to resupply at Lowestoft. She patrols with the fishing fleet out of there."

Gordon, who was a student of history, commented, "Fishing boats were sacrosanct in the past, now everything is fair game."

"Indeed, U-boats will sink everything, but most at least let the crews get off."

The admiral returned to his desk and sat down. Gordon was focused on the task ahead. "That is their weakness. It gives us a chance to get in close," he said.

"Indeed, the panic party tactic is proving to be effective — but do not be complacent. The German captains are smart and any hint that you are other than a merchantman and they will avoid you like the plague."

"Understood, sir."

"Do you need anything else?"

"No, June's getting us a radio and the shore accommodation, so we are all but ready to go."

The radio was fitted in a day with the antenna run up the forward mast. Its wires were painted the same brown as the mast stays so it did not stand out; the antenna was set along the line that connected the fore and aft mastheads. The set was put in a cleaned-out locker behind the bridge. But then Gordon realised he had a problem. He had no trained radio operator. He had his executive officer check the service records of the crew. While all of the officers knew Morse and semaphore, only one had experience with the set and of coding.

"Yes, sir. I learned Morse at Britannia. We were the first year to be taught it," young Hardy answered when questioned. He was shown the set. "That's identical to the one we used. Did they give us a code book?"

Fisher handed it to him. "I had to sign for it."

"I promise not to lose it."

Fisher grinned; he liked Hardy. "Cheeky beggar, your hide will be forfeit if you do."

The radio was to be used sparingly as the Germans had direction-finding equipment and the simple fact they had a set was a dead giveaway they were not just a tramp steamer.

* * *

A telegram arrived from Mary's mother.

> *CONGRATULATIONS, CAPTAIN CAMPBELL. YOU ARE THE FATHER OF A BABY BOY. DAVID. MOTHER AND BABY DOING WELL.*

Word got around the ship and, on the bridge, he was congratulated by his fellow officers.

"I say, sir, jolly good show," Midshipman Radcliffe said.

Barnes, Gordon's steward, brought a tray of glasses and a bottle of rum to the bridge. He poured one for every officer. "You as well, Barnes," Gordon said, and when Barnes had got himself a glass, Gordon raised his and said, "To my wife, Mary, and my son, David."

"Mary and David!" the officers cried and drained their glasses to heel taps.

At dinner that evening, Gordon spliced the mainbrace, and the men celebrated the addition to the Campbell family with cheers and songs.

As Christmas was fast approaching and the weather in the Western Approaches was appalling, the *Farnborough*'s crew got to stay in port for the festivities. There was no going home for Gordon, so he wrote an extended letter to Mary with a Christmas card expressing that he missed her and wished he could hold the baby. The locals made the navy men welcome and did their best, with typical Irish hospitality, to give them as good a time as possible. That meant the crew who were berthed ashore spent Christmas Eve and Christmas

Day morning in the local pubs. As they were in Ireland, the local tipple was a pint of the black stuff. Not Guinness, as that came from Dublin, but Beamish or Murphy's — both brewed by the River Lee in the city of Cork.

On Christmas Eve 1915, Gordon donned his uniform and headed into town; the admiral had invited him and the other Q-ship captains in port for lunch and some drinks. The admiral, or rather June, had chosen a pub called the Roaring Donkey, which served good food as well as beer, and was a short walk from the waterfront. When he arrived, he found three other captains and June, along with the admiral and his wife, in a private back room. The captains were Lieutenant Commander Arthur Wilmot-Smith of the *Baralong*, Lieutenant William Penrose Mark-Wardlaw of the *Prince Charles* and Gunner Ernest Jehan of the *Inverlyon*.

The landlord was a jolly man whose wife was a miracle worker in the kitchen. She placed a veritable cauldron of stew in the centre of the table. The stew was thick and rich, containing slow-cooked mutton, potatoes, onions, carrots and turnip, all flavoured with herbs. On the side was a large dish of buttered kale. The soda bread was hot from the oven and nutty. Dishes of rich Irish butter were set around the table so all present could slather their bread with it.

Gordon preferred beer to wine, and ordered a pint of Beamish to go with his meal; its rich roasted malt flavour and dark chocolatey undertones matched the stew perfectly. Gordon struck up a conversation with Ernest.

"The *Inverlyon* is an armed smack. How did she sink a U-boat?"

"Ah now, there lies a tale."

Applause rippled around the table when he finished. The admiral said, "And all without an engine!"

"A rare feat indeed," Gordon complimented Ernest. Then he spoke to the table: "As I am the only one who hasn't sunk a U-boat yet, would you like to share your experiences?"

The admiral nodded to Mark-Wardlaw, who looked a little abashed at having to tell his tale.

"It was luck, really. We gave her a good peppering and she surrendered but she was sinking fast and went down with eighteen of her hands."

Mark-Wardlaw looked a little pale at the thought of eighteen men going to the bottom, even though they had rescued fifteen, including the commander.

Last to go was Arthur, who admitted, "I was not on the *Baralong* when she sank the *U-27*, Lieutenant Commander Herbert was in charge then."

They all knew the scandal of that event, when Herbert ordered his crew to kill all the submariners fearing they would scuttle the steamer.

"However, I was in charge when we sank the *U-41*. She was sinking the SS *Urbino* with her guns — we opened fire, hitting the conning tower. Like William's U-boat, they dived but popped up again and two men jumped off before she sank."

All of this was very educational for Gordon, who took it all in gratefully.

When they had finished the meal, and the admiral and his lady had taken their leave, the rest went into the pub's public bar to finish the evening off. The locals were well into their evening and the black stuff was flowing. A small group of musicians were playing popular Irish folk songs. There was a drummer with a bodhrán, a fiddler and a man with a squeeze box. When the sailors came into the room they launched into a lively rendition of "Leave Her Johnny, Leave Her", which everyone joined in with.

Farnborough

I thought I heard the Old Man say:
"Leave her, Johnny, leave her!"
Tomorrow you will get your pay
And it's time for us to leave her

Leave her, Johnny, leave her!
Oh, leave her, Johnny, leave her!
For the voyage is long and the winds don't blow
And it's time for us to leave her

Oh, the wind was foul and the sea ran high
"Leave her, Johnny, leave her!"
She shipped it green and none went by
And it's time for us to leave her

Leave her, Johnny, leave her!
Oh, leave her, Johnny, leave her!
For the voyage is long and the winds don't blow
And it's time for us to leave her

I hate to sail on this rotten tub
"Leave her, Johnny, leave her!"
No grog allowed and rotten grub
And it's time for us to leave her

Gordon found himself next to June as they sang along, or listened to the locals sing songs in Gaelic. It was a wonderful night, and he walked her back to her lodgings.

"Will you be at the Christmas dinner in the wardroom?" he asked.

"No, I'll have lunch with my landlady's family."

"Then can I see you afterwards? We can go for a drink, there's bound to be a pub open somewhere."

She looked at him in a slightly quizzical way — as she knew he was married, and a new father — and answered, "All right, meet me here at three."

Gordon wrote to Mary daily but craved company other than the other officers, so dressed in civilian clothes and was at the door of June's lodgings at three precisely. It opened and June stepped out, wearing an overcoat and with her head covered in a scarf against the damp winter chill. He was likewise dressed to keep warm and dry, as Ireland was living up to its reputation for rain. They followed the sound of singing and entered a pub a couple of streets away.

There was a free table in a corner, which they took, and Gordon went to get them drinks — a Murphy's for him and a gin and tonic for her. As they sat and chatted, he learned that she was the daughter of an Irish father from Dublin and English mother from Liverpool. She had grown up in Dublin and became a secretary for the navy at the outbreak of the war. He told her of his past as the son of a navy captain, and his eyes glowed when he talked of king, country and the service as much as they did when he talked of Mary and his son.

Gordon noticed a priest looking at them from where he stood at the bar. He was an older man with grey hair and was sipping a glass of whisky.

Gordon asked June, "Why is that priest looking at us?"

She laughed. "That's Father Michael Horan. He knows me from

when I attend Mass and confession. He's probably wondering who you are."

Seeing that he was likely the subject of discussion, the priest moved from the bar to their table.

"Good afternoon, Father Horan," June said.

"June, I saw you at Mass this morning." June smiled and nodded. "And who is this fine young man you are here with?"

June answered formally: "Father Horan, may I introduce you to Commander Gordon Campbell?"

Horan held out his hand and Gordon took it. "Are you a Catholic, commander?"

"I'm High Church Anglican, Father."

"So, not so far from the Catholic way!"

"I believe not," Gordon said carefully. He hadn't been to church since well before the war except to get married. He decided to head off further questions.

"Can I get you a drink, Father?"

"That is kind of you, a wee whisky if I may."

Gordon left them to chat and headed to the bar. The landlord grinned as he approached and lifted a bottle from behind the bar. "For the Father?"

"Yes, please."

"By the time we close, he'll be drunk as a lord and sing hymns all the way home. Does it every Sunday."

"Better make it a double to help him on his way, then," Gordon said, and grinned back.

On their way back to June's lodgings, she told him that Horan advised her that the Church would not look kindly on a marriage between one of its members and an Anglican — whether he was High Church or not.

Gordon snorted. "Good grief, you didn't tell him I'm married?"

"Absolutely not — he would have been outraged."

"I suppose so. It's funny how priests are always ready to think the worst. He would never believe I just needed a break from all-male company with a friend."

"I told him we were just colleagues, and that the navy forbids relationships between officers and civilians in its employ. It seemed to satisfy him."

Gordon chuckled. "The nosy old—"

June stopped him. "Now don't you go blaspheming and deriding the people of the Church. You don't need to take risks — your job is dangerous enough as it is."

They parted at her door. They met again a couple of times as friends when their duties allowed, and spent New Year's Eve with many of their colleagues in the Q-force and regular navy, as Gordon couldn't get home.

The weather stayed excessively rough with one storm after another coming in from the Atlantic, and it was well into January 1916 before the *Farnborough* got to sea again. Gordon had picked up some tricks from the other captains and briefed the crew on these when they were in the Irish Sea.

He described the panic party tactic, and looked at the men's faces to see if they understood. "Good. Now, if they fire a torpedo and they miss we will keep going at the same speed to force them to the surface to make chase. Then play-act surrender."

"What if they hit us with their torpedo?"

"Then we act out the same panic scenario, which I want the crew to practise. When the bastards come in close to finish us off, we will let them have it. Hopefully the watertight doors will keep us afloat long enough to finish the job."

Submarine U-68

They set sail, destination Galway. They had gained a contingent of Royal Marines before they left, which added to their boarding power and gave them a small arms capability they had lacked before. From the outside, the *Farnborough* looked like any other tramp steamer: ill kept, a little rusty and hard used. Inside, she shone like a navy ship. Her guns were ready, the crew ready and … nothing happened. The trip to Galway was undisturbed by any type of action or excitement. Meanwhile, a convoy was attacked and ships sunk or damaged somewhere else. It was extremely frustrating.

They went into port and stayed for a couple of days to make it look like they had done some business. The crew explored the pubs along the waterfront and got into fistfights with the uniformed navy. Gordon had to bail out more than one of his crew before they sailed.

When the two days were up, they set sail for the four-day trip to Liverpool. Taking their time, as a tramp would. Whether it was the rough seas, or the U-boats were out in the Atlantic chasing a convoy, they saw nothing. More trips had the same result.

* * *

January and February passed and March crept in. They left Liverpool on 15 March 1916 and sailed down the Irish Sea, ten miles off the coast of Ireland. Again, the trip looked likely to be uneventful — until, that is, they spotted a steam drifter off the Fastnet Rock flying the Danish flag. They were going to ignore it but the lookout spotted a flashed signal from the Fastnet lighthouse. Radcliffe decoded it and passed the slip to the captain.

"The lighthouse keeper thinks there's something dodgy about that fishing boat. Let's go and have a look at it."

They flew the American flag and approached obliquely, so as not to spook anyone and to gain a good shooting angle before closing in.

"Bring us to action stations and be ready to put a shot across her bow, guns."

Sub Millard ran down to the starboard forward gun and had them load.

On the drifter *Obst*, the skipper Oberleutnant zur See Ingo Krämer thought it looked as though the tramp was going to pass their bow at least 600 metres inshore. He watched it casually; it was just another tramp taking coal to the west coast of Ireland. They would report its passing to the *U-68* that was on patrol this month. Their task was to monitor the shipping out of the southern entrance to the Irish Sea and report potential targets to the submarine that was patrolling the western approach to Ireland and Britain.

The tramp had got upwind of them, plodding along at around five knots, when suddenly there was a flash from the end of her bridge and a shell hissed past the bridge window. A voice boomed out, "Heave to and stand by to be boarded."

The American flag had disappeared, and a White Ensign of the Royal Navy had replaced it.

"Action stations!" Ingo yelled, and his men ran to man the 30-mm cannon hidden on their foredeck. They had it halfway uncovered when the tramp suddenly sprouted some large guns from behind panels that dropped down. The forward one fired. An explosion above his head told Ingo that they had taken his mast and antenna. A heavy machine gun opened fire and the gun crew had to dive for cover.

Gordon watched the crew of the drifter wave a white flag and line up along the side. The forward port gun had scored a lucky hit on the drifter's mast four feet up from the roof of the bridge. He had no idea they had taken out the antenna.

Someone threw a bag over the side.

"Lower a boat and send the marines across. See if they can retrieve that bag."

The marines were rowed over and soon scaled the side. Once they had control, Gordon brought the *Farnborough* alongside. He stepped down into the boat armed with a holstered Webley Mk VI .455-calibre revolver and two burly ratings, both with rifles, at his side. He was taking no chances.

He searched the bridge and found the radio, and the men searched the cabins. They found little except some German uniforms, but it was enough.

Gordon decided to take the crew members prisoner and sink the boat, and he was about to transfer back to the *Farnborough* when one of the boat crew approached him with a very wet canvas bag.

"It's the one they threw overboard, sir. They forgot to put a weight in it."

Inside they found a code book and a sheaf of papers apparently detailing Allied shipping.

Gordon sent a boat across to the lighthouse with a bottle of navy rum for the keeper and a message. *Thanks for the tip! Well spotted.* When it returned, he ordered, "Set a course for Queenstown — we need to get this to Intelligence. Blow the bottom out of that and send it down."

The 6-pounder gunners went to work with a will. This was a much more interesting target than some floating barrel.

Prisoners and papers having been delivered to Queenstown, they set out again immediately and resumed their trek around to Galway. They received a brief message by radio.

DRIFTER YOU INTERCEPTED TRANSMITTED A MESSAGE TO U-68 THOUGHT TO BE SOMEWHERE OFF W COAST IRELAND. CODE BOOK VERY USEFUL.

"We had better keep a good look out then," Gordon said, and smiled to no one in particular.

They were passing the Blasket Islands off the west coast of Ireland on 22 March 1916 when a lookout called, "Periscope, 1,500 yards, two points off the bow."

Gordon picked up his binoculars and scanned the sea.

"Action stations."

The crew went to their guns and extra ammunition crates were brought up from the magazine. The panels were left in place.

"Torpedo track!"

Gordon had seen it.

"Hard to port!"

The bow swung slowly ... ever so slowly ... but just enough as the torpedo sped past the bow, missing by a few feet.

"Bugger, that was close. Where is he?"

They scanned the sea, knowing that even at five or six knots they were going faster than a U-boat could do underwater.

"Periscope astern!"

He went to the walkway outside the bridge and saw the sleek grey hull of the U-boat rise up out of the water 1,000 yards astern. Soon men appeared on the conning tower and a group came out of a hatch on the deck to man the deck gun. Smoke burst from her exhausts as her diesel engines started up. She sped up and moved out to the *Farnborough*'s port quarter, the deck gun fired, and a shell whistled across their bow. A German-accented voice shouted through a megaphone, "Stop your engines and prepare to be boarded!"

"Stop engine, blow off steam, panic party away."

The *Farnborough* had an elaborate set of pipes installed around the base of the funnel that were fed by the boiler. If the cock was opened, they sent a spectacular amount of steam up around the funnel as if they had vented their boiler. The panic party went into action, making a proper show of abandoning ship. One boat full of men rowed away, then a second.

Gordon estimated how far they would drift before stopping.

"Hard to port."

The helmsman spun the wheel, and, with their remaining momentum, the ship eased to port to expose her side to the attacker.

At that point, something extraordinary happened.

Fisher stood staring out at the submarine, his face chalk white, his eyes wide. He was shaking and a wet patch had appeared on his trousers.

"Rodney? Are you all right?" Gordon asked.

He got no reply. Fisher's eyes were unseeing, his mouth open, his breath panting.

"Get him to his cabin, put him to bed and keep him quiet," Gordon ordered a lookout.

The U-boat, which had *U-68* stencilled on her bow, closed the range, eager to make the kill. At 800 yards Gordon shouted, "Raise the colours! Open fire!"

The panels crashed down as the White Ensign flew up and the two stern and the port forward 12-pounders swung around and into action. Shells spat from the barrels. The bridge 6-pounder joined in. They went for the U-boat's hull and were scoring hits, the gunners loading as fast as they could. A shell took out the deck gun, a direct hit on the mount killing the crewmen and rendering the gun useless. Another went right into the conning tower, hitting the periscope tube, knocking it askew and killing everyone on the bridge.

Gordon's blood was up! The submarine started to sink or dive; he knew not which. "Full speed ahead, steer us over her!"

The helmsman obeyed and the telegraph clanged, acknowledging the order. The propeller thrashed and they sped up. The guns kept up their barrage until they had completed the turn and were bearing down on the bubbles rising from the depths.

"Depth charges set to forty feet!"

Sub Norman Milford ran to the racks at the stern and checked the fuses.

"Ready!"

They were at full speed and the sub was passing below them.

"FIRE!"

It wasn't the correct command, but Milford understood, and charges rolled off the racks. Just five seconds later they exploded, sending columns of dirty water into the air. The submarine's bow followed, blown up and out of the water. The guns let loose again to score another five hits as she went down by the stern.

"Dead slow. Right full rudder, circle to starboard."

They made a complete circle, waiting for debris or survivors to come to the surface. Oil bubbled up, flattening the waves. A couple of bodies and debris appeared — the boats pulled the bodies and any identifying debris out of the water. After half an hour, Gordon sent a message to Queenstown:

ACTION AT 51°54'N 10°53'W. Q-05 SUNK U-68 WITH ALL HANDS. GUN AND DEPTH CHARGE ATTACK. NO SURVIVORS. ONE CASUALTY, LT FISHER.

Midshipman Radcliffe encoded it and sent it — his fingers, now well practised, tapping out the Morse at speed. Gordon ordered the crew to stand down and soon the empty shell cases were gathered up for storage, the guns cleaned and the panels restored to their usual positions. He heard the radio chattering as they increased speed to half ahead, heading to Galway.

"Message from Queenstown, sir." Radcliffe held out a flimsy with the decoded message on.

CONGRATULATIONS, Q-05. COME HOME.

It was close to the end of their patrol and Gordon decided to go the long way around. He hoped they might get lucky and find another target. They cruised up the west coast of Ireland until they reached Main Head, where they turned east, passing the Isle of Islay and easing south-east past Rathin Island and the Mull of Kintyre into the Irish Sea. They kept the coast of Ireland in view on the horizon as they passed Dublin, Wicklow and Rosslare Harbour to pass through Saint George's Channel and turn south-west for home.

They turned in past Roches Point and entered the Muir Cheilteach. As they rounded Spike Island, other Q-ships began sounding their horns and the crews manned the sides, cheering. By the time they were eased alongside by a solicitous tug, the admiral and June were waiting for them and came aboard as soon as the gangplank was put in place. The cheering continued.

The admiral saluted, then shook Gordon's hand. "Well done, me boy."

"Thank you, sir. The crew, especially the gunners, were outstanding."

"Gather your crew, I want to speak to them."

The crew gathered on the foredeck and the admiral stood on a crate so they could all see and hear him.

"I want to congratulate you all on your outstanding action in sinking the *U-68*. Not only did you score a kill, but this was the first time depth charges have been used in any kind of action. You have proven their worth and set the standard which all that follow will have to strive for. By sinking that boat, you have aided the war effort immensely by removing a threat to the ships that are keeping Britain alive. I believe that you deserve three cheers for yourselves."

The crew responded enthusiastically. Then the admiral joined Gordon on the bridge, where he had gone to watch the speech with June.

"Your crew is being granted two weeks' shore leave while the ship is serviced in the Haulbowline yard." He looked down at the side, where Rodney Fisher was being taken to an ambulance. "No moral fibre, some people." What he didn't say was Fisher had been torpedoed before and spent ten hours in a lifeboat before being rescued, seriously dehydrated and shocked.

Fisher would eventually be taken to Haslar, where he would be treated for shell shock. Gordon searched for a replacement and found Lieutenant Ronald Stuart, RNR, a qualified Anglo-Canadian mariner who worked with Canadian Pacific before being called up to serve in the Royal Naval Reserve. He was a persistent bugger by all accounts, having applied for transfer to an active command multiple times, and would suit the crew very well.

Gordon decided to spend his leave at home in Saltash in Cornwall. He got a local drifter to give him a lift and arranged to be picked up in twelve days' time. He was dropped off late into the evening, and cheerily greeted by several locals on his way up from the dock.

His home, Boisdale House, was in North Road between the town centre and waterside. It was of yellow-brick construction and was the former home of Admiral Sir Henry Jackson, the pioneering officer who worked with Marconi on ship-to-ship communication that now all navy ships were fitted with.

The house fronted the road and had a large rear garden. Gordon slipped his key into the lock and opened the door.

"Mary, it's me!"

Mary came from the direction of the kitchen, rushed into his arms and kissed him. He had sent a telegram ahead of his arrival.

"Darling, you're earlier than I expected!"

Gordon laughed and looked her up and down as he held her at arm's length.

"A fishing boat brought me. I probably smell of herring."

Mary sniffed his shoulder. "A little, but it will wear off."

Now she held him at arm's length and studied his face.

"What is it? Is there a spot on my nose?"

She laughed, then sobered.

"I was looking to see if the action had changed you."

"The action? I haven't told you about that yet."

She led him into the living room, where he found his son, David, fast asleep in a cot. He bent over him, marvelling at the first sight of his child. He gently picked him up and held him. The boy made a gurgling sound and opened his eyes momentarily before dozing off again. Once he put him down, Mary pointed to the occasional table, which had a pile of newspapers on it. "You're in today's papers and the *Gazette*. You are quite the local hero."

He read the highly redacted account and snorted, unimpressed. "Oh bugger. They didn't waste any time getting that out. I was hoping for a quiet time."

He was out of luck. Saltash was a small town and word soon got around that their local hero was home. It wasn't long before a reporter asked for an interview. Gordon agreed, and they sat under a pagoda in the garden, a pot of tea between them. Mary poured.

"This was not the first submarine to be killed," said the journalist, not entirely confidently.

"No, absolutely not. There have been several before us."

"Yet yours is the first that made the national papers."

"That's because we used depth charges."

"You were the first to use them?"

"In anger, yes."

"There is talk of you getting a DSO."

"I doubt that will happen!" Gordon laughed. "My ship didn't sink!"

The reporter asked many more questions, most of which Gordon couldn't answer for security reasons, including, "What is the name of your ship and what type is it?" To that he answered, "Don't be a bloody fool! If I tell you that, or what she looks like, the enemy will be all over us or — worse, avoid us completely!"

When Gordon and Mary went out in the town they found the experience ... different. They went to a local pub that served food and Gordon had to insist on paying for their meal. The drinks, however, came for free as the locals would bring fresh ones over any time they got near to finishing the glasses in front of them. Only by going across the River Tamar to Plymouth could they dine in relative anonymity.

Their days were spent catching up; they talked a lot and Gordon listened to the radio and read the papers. He read the version of his report that was printed in the *Gazette*. It was heavily edited, but it did mention that his was the first action that had used the new depth charges. Mary told him he had lost weight and fed him wonderful home-cooked meals. He went shopping and refreshed his stock of books. He bought Somerset Maugham's *Of Human Bondage*, a book of poems by Robert Frost, John Buchan's *The Thirty-Nine Steps* and *The Valley of Fear*, the latest Sherlock Holmes novel.

While on leave, Gordon received a personal letter delivered by courier from the First Lord of the Admiralty, Winston Churchill, praising his and his ship's action. Mary had it framed, and it now stood proudly on the dresser in the living room.

All too soon he had to meet the drifter that would take him back to Queenstown. His au revoir to Mary and David on the dock was truncated by the toot of the boat's horn, telling him that the small boat was on its way over to pick him up. He kissed his wife tenderly, but he did not promise to be careful.

"Good morning, Commander," chirped the first mate as he stepped aboard. The drifter was laden with herring, her holds full. They had had a successful trip and now needed to get it home, where it would be salted and packed in barrels. The weather was fine, and the drifter chuffed its way down the Tamar out through Plymouth Harbour and into the Channel. He would be back in Queenstown the next day.

Tedious Times

The *Farnborough* was in fine fettle. The service at the yard had been thorough and her electrical systems revised with a new generator and wiring to add twenty-four-inch searchlights fore and aft. These would aid them in a night encounter, illuminating a target out to 1,000 yards as their 12-pounders had no star shells. The searchlights could also be used for signalling.

The crewmen were rested and keen to get out to sea, their recent victory energising them. To a man they could have dined out on the story for the entire leave, but kept it secret. Their new executive officer, Lieutenant Stuart, joined and immediately made an impression on the discipline and efficiency of the ship. His experience as an officer in the merchant marine quickly proved invaluable.

They set out. Their patrol area had been extended to cover the entire west coast of Ireland and the Irish Sea, and they all felt there was an excellent chance of a kill. They had dirtied the outside of the ship to make her look more like a tramp than before and deliberately made smoke. The crew were now well practised at sailing merchant style and fell into the routine quickly.

Gordon decided to head north up towards Liverpool, then continue on past the Isle of Man to the east and out through the strait between the Mull of Kintyre and Antrim. Staying within sight of the coast, they circumnavigated the island down to Galway, where they called in for some fresh supplies. They were undisturbed.

They chugged down from Galway around the southern tip of the island into the Irish Sea. Still nothing. *Nil desperandum,* Gordon thought as they returned to Queenstown. He checked with Intelligence whether there had been any sightings, and was told that a U-boat had been sunk out in the Atlantic by the escorts of a convoy en route to Liverpool. He checked the convoy's position and planned to trail it into the Irish Sea as if he was a straggler.

They set out, travelling at full speed up the Irish Sea to intercept the convoy before it reached the northern entrance. They were just in time. At dawn, the convoy came into view spread out over a huge swathe of the ocean. Fifty ships in columns of ten, with escorts buzzing around the periphery like so many sheep dogs.

Gordon steered a looping course to bring them up behind the convoy, flashing their number and intention to the escorts. A corvette, a submarine hunter/fleet escort that was smaller than a destroyer, sent back: *Good Luck.* They joined the middle column then reduced speed to slow ahead, started making smoke and dropped back. The escort flashed for them to keep up. Gordon grinned at his exec and ignored it.

They were a mile behind the convoy when the lookout called, "Torpedo track, fine on the starboard bow."

Gordon snatched up his binoculars and scanned the ocean. There it was.

"Turn to starboard. Half ahead."

That reduced the chance of being hit while setting them on the opposite track to the torpedo. He planned to accelerate to full ahead as soon as the submarine surfaced.

"Submarine coming up dead ahead."

"Damn — he's facing away from us."

Twin puffs of smoke showed that he had started his diesel engines.

"Full ahead!"

It was no good. The sub had four knots on them at least and opened the range rapidly.

"Try a shot," Gordon ordered.

The 12-pounder in front of the bridge fired a ranging shot that missed by a wide margin.

"Stand down," Gordon said.

The next few weeks were much the same. They tried running close to the coast, far out from the coast, running directly out into the Atlantic before turning around and limping back in. Every idea was tried. Every idea failed. The admiral decided they needed a change of scenery and gave them the Channel patrol, the theory being that perhaps the Germans were identifying the *Farnborough*.

"At least we get some new scenery with Plymouth as our base," Ronald said.

Gordon silently agreed and looked forward to spending some leave with Mary.

While submarines were elusive, German surface ships proved vulnerable. They were sailing south from Hull, following the European coast, when they came across a steamer heading north.

"Man the guns," Gordon said as he watched the ship approach.

* * *

Farnborough

The Germans were far enough north that they were out of range of the British motor torpedo boats based in Belgium; there had been no reports of British U-boats either, so the German skipper felt safe to run on the surface in daytime. The ship approaching them flew a Dutch flag and closed without drama. His ship was not just a steamer, she was also used for intelligence gathering and he had a radio to report sightings of enemy ships.

"Watch her carefully. I have seen a ship like her using a false flag before," he told the lookout.

Gordon studied the approaching ship carefully, then spoke to the gunner of the 6-pounder on the starboard side of the bridge.

"I want you to take out his forward mast. Can you do that?"

"If we get close enough, Skipper."

"We will, just wait for the word."

Ronald was curious when he heard the order being given and studied the mast through his binoculars. He smiled when he saw why his captain had given the order. There at its tip was a poorly disguised antenna.

They aimed to pass the German at around 300 yards. The range closed and just before they crossed, Gordon shouted: "NOW!"

The concealing panels dropped, and the guns came to bear. The 6-pounder barked. Once, twice, three times ... and the mast shattered.

"HEAVE TO OR BE SUNK!"

The ship stopped her engines. Gordon sent the marines across, commanded by Sub Millard. The boat came back with the captain and crew, followed by the marines.

"Did you get his papers?" Ronald asked.

"No, sir. He threw them out of a porthole before we could stop him."

Ronald swore then asked, "What was she carrying?"

"Empty shell cases."

"Is everyone off?"

"Aye, Skipper. Even the ship's cat," Millard reported.

"Demolition charge set?"

"Aye." Millard checked his watch. "Three minutes to go."

"Excellent. Half ahead, course 1, 8, 0 degrees."

They all watched as the seconds counted down, then they felt rather than saw the charge go off. The sea sort of shook and the waves around the doomed ship seemed to flatten.

"She's going down!"

The *Seemöwe* was indeed getting lower in the water. Her captain came up onto the bridge at Gordon's invitation, to witness her end. She started going down faster at the stern and a gout of steam ushered from her funnel and her horn sounded forlornly. Then she was gone.

Gordon turned to the captain.

"You had a radio on board and threw your papers over the side. You were more than a cargo steamer."

The captain did not answer. Gordon didn't know if he did not speak English or was just refusing to talk, but he had him taken below and held in a cabin away from his crew.

Once they were underway, Gordon and PO Mike Strange went down to interrogate him. Strange had served on merchant ships out of Newcastle that traded with northern Germany, and he spoke German.

"Your ship was spying," Gordon stated. "You will be treated as a prisoner of war, rather than a civilian, and interned."

The captain said nothing.

"You know you could be shot as a spy?"

"I am not a spy."

That was a start.

"What is your name?"

"Gerhard Mueller."

"Captain Mueller, I am Captain Campbell."

"What is the name of your ship? It is a marine raider, no?" Mueller asked.

"Yes, it is." Gordon smiled. He had spotted a pipe in Mueller's breast pocket, so pulled out his own and stuffed it with tobacco. He pushed the pouch across.

"Help yourself."

Mueller took out his pipe and filled it. Gordon passed over his matches so he could light it.

"What was your ship called?" Gordon asked. "That's just for the record, you understand."

"The *Seemöwe*, we are out of Bremerhaven."

"Did you get a message off?"

"What if we did?"

"It would be inconvenient."

Mueller laughed.

Gordon could get no more out of him, so he shook the captain's hand. The man would spend the rest of the war in England as a prisoner of war.

On the way back to Plymouth, as they were passing Calais, the lookout called, "Torpedo track broad on the starboard beam!"

Gordon immediately ordered, "Full ahead! Hard to starboard!"

A tense thirty seconds passed as the torpedo came closer as they turned. It hit the stern obliquely with a loud *thunk*, but did not explode. They chased the torpedo's track back a good 2,000 yards, only to spot the submarine on the surface 1,000 yards away making fifteen knots away from them.

Gordon swore. This was becoming really frustrating.

Leave time came around and they docked in Plymouth for Christmas. The men went ashore and only a harbour watch was left on board. The year 1916 was coming to an end.

Gordon went home, and he walked up the North Road with a fine smattering of snow on the shoulders of his coat. It was one of the coldest winters on record. That morning they had experienced a frost of 12 Fahrenheit, which was bitterly cold and meant the *Farnborough*'s boilers would run continuously while she was in port to stop her freezing up.

He got to his house, where the soft glow of gas light spilled from the windows, which were decorated with lace and boughs of evergreen. He stopped, his breath steaming in the frigid air, and put down his bag. He looked around at his neighbours' houses, also lit and decorated. You would not know a war was happening just across the English Channel.

He sighed; it was so peaceful. Then the sound of laughter came from inside his house and he smiled as he pulled out his key and let himself in.

"Gordon, is that you?" Mary called as a small dog barked furiously at him.

"It is," he called back, as he knelt to invite the mutt to come forward for a pet. It was Mary's mother's dog; she must be joining them for Christmas.

Mary's father had died serving his country as a brigadier at the

Relief of Ladysmith in 1900, when he was shot by a Boer sniper. Her mother, a grand lady, lived near Exeter in Devon and had probably travelled down on the train. Mary came out and they embraced after he had shed his coat and hat.

"Come into the sitting room and warm yourself," Mary said, noting how cold his lips and hands were.

Inside the living room he was surprised to find not only Mary's mother but his own parents as well. His father, who stood in front of the fire, stepped forward and shook his hand vigorously. His mother stood and waited to embrace him. His father, who had been an excellent cricketer and a lieutenant in the Royal Artillery, was now an honorary colonel of the 1st Argyll and Bute Artillery Volunteers. He was a companion of the Order of the Bath and a justice of the peace. On top of all that, he was a personal friend of W. G. Grace and a member of the Marylebone Cricket Club.

As he was just one of sixteen children, Gordon wondered why his parents had chosen to spend Christmas with them. His brothers included Edward, the Vice Consul of Java and resident in the country; Ian, an officer in the Argyll and Sutherland Highlanders and now on the Western Front; and James, who was in the Royal Navy and probably at sea. He could only assume his sisters, with all their associated brats, were also occupied. Then it occurred to him that they had come because of David, their newest grandson.

Mary's mother was an older version of her and was the archetype of British reserve, with a strong sense of right and wrong. In contrast, Gordon's mother was the family matriarch, opinionated on many matters and not afraid to share those opinions. His father could silence her with a, "Not now Emilie," when she started.

"Where is your ship?" his father asked.

"Plymouth Harbour. We finished our patrol yesterday."

"See anything?"

"Only a German freighter, which we sank."

His mother sniffed and said, "They should all be sent to the bottom. Damn Germans."

Gordon decided to change the subject. "How is James faring? Have you heard from him?"

His father frowned. "He's still commanding the *Constance* and was at Jutland. Not sure if they fired a shot, they certainly weren't damaged."

The *Constance* was a light cruiser and part of the 4th Light Cruiser Squadron. At Jutland the Royal Navy lost three battlecruisers, three armoured cruisers and eight destroyers/torpedo boats. The Germans lost a battleship, a battlecruiser, four light cruisers and five destroyers/torpedo boats. It was counted as a British victory at home, but that was debatable.

The Western Front had ground to a halt with both sides entrenched. Gordon's brother Ian was there and the newspapers gave lurid accounts of what could only be described as hell on earth. The subject that would not be mentioned during the festive season. The war was grinding on.

Mary got him a pink gin, which he sipped gratefully as he sat on the sofa next to her. His mother had a sweet sherry and his father a whisky and soda. Mary's mother sipped a glass of Madeira. The Christmas tree stood in the corner, decorated with a mixture of classic glass and home-made ornaments. Presents lay underneath. He would add those he had bought for Mary while he was in port later, after everyone else had gone to bed.

The conversation wandered around until dinner time, when Mary produced a wonderful steamed steak and kidney pudding. Food was abundantly available in the south-west of England, which had a rich farming tradition and many market gardens. His father commented, "You're lucky down here — we have to queue for our food." His mother snorted a laugh — her husband never queued for anything in his life. Gordon knew that but said, "I read there were food shortages in London."

His father put on a knowledgeable look. "In parts. The distribution is inconsistent, and prices are generally rising. The government is looking at rationing as a solution."

"Across the whole country?" Mary asked.

"Only in London by the end of next year, at least to start with. It may be expanded later."

"The locals are complaining about the new pub opening hours," Mary said.

"Why? And what are those?" Gordon asked.

"It's to ensure the workers stay sober!" his father said, and laughed. "Only five and a half hours' opening time a day, closed by nine and no opening on Sundays. The beer is watered down as well, and buying rounds is banned."

"Good Lord, I'm not surprised they're complaining."

Mary's mother piped up: "They've also banned feeding the ducks in the parks."

Gordon shook his head. "What is the world coming to?"

Christmas passed, as it does, and a goose was consumed. They attended church and prayed for peace — after they prayed for victory. Presents were given and received. The parents went home before New Year's Day, by which time Gordon had seen enough of them all. His father was starting to make suggestions on how to improve the house, and his mother had started interfering with Mary's running of it.

Once they were gone, Gordon and Mary started attending parties held by their neighbours and he rediscovered a love of dancing at a ball in the town hall, which was thrown by the mayor to see the old year out and the new year in. At midnight they sang "Auld Lang Syne", which had become a tradition all over Britain.

They also paid a visit to HMS *Vivid*, the Royal Navy barracks in Plymouth, to attend a dinner thrown by the resident commissioner, Captain William Shield. This was for officers and their wives or girlfriends only and all officers with ships in port were invited. As it turned out, only the land-based officers and a very few ship's officers had wives or mistresses they could bring. Consequently, the women that were there did a lot of dancing — and Gordon suspected that one or two of the so-called girlfriends were professional escorts.

They walked home. Mary was happy but a little footsore, and that night their second child was conceived.

1917 came in quietly. Their patrol had been switched back to the Western Approaches and Gordon said goodbye to Mary at the house when a navy car came to take him to his ship. Once at sea he sat with his executive officer to discuss tactics. Gordon opened the conversation.

"From what I've heard from the other Q-ship commanders, the Germans are reluctant to follow up unsuccessful torpedo attacks with a surface attack. It seems the Germans have concluded that British merchantmen are all armed nowadays and they need to keep their distance. They're shooting from further out, as well."

Ronald agreed. He had heard the same while drinking with a bunch of merchant captains. "That makes life difficult. Guns are rendered useless and any attack with depth charges is hit and miss as we largely drop them blind."

"Hmm, and by the time we follow the track back to the point of origin they've gone," Gordon muttered.

"If it lasts that long."

Gordon sighed and rubbed the bridge of his nose. What were they to do? The discussion was going nowhere as they had no new ideas. Gordon wondered, *Are we avoiding the obvious solution?*

Queenstown was quiet. It had recently snowed and a decent layer was left on the ground. Children made snowmen and had snowball fights. Adults got on with the war and their lives. Gordon had a meeting with the admiral and, after reporting on the state of the *Farnborough*, he broached the subject of tactics.

"I've had two encounters with submarines in the last six months, both of which led to nothing. The submarines fired shots at long range, which I easily avoided. They then surfaced and escaped before we could get to them."

The admiral looked resigned. "Yes, others have reported the same. I don't have an answer."

Gordon considered his next words carefully: "I think I do, but I don't think you or the Admiralty will like it."

The admiral looked at him over his glasses, and his eyes narrowed as he said, "Go on."

"The Germans won't attack on the surface day or night unless their target is crippled or disabled, and they're unlikely to fall for any kind of deception."

"Yes."

"Well, I propose to allow a torpedo to hit, draw the sub up by feigning a panicked abandon ship, leaving only two men in the engine room, me and the gunners on board. We counter-attack when he comes in to finish us off."

The admiral thought about it for a long, silent moment. He got up and paced, turned to say something, then changed his mind and continued pacing. Then he stopped and faced Gordon.

"You could lose your ship."

Gordon was ready for that.

"I could, but it would be one less sub out there. In any case, it's a trade of one old steamer for a submarine and crew."

The admiral paced some more. "If you fail to sink the submarine and lose your ship, your career could be over."

"I'm prepared for that."

The admiral slumped into his chair. "It could be suicide."

"Or it could work wonderfully and we get a sub for a bit of damage."

The admiral gave him a hard look.

"You and I have not had this conversation — because if I had, I would have to tell you not to be so damn stupid and order you not to do such a rash thing. But God help me, if anyone can pull off a move like that, you can. Now, get out of my office while my memory is bad."

Submarine U-83

They left Queenstown at dawn on 11 February 1917 — a cold, blustery morning — and headed north to circumnavigate Ireland anticlockwise. The wind was from the north and bitterly cold; ice formed on the upperworks. As the day progressed the sun shone weakly through a thin overcast but did nothing to warm them. Everyone was wrapped up in heavy coats, scarves, hats, gloves and at least two pairs of socks inside their sea boots.

The second day dawned, and they were surrounded by fog that froze to everything it touched, forcing the men to hammer it off the upperworks.

"Can it get any worse?" Ronald Stuart said.

"I suppose we could run into an iceberg," Gordon joked.

The horn blared out. They were barely making headway and steering on the compass.

"The only way a submarine will find us in this muck is by tripping over us," Ronald quipped.

Midshipman Radcliffe, who had been in the radio room training a hand in Morse and communications, came onto the bridge.

"Captain, we've picked up radio messages that a submarine is active to the south. A convoy was attacked coming into the Irish Sea."

Gordon blew out his cheeks. "Well, there's bugger all we can do about it until this clears. Thank you, Mr Radcliffe, please keep monitoring."

The fog didn't lift until midday and when it did they sped up to half speed and started rehearsing the panic party performance. They even got Radcliffe dressed in a woman's dress and blonde wig to make it look as if they were carrying passengers.

On 15 February, as they were passing Dingle, the lookouts spotted something in the water. Gordon was called from his day room.

"Slow ahead, let's see what it is."

It was quickly identified as wreckage, and they stopped to put a boat over. There was little chance of finding survivors, for the water was so cold anyone who was in it would be dead in less than ninety minutes.

"We found a life vest. It came from SS *Colemere*," the bosun who had commanded the boat reported when he returned.

Gordon, who didn't want to hang around any longer, ordered "Half ahead, resume course. That proves that U-boats are operating in the area." Then he went to the chart table and ran his finger around the southern tip of Ireland. "The convoys come in on this track. What I want to do is swing out and come in as if we're a straggler. Mr Radcliffe, plot us a course, if you would be so kind."

Radcliffe quickly handed a course correction to his captain, who ordered, "Course 2, 2, 5, full ahead."

The bow swung, then steadied on the new course; the engine vibration increased as they sped up.

"Course 2, 2, 5, sir," the helm confirmed.

"We will maintain this course for twelve hours then turn to 0, 9, 0 and reduce to half ahead."

Gordon called Radcliffe to him. "When we change course, I want you to broadcast a message in plain language that the *Farnborough* has made repairs and is underway to dock at Cork. Send it as if it came from a destroyer."

"Aye-aye, Skipper."

The executive officer doubled the lookouts on his own initiative, aware that one never knew when or where the U-boats would strike.

The ship was tense as the word got around and the men started the preparations for action stations without being told. As Gordon watched them bring ammunition to the guns, a crew man looked up and grinned. *They are good lads,* he thought.

The next day they steamed a steady course. They did not zigzag, although that was the latest technique for avoiding U-boats and the sensible thing to do. Gordon thought that a skipper who had got away with making repairs at sea and getting separated from a convoy would want to make port as fast as he could.

At the end of the day, when nothing had been spotted, he had Radcliffe send another message telling his owner that they were one day out from Cork. Gordon did not sleep that night; all his instincts were telling him that he was being stalked.

Dawn rose, weak and watery but clear. The sea was running just a light swell from the west. They were making more smoke than usual and maintained a steady course. Then: "Deck, there's something on the horizon — 1, 4, 0 degrees," the lookout positioned on top of the superstructure called down.

They were due to make a course change towards Cork.

"Maintain course. Call the captain," Sub Millard, who had the watch, ordered.

Gordon came out onto the bridge from his day cabin. "Where is it?"

"1, 4, 0 degrees about four miles out," Millard said.

Gordon wanted to make them as easy a target as he could.

"Start easing our course around to 0, 2, 0. Slowly."

After a tense ten minutes the lookout reported, "U-boat closing fast. It's one of the big new ones. Range 4,000."

The data on the Type U-81 class of submarine said they were 230 feet long and could do around seventeen knots on the surface. They could make nine knots submerged. She would have two bow tubes, two stern tubes and a 4-inch deck gun.

Come on, my beauty, keep coming.

It was not long before a rather tense voice called, "Torpedo track — 1, 3, 5 degrees."

"Steady men, brace for impact," Gordon said, and sounded the collision alarm.

As per their practice sessions, every watertight door was closed and locked. The only crew below decks were Loveless and Boyd in the engine room, and they would evacuate as soon as they had stopped the engines if there was flooding aft.

Gordon watched the torpedo approach; it had been fired at around 4,000 yards and was moving at thirty-six knots. It was heading just aft of the middle of the starboard side, which was about the most survivable place it could hit, since that was a hold full of wood.

The explosion was tremendous as 463 pounds of hexanite made quite an impact, and the torpedo exploded just after it punched a hole on the side.

The ship's stern started to settle.

"All stop! Clear the engine room after starting the pumps. Panic party away! Radio, send a mayday."

Down in the engine room, Angus Boyd ordered his men to evacuate up to the main deck. He stayed and kept the boiler running to power the generators that ran the ship's pumps. He would only leave when he was up to his waist in water.

The panic party dropped four of the ship's lifeboats and threw a couple of life rafts over the side. They made a fine show of abandoning ship in a disorderly fashion. The *Farnborough* settled, her stern low in the water. Gordon and Ronald stayed on the bridge. The gunners were at their stations, the trap was set.

Ronald had an idea. "I'll shine one of the spotlights on them to dazzle their gunners once we're ready to go."

"Good idea," Gordon said. "Get ready but stay low, do not get shot."

The submarine was approaching fast, but at 1,000 yards it slowed. Her skipper was wary. The *Farnborough*'s boats had scattered, getting well out of the line of fire.

"Steady, lads," Sub Millard told the foredeck gunners, as did Midshipman Radcliffe on the afterdeck. The men were ready, the guns loaded and swung around as far as the panels would let them.

The *U-83* closed. Kapitänleutnant Bruno Hoppe wanted to get in as close as possible to make sure all hands had abandoned ship before he ordered his deck gun to end her. The ship was sinking by the stern, and it wouldn't take much to finish her off. He swung around in an arc to bring the *U-83* alongside. This was his second patrol, and he already had six kills under his belt for 6,450 tons of cargo sunk. He was confident and a little arrogant.

Gordon watched what he now knew was the *U-83* — he could clearly see the number on the bow — make an arc to come alongside. The U-boat's skipper was in the conning tower, looking up at him. Gordon saluted him — and then pressed the button that set off the claxon to signal the guns to fire.

The panels crashed down and the guns swung rapidly around and down. The first gun fired. The 6-pound shell from the bridge gun took the head clean off of Bruno Hoppe, and his body dropped to the deck of the conning tower, his blood dripping down through the open hatch. The Maxim and Lewis guns roared into life at the same time; they decimated the deck gun crew and left the conning tower looking like a sieve. The 12-pounders opened up and poured fire into the now stationary submarine just ten yards off the *Farnborough*'s beam. Gordon urged them on. The continuous fire soon reduced the U-boat to a battered wreck, and she started to sink. Men threw themselves overboard into the freezing Atlantic water.

Eight German sailors escaped the *U-83* before she sank, and the boats managed to pick up two of them. The rest perished in the freezing waters.

Gordon asked the radio operator to send a message.

Q-5 ENGAGED AND SANK U-BOAT U-83 AT 51°34'N 11°23'W, TWO SURVIVORS.

He and Ronald then did a survey of the damage. His own ship was clearly sinking, albeit slowly, as the pumps could not keep up with the inflow of water. He decided to leave the men in the boats and sent a second message:

Farnborough

Q-5 SLOWLY SINKING, RESPECTFULLY WISHES YOU GOODBYE.

The message was received by the destroyer *Narwhal* and the sloop *Buttercup*, both of which were nearby. The *Farnborough* soon received a reply.

HMS NARWHAL *ONE HOUR AWAY. HOLD ON, CHAPS.*

They would easily survive an hour, so Gordon ordered the gunners to abandon ship, keeping twelve men aboard to try and stem the flood. With help on the way and the boiler still burning and powering the generator they would strive to keep her afloat. As a precaution he destroyed all confidential papers, including the code book. The *Buttercup*, an Arabis-class sloop, arrived first and picked up the men in the boats. She was a minesweeper and had been the closest ship to them. The *Narwhal* arrived a short time later and immediately fired a line across so that they could send a cable over and be towed to land.

Gordon called across using a megaphone: "Much appreciated! I think we'll have to be beached."

The *Narwhal*'s skipper called back: "We'll take you to Mill Cove. There's a beach there and deep water for us to get in and out."

All was going well as night fell. The tow was slow, but they were holding their own. Gordon was on the bridge watching the stern light of the destroyer when there was an enormous *bang* that shook the ship from end to end. One of their depth charges had exploded. The tow was dropped, and he ordered, "All hands abandon ship."

As they left in the remaining boats, he started to make a final survey of his ship. He went towards the stern, moving slowly and deliberately down the sloping deck. He was still beside the 12-pounder behind the funnel when a second depth charge exploded. He was knocked to the deck but got up and was able to peer around the corner. The afterdeck was a scrapyard, but forward of the debris the ship was still intact.

He made his way forward. The generator was still running, and he still had lights, so he decided to go to the bridge and inform the *Narwhal* accordingly by lamp signal. Suddenly, ahead of him, he spotted a lone figure. As he got closer, he saw it was Ronald.

"Lieutenant, why are you still aboard?"

Ronald grinned at him.

"Making sure my captain didn't go down with his ship, sir."

Gordon slapped him on the shoulder,

"Then make yourself useful and tell that destroyer to send over a line."

The *Farnborough* was beached at Mill Cove, but she was never to sail again. A salvage team would remove her ordnance and anything useful and she would be reduced to scrap. Her crew got back their personal belongings and were assigned to new ships.

Gordon, Len and Ronald were summoned by the admiral as soon as the *Narwhal* dropped them off at Queenstown. June met them in the outer office. Gordon noticed that Q-5 had been removed from the active list.

"Well, I must say — for shipwrecked sailors you all look to be in amazing health," June said with a smile.

"We were lucky we didn't lose anyone and only a couple were wounded," Gordon replied.

"The admiral will see you right away."

June knocked on the door to his office and announced them.

"Gentlemen, please be seated."

They took seats around a meeting table that had been added to the office since their last visit.

"Firstly, congratulations on the sinking of the *U-83* and getting the *Farnborough* to shore. It is a shame that she will never be refloated, but she will always be remembered. Your crew will receive £1,000 in prize money. You three will be kept together as inspectors of shipping until you can find another vessel that is suited to join the Q-fleet."

That was welcome news and the three all smiled in joy.

"I am also informed by the Admiralty that you, Commander, will be put forward to receive the Victoria Cross for your actions."

Gordon sat back in his chair, shocked. "Good God," he gasped.

"Well done, Skipper!" Len and Ronald congratulated him.

"Not so fast, you two." The admiral smiled. "You are both getting DSOs for your part."

Now it was Gordon's turn to congratulate them.

A month's shore leave followed, and Gordon went home. It was Easter and he and Mary attended church and enjoyed each other's company. She was by now visibly pregnant. A letter arrived from Buckingham Palace summoning him to receive his VC. The citation, which benefited from the *Farnborough* being no more, read:

On 17 February 1917, in the north Atlantic, Commander Campbell, commanding HMS Farnborough *(Q-5) (one of the 'mystery' Q-ships) sighted a torpedo track. He altered course and allowed the torpedo to hit Q-5 aft by the engine-room bulkhead. The "panic party" got away convincingly, followed by the U-boat. When the submarine had fully surfaced and was within 100 yards of Q-5 — badly damaged and now lying very low in the water — the commander gave the order to fire. Almost all of the forty-five shells fired hit the SM U-83, which sank. Q-5 was taken in tow just in time and was safely beached. On 22 March 1916, another U-boat, SM U-68 was sunk by Farnborough.*

They travelled up to London by train and were met at Victoria station by his mother and father on the day before the investiture. They all stayed at the Strand Hotel that night and were at the palace in good time the next day. As only one guest was allowed to the investiture at the palace where he would receive his medal from the king, they would wait outside for him.

Gordon was dressed in his number one dress uniform, complete with ceremonial sword. Mary wore a very smart dress of Royal Navy blue with a corsage and a pretty hat. All four of them were admitted to the palace grounds and directed into the quadrangle. A covered area was set aside for the families of the recipients and Gordon and Mary were directed through the grand entrance to the green drawing room. When his turn came, they were summoned by a secretary, who took them into the throne room.

Gordon had been told what he must do and followed the protocol precisely. He found himself standing in front of King George V — who was dressed in military uniform festooned with honours — and bowed. The king was handed the VC by an equerry and stepped up to Gordon.

"I have read your citation and I congratulate you on sinking two submarines and for your gallantry in fighting while your ship was sinking," the king said as he pinned the medal to Gordon's chest. Then he stepped back and saluted him army style — an action that

Gordon returned navy style, with the palm down. The king shook his hand, and it was over. The secretary showed him out through the same green room and handed him the box that the medal and its ribbons could be stored in. An official photographer was set up in the quadrangle, where Gordon was photographed alone then with Mary and David.

"I will see prints get sent to you, sir. How many of each would you like?" the photographer asked.

Gordon looked to Mary, who answered: "Is it possible to have five of each?"

"That will be no problem. They will be sent through the navy office."

The five of them left together and walked out of the main gate set in the railings that separated the palace from the Queen Victoria Memorial. Several people congratulated him, and service men saluted. Then they walked across St James's Park to the Ritz for a celebratory meal.

All too soon, Gordon was back on duty. It was shore duty, admittedly, based at Plymouth so he could live at home, but as inspectors of shipping he and his shipmates would be travelling around the ports looking for suitable ships to convert to Q-ships. That meant they would visit not just the main ports but all ports where tramp steamers and larger fishing boats docked.

They were given a navy staff car and a rating to drive it. Gordon summarised their approach: "We will start in the west and work our way east. There are more ports along that stretch of coast than anywhere else in England."

They started at Padstow, which lay on the River Camel that emptied into the Atlantic. This north Cornwall town was a famous fishing and commercial port and was the main destination for coasters delivering coal to north Cornwall. It was busy, and a couple of deep-sea trawlers caught their eye but turned out to be too new and reserved. That is to say, they had a government licence that kept them out of the navy's hands.

They moved on to Newquay, but there were only small boats there; the same was true of St Ives. They moved down to the south coast and Penzance. This was more like it, and they found a deep-sea trawler that was steam powered and old enough not to be on the reserved list. They talked to her skipper.

"Are you the owner of this boat?" asked Gordon.

"I am, what of it?" the man said bluntly, clearly not trusting the men in Royal Navy uniforms.

"I am Commander Campbell and we are shipping inspectors. We want to requisition her," Gordon answered, knowing that dissembling would get him nowhere with blunt-spoken fishermen.

"She's my livelihood. You can't."

Gordon smiled at him. "You will be compensated, of course."

"What, at 10 shillings to the pound?"

"Actually, as fishing is seen as vital to the war effort you will be given enough to set you up with a new boat, and that one will fall under the reserve list," Ronald pointed out.

"The *Rosy*'s been in my family since she were built," the skipper said. "What do you want her for?"

Gordon leaned in conspiratorially. "We are going to make her into a Q-ship to sink enemy submarines."

"Oh." The fisherman took out a pipe and stuffed it with some short-cut shag tobacco. He lit it and it gave off a cloud of pungent smoke. "To sink subs, you say." He puffed and thought for a while. "All right, you can have her — but let me know when she gets one."

Their next stop was Falmouth, home of the packet ships in days gone by. The harbour, which was on the Penryn river, had been known in the past for being accessible when the wind was in any quarter except east by south-east — which meant almost never. The Carrick Roads provided a safe anchorage for many large ships making the transatlantic crossing.

Falmouth harbour was empty of large fishing boats because the fleet was out, so they hired a small one to take them to the Roads. As the weather was fair, the Roads was relatively empty, but one ship stood out.

"Can you take us around that one?" Gordon asked their skipper, who leaned on the tiller.

The ship was old and crusty with rust. She had seen better days but floated high in the water, showing a relatively clean bottom. The name painted on her stern was SS *Vittoria*, and she was out of Hull.

Ronald had a register of shipping, a weighty tome that contained the names of the owners of all ships registered in Great Britain and Northern Ireland. He looked her up.

"SS *Vittoria*, registered in Hull in 1902, owner is the Leith Hull and Hamburg Steam Packet Co."

"She looks the part, doesn't she?" Len said.

"Take us around to the ladder," Gordon said.

As they pulled up, a face appeared at the top of the rope ladder that hung down from the entry port.

"Who are you? I been watching you goin' roun' my ship," the broad Cornish voice of the man called down.

"Royal Navy shipping inspectors, can we come aboard?"

The man looked at them suspiciously then shouted, "Come on up."

The climb was precarious — the rope ladder steps were slippery at the bottom.

"Commander Campbell, pleased to meet you," Gordon said and held out his hand.

"I'm Captain Pedrick, what can I do for thee?"

"We would like to inspect your ship," Gordon said.

Pedrick looked at him quizzically. "Help yourself, it's your time you be wastin'."

Gordon checked out the bridge while Len inspected the boiler and engine rooms. The deck was teak and relatively unencumbered. Len bent to take a closer look at it.

"Solidly built, should take gun mounts with no problem."

Her foredeck was slightly raised behind hull plates that extended up around three and a half feet. Gordon could envision two centre-mounted 12-pounders that could fire either side. Behind the bridge and funnel was another open area of deck that, when he paced it off, he discovered would easily take a pair of torpedo tubes, and behind that was a raised section that could carry a 4-inch gun. She had a nice gently rounded stern that was ideal for a couple of depth charge racks.

Len came up from the engine room. "Her engine is old and coal-fired but in good condition. She seems tight and well maintained. She has a saltwater boiler that has been cleaned recently."

She would do nicely.

They returned to port and sent a telegram to the admiral telling him of their progress so far and about the two ships they wanted to requisition. They continued on, reaching Bridport before they found their third candidate.

Farnborough

The estuary of the River Brit had a relatively deep-water harbour that was well protected by a stone sea wall that doubled as a pier. Inside, the fishing fleet was in port and some fifteen or so boats lined the dock, stern on. Gordon and his colleagues walked along the line looking at each ship in turn, receiving hostile stares from crewmen as they did so.

"Do you think the word has got around?" Ronald said.

"Probably. Fishermen are a tight bunch," Gordon replied, then stopped at a steam drifter. She was around eighty-five feet long and eighteen feet across the beam. Wooden hulled and, by the look of her, more than ten years old.

"Perfect," Gordon said.

"She is, isn't she?" Ronald said

"Absolutely," Len said.

The *Dorset Maid*'s fate was sealed.

HMS Pargust

The *Vittoria* was brought in and sent to Queenstown. She was, Gordon thought, the perfect Q-ship. She was old and rusty but otherwise sound. Coal-fired with plenty of free deck space for concealed weapons. She was renamed *Pargust*. Most of the men from the *Farnborough* who were still ashore volunteered to join them.

During May 1917 she was fitted out at Haubowline with a single 4-inch gun, two QF 12-pounders, two Maxim machine guns, a pair of 18-inch torpedo tubes and depth charges. She also got the latest Marconi radio set and a pair of 24-inch carbon arc spotlights. A petrol generator was mounted on the main deck, to power the new electrical circuits for the radio and search lights independently from the engine. A dummy 4-pounder was mounted on her stern to make her look like a regular, lightly armed cargo ship. Gordon and the two lieutenants oversaw every step and were joined by Lieutenant Francis Hereford as it neared completion. Hereford was their torpedo officer, which meant he was also responsible for the electrical systems and communications. He came with a leading torpedo man, a PO and a seaman gunner torpedo man first class, who were also electricians.

"Make sure all wiring is concealed," Gordon told them. "Especially the antenna and its feed."

The torpedo tubes were mounted aft of the funnel and could be turned to both sides of the ship. They were thirteen feet long and the torpedo was ejected using a black powder charge. Hereford spoke to Gordon about these.

"The concealments on both sides have to be dropped to give us space to swing them. I would like to install a common release for them. I also need a watertight locker for the instruments."

Gordon knew what he meant by *instruments*. Calculating the angle of launch relative to the ship's speed, target range, course and speed was complicated and needed a quadrant to measure angles and a slide rule made especially for the job.

"Make it happen, Mr Hereford. Anything else?"

"Yes, there is, actually. The depth charge racks are covered by a tarpaulin, which I'm pretty sure any half decent submarine commander will see through in an instant."

Gordon knew what he meant. The problem was that the racks, which hung over the stern, were long and wide and hard to conceal.

Hereford had more to say. "They're mounted side by side in the centre of the stern, which makes them harder to hide. If they were mounted further outboard, we could disguise them individually as deck lockers or cargo."

Gordon liked the way he thought. "That is excellent thinking. Get them moved and disguise them as stacks of lumber. It makes more sense to have something like that hanging over the stern."

By 5 June, armed and ready to go, the *Pargust* left Queenstown and headed down into the area where they had sunk the *U-83*.

"Gentlemen, if we get lucky, we will be one of the most successful submarine-hunting crews in the navy," Gordon had told the crew prior to departure, and he was right. Few others had sunk two, let alone three submarines.

The engine ran smoothly, giving out a nice tell-tale ribbon of smoke that could be seen from miles away. They "poodled", as Gordon put it, travelling at no more than five knots. Gordon was fishing, and now presented a juicy morsel for a greedy grey metal shark to devour.

"Skipper, we have received a mayday. Cargo ship *Andromeda*, forty miles south of here," Midshipman Radcliffe reported.

"Thank you, Hardy. Have you plotted a course?"

"Aye, Skipper. Steer 1, 8, 7 degrees magnetic. At full speed we should be there in just over five hours."

"Helm!"

"Aye-aye — 1, 8, 7 degrees, full ahead."

Gordon grinned; they worked as a well-oiled team.

The old ship creaked as she sped along at eight knots, leaving a phosphorescent trail in the sea. It was getting dark when they arrived at the location of the sinking.

"Launch the boats, pick up survivors. Get a net over the side," Gordon ordered.

A short search found survivors both in the water and in a lifeboat; there was no sign of the ship, just an oil slick and debris. The *Andromeda*'s skipper came up on the bridge and introduced himself.

"Captain MacKeigan. Thank you for picking us up, Captain!"

"Call me Gordon. You're more than welcome ... but you may not appreciate it in the long run." Gordon nodded at the main deck.

MacKeigan looked down at the deck and the concealed weapons.

"You're a Q-ship?"

"Yes."

MacKeigan was philosophical about it. "Well, we might be getting wet again. But at least this time we can fight back."

Gordon smiled and offered him his tobacco pouch, as he noticed a pipe sticking out of his top pocket.

"Don't mind if I do." MacKeigan grinned. They had just lit their pipes when the horizon was lit by a flash.

"Seems our German friends are busy this afternoon," Gordon said and nodded to the helm, who steered straight for it.

The second ship was a tanker, and she was burning ferociously. The U-boat had torpedoed her without warning and survivors were in the water, covered in oil and in danger of being burned alive. The *Pargust* hove to and lowered a pair of boats, her men displaying exceptional courage by rowing close to the burning oil to pull men out of harm's way.

Gordon watched and pondered that they were a sitting duck outlined against the flames as they were. The gun crews were at the ready, torpedo men at their station. Everybody was tense, waiting for the explosion that would announce they were under attack.

Gordon called to the radioman, "Send a message: *Q-19 has rescued two sets of survivors, some in urgent need of medical care. Returning to Queenstown.* Give our position."

They steered for Queenstown, and as soon as they docked the survivors were taken ashore to a fleet of ambulances and from there to the hospital. As soon as all were in safe hands, they set out again.

The following morning, twenty miles off the southernmost tip of Ireland, they responded to another mayday. German activity in the area had increased, so they were on full alert and expected to be attacked at any time. This time the ship was the *Liverpool Rose*, a relatively new cargo ship. The mayday said they had been torpedoed and shelled — meaning the submarine had surfaced to finish them off.

This was a brave submarine commander, prepared to take a risk. Just what Gordon had been hoping for. A two-hour sail took them to the wreck. The lifeboats were not far from their capsized ship and full of men. They brought them alongside.

"Cargo nets over the starboard side, help them aboard," Gordon called.

The boats came alongside, the wounded handed up first, then the able-bodied. Gordon asked the cook to prepare Bovril laced with rum for the survivors and asked the skipper to come to the bridge.

"Thank you," Captain Edward Monkton said, as he clasped his mug in his hands to warm them.

"Tell me about the attack," said Gordon.

"We were hit by a torpedo amidships from relatively close range. We started to list almost immediately, but I felt that we had a chance of saving her. That's when he surfaced astern of us about 500 yards away. He circled us and signalled that we were to abandon ship. He said we had fifteen minutes to get everyone into the boats and away. We had already sent a mayday by that time, so I ordered the abandon ship."

"Then he shelled her?"

"He did, but he could have saved his ammunition. Without us on board to make repairs she would have capsized anyway."

This was all good information and Gordon soaked it up.

The lookouts were vigilant and there was one possible sighting of a periscope. However, they weren't attacked and they left the sinking hulk behind.

Later that day they spotted yet more survivors in the water, from a separate attack. They were extremely lucky, as they had not sent a mayday before abandoning ship. There were only four people alive in a boat that had lost its oars and was adrift. They had been in the water for fifteen hours or more. Their new guests told them they were all that was left of a steamer with a crew of nineteen.

The day closed with the *Pargust* back in port offloading their guests. The admiral visited that evening. "That submarine is still out there."

"We're going fishing tomorrow," Gordon replied.

The admiral chuckled. "With you as the bait. Do you think you can get him?"

Gordon shrugged. "I'll make us as attractive a target as he's ever seen — the rest is up to him."

The admiral nodded. He appreciated the risk they had to take and knew how far Gordon was prepared to go. The crew stayed aboard, and she slipped back out at midnight.

7 June 1917 dawned misty, with a choppy sea and fresh breeze that did nothing to clear it. Visibility was down to about 200 yards. They were sailing west, sounding their horn regularly, when, as Lieutenant Loveless described it later, "the world went to hell in a handbasket".

At 08:00 a torpedo hit them from very close range on the starboard quarter. Gordon was on the bridge and knocked off his feet. The damage was immense: the boiler room, engine room and No. 5 hold immediately flooded, and the starboard lifeboat was blown to matchwood.

"Action stations! Damage report!" Gordon barked as he picked himself up. Men ran to their stations.

"No answer from the boiler or engine rooms, Skipper," Lieutenant Stuart reported. We are holed at the waterline."

Gordon reacted as all expected.

"Panic party away!"

Loveless and Boyd tried to reach their men in the boiler and engine rooms but it was hopeless — the water was up to the deck. They banged a spanner on the deck to see if the men were trapped in an air pocket. There was no response. PO Arnold Smith and the stokers, Frampton and Carley, were all dead.

The starboard-forward 12-pounder gun crew was getting the gun ready when the gun port broke loose, threatening to give the game away. Able Seaman William Williams spotted the danger and moved fast. He threw himself under the port that was swinging down and by sheer strength pushed it back into position, his muscles straining as the steel panel dug into his back.

"Lend a hand!" he cried.

The gun crew rapidly came to his aid and used timbers to shore up the port. Williams practically collapsed after the load was taken off him. The port weighed close to half a ton.

The *UC-29* was a Type-UC II minelaying submarine. She had two forward-facing torpedo tubes mounted externally on the hull and one internal tube mounted aft. She had no reloads for the forward tubes and seven for the aft.

"It's a good hit, Heinz," said her captain, Ernst Rosenow, to his number two. "She's disabled and down at the stern."

"Should we finish her off with the stern tube?" Heinz asked.

Rosenow was cautious but didn't want to waste torpedoes. However, he was well aware of Q-ships and wasn't going to take any chances.

"Stand us off at 400 metres."

He watched the panic party through his periscope. One of the boats was hung up at an angle with the men desperately trying to free a jammed tackle. He gave a running commentary.

"They're making a good show of being disorganised. Either that, or we scared the shit out of them. They've launched three boats so far. There's an officer in each."

The crew in the control room laughed.

"They've launched another boat."

"That's four — how many do they carry?" Heinz asked.

"We destroyed one. I don't see any more on the deck."

He watched as the fourth boat, with an officer in a uniform coat at the tiller, rowed away.

"Take us up close behind her. There are no threats on her stern."

The submarine surfaced fifty metres behind the ship and started to follow the boats, a machine gunner having been told to keep them in his sights. Ernst homed in on the fourth one as he assumed she carried the captain. He wanted to interrogate that man.

In the boats, Lieutenant Francis Hereford, in charge of the panic party as his torpedoes and depth charges had been rendered useless by the torpedo hit, realised he was being followed and ordered the boats back to the ship. "If that bastard wants to follow, let him follow us there. Anybody got any idea what he's shouting?"

"He wants to know if any of us know the way back to Germany. He's lost," quipped Leading Seaman Parmeter, and all the men laughed.

* * *

"They are trying to regain the ship!" Rosenow shouted angrily and waved his arms at Hereford, who stoically ignored him.

The game was not played out yet, and Hereford and his men were key players.

"Get us between them and their ship," Rosenow ordered, then turned to the conning tower machine gunner. "Put a burst across his stern."

Gordon watched from his position on the bridge. He was hidden from the submarine's view but could observe them through a scuttle. "Oh, well done, Hereford! Got you, you bastard. OPEN FIRE!" Gordon cried as the sub slid into the perfect position for his guns to attack.

The gun ports dropped, the forward one clanging to the deck as the timbers were kicked away and every gun opened up. The gun captains urged their gun crews to extraordinary efforts and poured fire into the submarine at a rate better than fifteen rounds a minute.

"POUR IT ON!" Gordon shouted from the bridge.

Numerous hits made the *UC-29*'s conning tower into a sieve, and Rosenow was killed — cut in half by a shell. The sub had been caught completely off guard and now oil squirted from holes in her side. Crewmen poured out of the hatches and conning tower, their hands held aloft. They looked to be surrendering.

"Cease fire!" Gordon ordered.

As soon as the guns stopped, they heard the U-boat's diesels roar and she started to move away, increasing speed, trying to escape in the mist.

They had been played.

Gordon was outraged. "FIRE! SINK THE DEVIOUS BASTARDS!"

The guns didn't hesitate. The Maxims swept the deck. The big guns opened up, the loaders working as fast as they could. Suddenly there was an enormous explosion, and the submarine lifted out of the water.

"Good God, she's split in half!" Ronald gasped.

"We must have hit one of her mines," Gordon replied with a satisfied smile.

As peace settled over the ship, the boat crews made a valiant effort, pulling against the wind and tide, to save any survivors. They only succeeded in pulling one officer and a crewman out of the water.

Gordon turned his attention to his ship and crew. "Is the generator still running?"

"It is," reported Ronald.

"Send a message."

Q-19 SERIOUSLY DAMAGED. IN NEED OF ASSISTANCE. POSITION 51°27'N 10°70'W. SUBMARINE UC-29 SUNK WITH TWO SURVIVORS.

Help arrived in less than an hour in the form of USS *Cushing*, an American destroyer, and the sloops *Crocus* and *Zinnia*. All crew were transferred to the *Zinnia* except for Ronald and a skeleton crew of three men. Gordon had slipped on the sloping deck and sprained his ankle so badly he couldn't stand, and his exec made the decision for him. A line was fired across from the *Cushing* and a towline hauled aboard. Another came across from the *Zinnia*, and a third from the *Crocus*. The *Pargust*, still taking on water, was getting heavier by the hour.

They reached Queenstown after a hard two days with the *Pargust* so low in the water that the skeleton crew had to be taken off.

The tow was taken over by tugs, which had high-volume pumps to keep her afloat.

As the *Zinnia* came alongside the dock, Gordon saw a group of officers, including his admiral, gathered waiting for them.

"Admiral Sir Lewis Bayly is among the greeting party. Get the men into parade order as they get ashore," Gordon told his exec. In naval tradition he would be last to leave the ship, and in any case, his ankle had him walking with the aid of crutches.

As the last man descended the gangway, Gordon shook hands with the captain of the *Zinnia*, who left the ship ahead of him. Then he hobbled down the gangway, refusing any aid. He made his way to the front of the parading men and joined his exec. The two stood before the admiral and Ronald ordered, "Parade *at-ten-shun*!"

Bayly stepped forward and saluted Gordon and the crew. "At ease, men." He held out his hand to Gordon. "Another bloody good show, Commander. Your third?"

"It is, sir." Gordon shook his hand.

"I am informed that your crew will receive £1,000 as a reward. I am absolutely certain your officers will be rewarded with awards as well."

It was not until November 1918 that the full account of the action was published, as the secrecy of the Q-ships was paramount. Even then, the *Pargust* was not mentioned by name until the files were eventually declassified. The Admiralty was in a quandary; every member of the crew had been equally valiant during the action, and they couldn't decide who to nominate for Victoria Crosses as only two would be awarded. In the end, they let the men decide which officer and enlisted man would get the medals. The crew and officers held a ballot and William Williams and Ronald Stuart were chosen. Stuart was the first Anglo-Canadian to receive the honour. Fourteen other crewmen received medals and Campbell and Hereford received DSOs. In addition, Stuart was promoted to lieutenant commander and given his own command, HMS *Tamarisk*.

The award of the Victoria Cross alone, without any details, was announced in the *London Gazette* of 20 July 1917. The actual citation, held at the Admiralty and not released publicly until declassified, read:

To receive the Victoria Cross.
Lieut. Ronald Neil Stuart, DSO, RNR
Sea. William Williams, RNR, ON, 6224A

Lieutenant Stuart and Seaman Williams were selected by the officers and ship's company respectively of one of H.M. Ships to receive the Victoria Cross under Rule 13 of the Royal Warrant dated 29th January, 1856.

On the 7th June, 1917, while disguised as a British merchant vessel with a dummy gun mounted aft, HMS "Pargust" was torpedoed at very close range. Her boiler room, engine room, and No. 5 hold were immediately flooded, and the starboard lifeboat was blown to pieces. The weather was misty at the time, fresh breeze and a choppy sea. The "Panic Party", under the command of Lieutenant F. R. Hereford, DSC, RNR, abandoned ship, and as the last boat was shoving off, the periscope of the submarine was observed close before the port beam about 400 yards distant. The enemy then submerged, and periscope reappeared directly astern, passing to the starboard quarter, and then round to the port beam, when it turned again towards the ship, breaking surface about 50 yards away. The lifeboat, acting as a lure, commenced to pull round the stern; submarine followed closely and Lieutenant Hereford, with complete disregard of the danger incurred from the fire of either ship or submarine (who had trained a Maxim on the lifeboat), continued to decoy her to within 50 yards of the ship. The "Pargust" then opened fire with all guns, and the submarine, with oil squirting from her side and the crew pouring out of the conning tower, steamed slowly across the bows with a heavy list. The enemy crew held up their hands in token of surrender, whereupon fire immediately ceased. The submarine then began to move away at a gradually increasing speed, apparently endeavouring to escape in the mist. Fire was reopened until she sank, one man clinging to the bow as she went down. The boats, after a severe pull to the windward, succeeded in saving one officer and one man. American destroyers and a British sloop arrived shortly afterwards, and the "Pargust" was towed back to port. As on the previous occasions, officers and men displayed the utmost courage and confidence in their captain, and the action serves as an example of what perfect discipline, when coupled with such confidence, can achieve.

The *Pargust* was refloated and repaired sufficiently to keep her on the surface, then towed to Devonport. She underwent extensive repairs to rebuild her stern. The US Navy decided that they wanted to get in on submarine hunting, and *Pargust* was one of two ships assigned to them in October 1917. However, her repairs were not completed in time, and so she was returned to the Royal Navy. In May 1918 she was renamed *Pangloss* and sent to Gibraltar. There she joined a special service force that patrolled the mid-Atlantic region, where German Type-139 U-cruisers — large, long-range U-boats — were operating. She saw no further action before the end of the war and returned to merchant service as SS *Johann Faulbaum*. Ironically, she was sunk by RAF aircraft near Kirkness on 13 May 1944.

Home Leave

Gordon was awarded some time off and went home to Saltash in June 1917 to spend it with Mary and David. His Victoria Cross and DSO made him a local hero, and while it wasn't regulation to salute a VC holder, the tradition was to do so. The only way he could go anywhere and not be bothered was to go in mufti.

Mary was naturally delighted to have her husband back, and he kept her blissfully unaware of his adventures and brushes with the Grim Reaper. Baby David was a good child and they didn't employ a nanny.

A letter arrived, written in green ink and with the fouled anchor seal, which is the seal of the Lord High Admiral of the United Kingdom.

"What is it? More orders?" Mary asked.

"No, I'm promoted to captain!" Gordon replied and handed her the letter.

Mary read it and noted, "There's no mention of a ship."

"No, I noticed that. That will come later, I expect." He was happy for now. Promotion came with an increase in pay as well as responsibility and he suspected his days with the Q-ships would be limited.

"We should celebrate!" Mary grinned.

By then there was a general ban on cars unless one had a special dispensation, and for official business Gordon had the use of a staff car and driver. So for local journeys they would walk, or Mary would ride a rather old bicycle. To go further, they would take the train. There were taxis to be found at ranks in the towns nearby, or one could hitch a ride with a lorry. In this case, they caught the train at Devonport to go to Exeter for the day. The seven o'clock train from Devonport arrived in Exeter at nine and they bought second-class return tickets. Little David travelled for free in his push chair. They found a café in the high street serving breakfast, bread and butter with bacon and eggs and a mug of good strong tea. A queue was forming across the road and Gordon asked Mary why.

"Oh, that's for margarine. There will be a queue at the pork butcher's too, with the price of poultry being so high."

Living in Saltash, they had not experienced this, as local farmers sold direct to the local shops and the butchers always had rabbits and pigeons as well as beef and pork. Chickens were commonly kept in back gardens, so eggs and chickens for roasting were readily available. The same could not be said for the cities.

"How much does a bird cost?" Gordon asked.

"Well, turkey is two and six to two and nine a pound, goose is anything up to two and six, and chickens are twenty-four bob a brace!"

"Good Lord! That's a fortune, how can the people afford it?"

Manual labourers only earned between thirty-five and fifty shillings a week and even qualified men like engine drivers only earned sixty-eight to eighty-three shillings per week. Most families had three or more children; the official average was three and a half children per family, with the poor having more. Out of that they had to pay rent, as most lived in rented houses — only ten per cent of people in the UK owned their own house. Coal was the main fuel for heating and cooking and cost fifteen shillings and seven pence per ton. The average household used two to three tons a year. Lighting was by oil lamp or candle for the poor, with gas lamps in the better parts of town.

The waitress wandered off to serve someone else and they finished their breakfast.

"Let's visit the cathedral," Mary said.

Exeter Cathedral was in the centre of the city and surrounded by the Cathedral Green. It was a peaceful place where people could go and simply sit quietly or let their children play. The cathedral was founded in 1050 in the reign of Edward the Confessor and rebuilt in the gothic style in the thirteenth and fourteenth centuries.

They walked across the green, side by side, with Gordon pushing the pushchair and enjoying the sun. Gordon stopped and looked up at the imposing building before them. "How did they manage to build this in the time of William the Conqueror?" he pondered aloud.

"With a lot of stone masons, I expect," Mary said, and laughed.

"That tower is impressive," Gordon said.

"Not as impressive as the spire in Salisbury — that's the tallest in Britain."

"Well, they must have longer arms in Wiltshire," Gordon joked.

They went inside through the west door, and discovered that inside, the cathedral was cool to the point of being chilly. The light from the stained-glass windows made coloured patterns on the floor. Little David slept.

They went to the astronomical clock. "It's hard to believe this was made in the fifteenth century," Gordon said, as they looked at the mechanism that ticked gently in front of them. A bell rang the quarter hour. The main display showed the current hour, day of the lunar month and phase of the moon in a series of concentric circles. A fleur-de-lis representing the sun indicated the hour of the day on the outer circle; the tail of the fleur-de-lis pointed to the day of the lunar month on the inner numbered circle. A half-black, half-silver moon showed the phase of the moon, and the earth was depicted as a golden ball in the centre. It was highly impressive.

Mary was duly impressed too, but not as mechanically minded as her husband, and they moved on to look at the tombs. These were mostly former bishops and a few local aristocrats from days gone by.

The family walked quietly around the building, soaking up the peaceful atmosphere. A service started and they took seats to listen. The organ started playing the requiem and an angelic contralto sang, filling the cathedral with a wondrous sound.

They lunched in a café in Little Castle Street that served sandwiches and cakes, then visited the ruins of Exeter Castle. It was built by William the Conqueror in 1068, but all that was left was the gatehouse with its circular arch, some of the original walls and a couple of towers. The Campbells walked atop the most intact section of wall, which gave them a magnificent view over the city.

All too soon it was time to catch the train back to Devonport and they were making their way towards St David's station along Howell Road when they came upon a bicycle shop. Gordon stopped and looked at a display of Raleigh bicycles for ladies and gentlemen. They had rim brakes as well as comfortable-looking saddles.

"What do you think? Your old bicycle is worn out and I don't have one," said Gordon.

Mary looked at the lady's model, which was described as an "all-steel lady's roadster" and priced at eleven pounds, ten shillings. The sprung saddle looked a whole lot more comfortable than Mary's current one, and the shop had baby seats that could be fitted behind the saddle

"With the hills in Cornwall it would be nice to have one with gears."

The owner of the shop noticed them and came out to chat. "Good afternoon," he said cheerfully. "Are you interested in a new bicycle?"

"Two, actually," Gordon said, taking out his pipe and filling it. "Do you have any with gears?"

"I have hub-geared wheels I can fit to any bicycle. Which ones are you interested in?"

Gordon had puffed his pipe into action and used the stem to point to two bicycles. "Those — with gears and a basket and a baby seat for the lady's cycle. If we can take them today."

The shop keeper rubbed his hands together and assured them, "I can have them ready in an hour."

There was a pub just down the road and the last train would leave in two hours, so they went to have a drink.

"That smells divine," Mary said as another customer was served a steaming plate of steak and kidney pudding and mashed potatoes.

"I am rather hungry," Gordon said, and beckoned the barmaid over. It had been some time since lunch and he was used to three square a day. "Can we have two of those, please?"

"Sorry, love, but we're only serving food to servicemen," she replied, seeing they were dressed as civilians.

Gordon got out his service card and showed it to her.

"Thank you, Captain, two meals coming up!" the waitress replied, including Mary in the order.

The steak and kidney pudding was made with a suet pastry that had been steamed for at least an hour and was rich with onions, carrots, tender beef and chunks of kidney. It was served with buttery mashed potatoes and broccoli. They finished it off with apple pie and custard.

The bikes were ready when they returned, and Gordon paid the man the £25 he asked for. They rode to the station with David on his seat and the pushchair tied to the back of Gordon's bike. When the train arrived, they loaded their new steeds into the guard's van. When they arrived in Devonport, they retrieved the bikes and rode home in the dark. They had dynamo-powered lights which dimly lit the road ahead, but the only cars were military or taxis and those were very few and far between.

The following days were spent cycling through the countryside and picnicking on the cliffs and hills of Cornwall and West Devon. It was the best of times and gave Gordon a period of peace to recover from the mayhem of the Q-ships. A neighbour's teenage daughter babysat for them and they went to the cinema in Plymouth and watched the latest Charlie Chaplin film, *The Immigrant*. Gordon laughed so hard, tears ran down his face.

They took their bikes to Tavistock on the train and rode up into Dartmoor. They passed across the western part of the moor to Merrivale, which consisted of a farm, a pub and a quarry. A short diversion found Bronze Age megaliths and some of the famous Dartmoor ponies. The weather stayed fine as they continued across the moor to Dartmeet. Then the moor performed one of its infamous tricks; the weather closed in and a thick fog descended.

"Good grief, where did this come from?" Mary said, as the visibility dropped to fifty G and the temperature with it.

"It's not far to Ashburton, we need to keep going. We can find a pub and have lunch there."

Gordon was right. As they emerged from the fog bank and entered Ashburton, the White Hart pub was right in front of them. Fresh bread, cheese and local ham washed down with the local beer refreshed them.

"This must be better than you get on board," Mary said.

"Our ship is not like a destroyer or a battleship, you know. We don't eat preserved meat as we can restock every time we're in port," Gordon replied with a grin.

Finally, they rode to Buckfast to visit the abbey. It was the home of a group of Benedictine monks who were restoring the once-splendid buildings to their former glory. Gordon approached one and said, "Good morning, can you tell me how many monks are here?"

The monk smiled and replied, with a distinct French accent, "There are just us four and the Abbot."

"You are restoring the church yourselves?"

"Every stone is laid by us."

"How do you fund it?" Gordon asked.

"By the will of God, donations pay for the stone and mortar."

Gordon looked at the wooden scaffolding and the manual hoists and took his wallet from his pocket. He took a ten-bob note from it and handed it to the monk. "This should help, brother."

The monks also made a rather good mead from their own honey and a bottle found its way into Mary's basket.

A railway branch line operated from Buckfast, and got them back to Plymouth and home.

As he spent more time cycling and walking with his family, Gordon knew that he was getting fitter. Indeed, he was starting to think he should get his uniforms taken in when he received new orders via a telegram from the admiral.

Farnborough

Captain G. Campbell, VC, DSO, RN
Report to HMDY Portsmouth to take command of HMS Dunraven *by July 1. Your old crew will join you.*

That still gave them a few days and they made the most of it. But all good things come to an end, and Gordon was soon packing his sea chest. A taxi would pick him up and take him to Dartmouth station, where he would get a train to Portsmouth.

HMS Dunraven

Gordon was stiff after the four-hour railway journey that was only broken when he changed trains in Salisbury. When he walked across the bridge over the tracks to change platform, he noticed the spire of the cathedral to the south-west. *Mary was right, it is impressive,* he thought. The train pulled into Portsmouth station on time, and he looked for a taxi. His sea chest was not the easiest to carry and he didn't fancy walking to the docks. He found a cab on a short rank outside the main entrance and asked the driver to drive him to the dockyard.

"Going to sea, Captain?" the lady driver asked. She was dark-haired and looked to be in her early thirties. Many of the jobs normally held by men had, by necessity, been taken over by women.

"Soon," he replied.

She smiled at him in the mirror.

It was just a few minutes' drive to the dock gates, where they were stopped by a marine. "Papers please, sir."

Gordon handed over his card and orders, which the marine scanned thoroughly and compared to a list he had pinned to a board in the guardroom.

"The *Dunraven* is on dock six, the taxi can take you all the way to her."

Before the taxi pulled away, the marine smiled at the driver. "Evening, Martha. You singing in the Six Bells tonight?"

"I am Freddy, see you there."

She engaged the gears and pulled away.

"You're a singer?" Gordon asked.

"I sing for my supper."

Gordon assumed this meant she got paid with a meal. Soon the dock came into view, with an old cargo ship tied up alongside.

"That's your ship?" Martha asked, surprised.

"It is," Gordon replied, hiding a grin.

"Who did you upset?" she said, then laughed.

Gordon didn't answer; he simply swung his sea chest to his shoulder and walked towards his latest charge.

You could tell the new men from the old hands; the former were dressed smartly or in uniform. Gordon had called the men to the foredeck to see what he had been given. He recognised many of his old crew, who were now bearded or unshaven and dressed like cargo steamer hands. He was pleased to see his gunners aboard.

"You new men, go into town and find second-hand clothes shops. Get clothes that are well made but shabby, like those our brothers in the merchant service wear. Do not tell anyone why you're buying them and do not talk about the ship to anyone or even among yourselves ashore. The Germans are good at spotting Q-ships and finding out which ships to avoid."

He let that sink in, then continued: "As we are coming out of Portsmouth, we will be watched, so no saluting and no navy ranks are to be used. I am the skipper or master, the executive officer is the first mate and all other officers are the second to fourth mates; CPOs are bosuns. Everyone in the engine room is an engineer, including the stokers."

He noticed the gunners looking smug.

"Gunners do not exist, nor do torpedo men. They have no place on a merchant ship, so are just hands. If we go ashore, you are to behave like merchant navy men and avoid pubs where members of the Andrew go. I do not want to have to bail you out of jail. Does everyone understand?"

A ragged, *Aye, Skipper*, interspersed with a few *Aye, Captains* was the response.

"Try that again."

This time they all got it right.

He needed to ballast the ship to make it look as though she was carrying cargo, but at the same time wanted to improve her buoyancy to keep her afloat if she was torpedoed. Part of the ballast problem was solved when Gordon heard that a friend had been killed on a Q-ship by a splinter passing through the wooden bridge wall. To avoid a similar incident, he had armour plating fitted inside the walls of the bridge. Another innovation was a perforated steam pipe that wound around the upper works with a valve on the bridge that could release steam whenever he liked, simulating a hit on the engine room. The guns also helped *Dunraven*'s trim as she had a 4-inch gun, four 12-pounders, two 14-inch torpedoes and depth charges. She also carried the standard merchantman's 2.5-pounder, proudly displayed on the afterdeck. Simulated deck cargo helped to hide the guns and torpedo tubes and included four well-crafted railway trucks made from wood and canvas. Gordon solved the buoyancy issue by loading wood in the hold. It added weight to the ship while providing buoyancy.

As Ronald Stuart had been given his own ship, Gordon needed a new executive officer/first mate. Charles Bonner, who had served with him on the *Pargust*, and earned a DSC there, was chosen; he knew the drills and how the Q-ship should work. Discipline and courage would do the rest.

Gordon initially planned to revisit his old hunting grounds to the south of Ireland, but a swathe of reports changed his mind.

"Look at these," he said to Charles Bonner. "They're all from the Bay of Biscay."

Charles leafed through the flimsies that had come from the radio room. "Looks like a sub is very active down there, maybe more than one," he replied.

"My thoughts entirely. I think we should go down and see if we can catch one."

"I'll get Radcliffe to plot a course."

It was 4 August 1917. Midshipman Radcliffe had been promoted to sub lieutenant after the sinking of the *UC-29* and was now their official navigator. He plotted a course to take them through the middle of the reported attacks.

"Course 2, 4, 0 for two days at eight knots, then 1, 8, 0 to take us past the Bay. That way we look like we're heading to the Middle East," Radcliffe said.

"Excellent," Gordon said, rubbing his hands together.

The *Dunraven* chugged out of Portsmouth waters into the English Channel, set her course and did what any good merchant ship would do — zigzag. The zigzag added a little to the distance but made it harder for any U-boat to set up a shot. However, Gordon didn't want to make things too hard for them, so the zigzag was very regular. The weather was good, with visibility clear to the horizon.

"Perfect hunting weather," Gordon said.

They were disguised as a collier and sailed under the name *Boverton*. Regular inspections made sure that all the disguises would drop perfectly when they needed them to, including the fake lifeboat that hid the 4-inch gun astern. The mock-lifeboat was hinged down the keel like a pair of clamshells and dropped down, exposing the gun. The gun had been named Venus by some wag with a better-than-average education, and the name was written on the barrel in white paint.

They steamed west to Falmouth before turning south. The trip down to Ushant took two days and from there they were in their hunting territory in the Bay of Biscay. A day later, on 8 August 1917, they were 130 miles south-west of Ushant when they spotted a U-boat on the surface. It was the *UC-71*, commanded by Reinhold Saltzwedel.

Oberleutnant zur See Reinhold Saltzwedel was an experienced U-boat commander. The *UC-71* was his fifth command; his track record was excellent, with a score of one hundred and ten vessels sunk for 172,000 tons. He was so successful that the 2nd U-boat Flotilla of the Kriegsmarine in Wilhelmshaven was named after him. He was twenty-seven years old, tall, blond, good looking and professional. His men adored him and would follow him to hell and back.

The *UC-71* was on the surface when the lookout called out, "Smoke on the horizon." Reinhold scanned the northern horizon with his high-powered Zeiss binoculars. He spotted the lone ship and guessed it was a cargo ship of some sort heading south.

"We will close with her, ahead full."

He manoeuvred to get ahead of the ship so he could submerge and have her come to him.

"Herr Kapitän, it is a collier and is flying the British flag," his executive officer said.

Heading to Alexandria or Gibraltar.

"Dive the boat," Reinhold commanded.

On the *Dunraven*, the crew started their well-practised routine of response to a U-boat sighting. The guns were manned, and the panic party was readied. Gordon was confident they could gain another victory. The men were excited but disciplined. He turned to Charles and said, "We will not try to avoid a torpedo."

"I didn't think we would. It's not a bad trade, a tatty old collier for one of their shiny new submarines."

As so they waited, scanning the sea for the tell-tale silvery track of an incoming torpedo.

Through his periscope, Reinhold watched the ship approach and decided on his plan of attack. "Let her pass over us and we will surface behind her. It will be a gun action — I will not waste a torpedo on her."

The throb of the ship's engines as she passed overhead echoed through the hull. The gun crew were ready at the ladder to the hatch. They would be first up to clear the gun for immediate action; Reinhold would follow and command from the conning tower. His men were the best in the submarine fleet and operated as a well-oiled machine. The ship was 1,000 metres off. It was 11:43 in the morning.

"Battle surface."

The engineers blew all the tanks, and the bow planes were put to full up. The boat shot to the surface, and as soon as the conning tower was clear the hatch was sprung and the gun crew poured out. By the time Reinhold was on the bridge, they were firing their first shot.

Immediately, the target ship made smoke and a boat was lowered. The gun crew got the range and shells started hitting the stern of the ship. There was a huge explosion.

"What the hell … ? What caused that?"

Then a shell hit the aft lifeboat on the stern deck, smashing it to pieces and exposing Venus.

Reinhold's response was immediate. "That's a gun! It's one of their decoy ships! Clear the deck! DIVE!"

Once he was in the conning tower control room he ordered, "Prepare for torpedo attack."

Things were not going to plan. The depth charges had started a fire astern, and the 4-inch gun had been blown away, killing one of the gun crew and wounding the others. Their cover was blown. Now the submarine was diving.

"Send away a second panic party — put the wounded in with them," Gordon ordered.

The boat was launched and moved away.

"Periscope 700 yards off the port quarter. Moving abeam."

Time seemed to stand still as the U-boat got itself into position. The *Dunraven* had no depth charges now, so could only sit and wait.

Reinhold was not in a hurry. The ship was going nowhere, and they had picked up no replies to her mayday. He manoeuvred the *UC-71* into the perfect firing position.

"Open outer door, torpedo one."

He started his firing solution.

"Angle on the bow, zero degrees. Range, 680 metres."

"Torpedo ready," said Andre Schmitz, his executive officer.

"Shoot!"

"Torpedo track!"

Gordon watched as the torpedo came straight for the side below the bridge. He moved to the other side just as it hit. The coal bunker was holed, and the port boiler room was flooded. He ordered the engineers up on deck and sent a third panic party off. This left just him, the torpedo men and the gunners of the two forward guns aboard.

The submarine surfaced again and started shelling them, and the *Dunraven* replied — ineffectually, although it did force her to submerge again. As she started to go down, Gordon shouted, "Fire torpedoes!"

With dull thuds the two torpedoes flew into the water and headed for the submarine.

Reinhold heard the torpedoes and called out, "Take us down to twenty metres."

The torpedoes passed above and forward of the control room.

"Periscope depth."

He sat and observed his quarry for some time. In his estimation she was sinking and would go down in a couple of hours. She was still armed, and he didn't want to waste another torpedo on her — nor did he want to get into a gunfight.

He checked his watch. It was 3 p.m. "Radio, have you heard anything?"

"A ship has answered his mayday."

That decided it.

"Steer course due east, half ahead. We will leave this ship to sink in its own time."

On the *Dunraven*, Gordon knew they were doomed and he ordered the remaining crew to abandon ship. An hour later, she was still afloat when HMS *Christopher* came into view. The destroyer was one of the most welcome sights Gordon had ever seen.

The men were picked up by the *Christopher* and Gordon met her captain, who suggested trying to tow the *Dunraven* back to Plymouth. Gordon's first lieutenant, Charles Bonner, RNR, insisted on being the one to return to the ship to steer her and he was accompanied by four men who would attach the tow.

Gordon had brought his log with him, and when he had a moment he sat and wrote:

It was a fair fight, and I lost it. Referring to my crew, words cannot express what I am feeling. No one let me down. No one could have done better. Their bravery and commitment to the principles of the Q-ships was without question.

At 01:30 on 10 August, just to the north of Ushant, Charles signalled that the *Dunraven* was going down. They cast off the tow and returned in their boat to the *Christopher*. The *Dunraven* slid beneath the waves.

When they returned to England, Lieutenant Charles Bonner was awarded the Victoria Cross and the crew members were balloted for the award of a second. They chose PO Ernest Pitcher. Gordon received a second bar to his DSO — and had reached the end of his Q-ship service.

In September, Gordon and Mary's second child was born. A girl, whom they named Flora.

Gunner Billy

William Edward Sanders, commonly known as Gunner Billy, was born in Auckland, New Zealand on 7 February 1883. He worked on steam ships before transferring to sailing ships to improve his career prospects. Billy earned his master's certificate in 1914 and when war broke out, he served on troop ships in the merchant navy until 1916, when he was commissioned into the Royal Naval Reserve. In December of that year, he went to England for training.

July 1916 — HMS Excellent *(RN training establishment), Whale Island, Portsmouth*

"What do you want to do, now we've finished training?" Sub Lieutenant Archy Smith asked Billy.

"I don't really know. The navy doesn't use sail anymore, so I suppose it will have to be a steamer," Billy replied. "I think they'll tell us once we graduate."

They were dressing in their new uniforms to parade for graduation and they checked each other over carefully, brushing any lint from the jackets. A fleet chief came into the barracks, shedding water from his hat and greatcoat. "All right, you lot. Report to the parade ground, two ranks. Oh, and you can wear your overcoats. It's raining."

Billy smiled at the unnecessary information. The water had been running down the window for the last half hour.

The training had only lasted three months, but it had instilled in them Royal Navy traditions going back hundreds of years and given them a good grounding. They knew what they had to do, and how to do it the navy way.

By now the pouring rain had reduced to a dense mizzle, the typical misty sort of drizzle that soaks everything and gets everywhere. The graduation parade went ahead regardless, and after all of the men returned to their barracks, they headed to the wardroom to get a wet and warm up.

"Sanders," the commander said as Billy walked into the wardroom, "I have your orders."

"Do you, sir? Where are they sending me?"

"You're being deployed to the Q-ship flotilla. They have need of your sailing skills."

"Q-ships?" Billy had never heard of them.

"Special operations, all very hush-hush. Here are your orders."

Billy was handed an envelope, addressed in green ink and closed in the old way with a wax seal. He put it in his pocket. If this was a hush-hush outfit, he had better open it somewhere private.

Billy arrived in Queenstown in Ireland at the end of July. His orders were to report to a ship called the *Helgoland*. When he enquired at the gate of the docks, he was told to report to Haulbowline Island.

This is all a bit rum, he thought, and found a navy cutter that ferried people to and from Queenstown. When he got there and asked where the *Helgoland* was berthed, the marine guard replied with a grin, "The Dutch-built *Helgoland*? She's in the inner dock. You can't miss her."

He was right. The *Helgoland* was the only sailing ship in the dock. Billy looked her over. She was a Dutch-built brigantine with two masts and a long bowsprit. The forward mast was sparred for square sails, and the aft mast for gaff-rigged. She looked able to carry two or three jibs as well. She had cabins amidships.

He walked to the bottom of the gangway. "Permission to come aboard?" he called.

A voice with a New Zealand accent replied, "Come on up."

Billy was met at the rail by a lieutenant, who returned his salute and said, "You must be William Sanders. I'm Blair, commander of this ship."

"Pleased to meet you, sir."

"Call me Skipper. We only wear uniforms in port. Do you have a set of regular clothes?"

"Only a seaman's jumper."

"Well, let's get you settled in, then you can go shopping in Queenstown."

Billy put his gear away in his berth, a ten-by-six-foot cabin with only a tiny porthole, and changed into working overalls before reporting back on deck. "What are we doing, Skipper?" he asked.

"Converting this tub into a Q-ship." Blair saw Billy's confusion. "A Q-ship is a decoy ship intended to look like an unarmed merchantman but one that has hidden guns to sucker in U-boats."

"That sounds like fun. Do we have an engine?"

"No, we only have sails — which is why you were selected. We'll mount a 12-pounder amidships and a Maxim on top of the cabin. Both need to be hidden with something that can be dropped at a moment's notice."

Billy understood. It was like fishing — you needed to attract them with bait into the area where you cast your hook. A steel plate was fixed to the deck. This formed the base of the gun mount, which was bolted through into the timbers below. The 12-hundredweight gun sat on the mount, which gave it 360 degrees in azimuth and minus ten degrees to plus ninety degrees in elevation. It had a shield to protect the five gunners, was ten feet, three inches long and, with the barrel in the rest position, over six feet high. Billy thought about it. What they needed were screens around the gun that looked like deck cargo, and which could be dropped at the pull of a single lever. His gaze drifted to the docks and there, sitting right in front of him, was the answer. *The crates the gun had been delivered in!* He sketched his idea and showed it to the skipper.

"If we make twelve-foot-long steel shutters for either side then face them with the wood from those crates, then make an eight-foot front end plate, we can hinge them to the deck so they drop when we pull these pins."

"Why no screen at the back?"

"The gunners need to get into position as soon as we see a submarine. They get in through a strip of canvas strung from the bar that runs across the back."

Blair nodded; it looked simple enough. They would only need to remove three pins to collapse the whole thing outwards. The steel sheets would also provide a bit of protection against machine gun fire. A simple crate concealed the Maxim.

As preparations continued, Billy went shopping and found a tweed suit in a second-hand shop. It was hard-wearing, water-resistant and a decent fit. He bought a flat cap to go with it, and a couple of civilian shirts. He was about to leave when he realised that he was wearing navy-issued vest and drawers. *That won't do. Any military captain would spot them a mile off.* The woman who ran the shop grinned as, blushing, he bought three sets of underwear as well.

Conversion completed, they set out on their first patrol in September 1916. They left Queenstown and headed up the Irish Sea, and had reached St George's Passage when they spotted a U-boat on the surface in a fire fight with a trawler downwind of where they were sailing. They hauled the sails around and sped with the wind on their stern.

"Ready the gun, drop the screens," Blair ordered. When they got to 700 yards: "Hard to starboard. Gun engage, port."

They got two shots away that landed close to the submarine, which decided discretion was the better part of valour and sped away. The trawler had taken several hits but was seaworthy enough to reach port.

"Do you need help?" Billy called across when they got within hailing distance.

"We're fine, thank you. Only one injured and the engine is working."

Billy waved as they sailed past, turning north again.

Three days later, they saw another submarine on the surface.

"Is it the same one?" Blair asked.

Billy studied it with their big, high-powered telescope. "I didn't see the last one's number, so I can't tell. They all look the same."

The submarine had either spotted them — as they had a full set of sails up — or it had recognised they were more than they seemed. Either way, it avoided them by sailing upwind.

Their second patrol, in October, started out fairly well. But then the worst thing that could happen happened.

"Wind's dropping, Skipper," Billy reported to Blair, who was off watch in his cabin.

Blair could feel the change in the ship's motion. She was rocking more as she lost headway. "Are we making steerage way?"

"Hardly, we're all but becalmed."

They went up on deck. The sails hung limply, occasionally fluttering as a pitiful gust ruffled them. Blair said, "Lookouts keep a careful watch. Damn, this never happens in October!"

They had sat, becalmed, for an hour when a lookout called, "Submarine on the surface bearing 0, 7, 5 — 3,000 yards."

They watched as the submarine closed slowly. Its skipper was obviously wary.

"Do you get the feeling they might have rumbled that we're a Q-ship?" Blair said.

Billy just grunted as he thought it was a rhetorical question. The skipper was right; the submarine commanders had been warned that a brigantine in the Irish Sea was carrying a gun, so they were treating all sailing ships with caution.

Suddenly, there was a puff of smoke from the deck gun of the submarine and a shell howled across the deck. It was followed by another, and then a third, which exploded close enough to shower the bridge with water.

"Bugger, he's just going to stand off and blow us to pieces. Engage him with the gun!"

The screens dropped and the gun went into action. The submarine commander didn't like that — especially as the Q-ship boys got the range after the second shot.

"He's submerging!" Billy shouted.

The submarine slipped below the waves. They waited.

"Torpedo tracks port side!" shouted the gunner on the bridge roof.

Two torpedo tracks approached at speed, heading straight for their port beam.

"Brace for impact!"

The silver trails disappeared under the side. Billy closed his eyes in anticipation of meeting the Lord …

Nothing.

"Bloody hell!" Gunner Price said. "They went right under us."

Billy looked to starboard and saw the tracks disappearing into the distance.

"Christ on a crutch, that was scary!" Billy breathed in relief.

The submarine gave them up as a bad lot and went hunting for easier meat.

The wind picked up and they made way again. The sailing was fair, with a steady south-westerly breeze of around ten knots. They were passing Dublin when they heard gunfire.

"Smoke to the north-east!"

They changed course to intercept and soon the lookout called down, "Steamer under attack by submarine, four miles, bearing 0, 4, 0."

There was no time to waste; they piled on all sail and raised the American flag.

"Action stations!" Blair shouted

They got to within 600 yards before the submarine turned its machine gun on them.

"Guns engage!"

Three of the panels dropped, but the one facing the sub stuck after moving about twenty degrees. Billy ran forward, bullets pinging off the panel and knocking chunks out of the rail around him. The panel had warped slightly, enough to jam it. He jumped up, grabbed the top edge and swung his weight on it. It gave, and he forced it to the deck. The gun opened up as soon as he rolled clear.

Again, when faced with an enemy that could fight back, the U-boat ran.

When they returned to Queenstown, Billy was called to the admiral's office in the Admiralty building. The admiral's secretary introduced herself as June. "Would you like some tea? The admiral is with another skipper at the moment."

Another skipper?

He accepted the tea and sat sipping it while she typed. On the wall was a very large chalkboard with the Q-ships on it. He had no idea there were so many and that they were so diverse. There were fishing boats, brigs, schooners, colliers, coasters, sloops and coastal patrol boats.

Billy had just finished his tea when the door to an adjoining office opened and a commander came out. The admiral was right behind him and said, "Sanders?"

Billy replied, "Yes, sir."

"Come in. You've had tea, I see."

Billy followed him in and was told to take a seat.

"I have read the report from Lieutenant Blair and must congratulate you on your bravery in getting that panel down."

"Thank you, sir. I think the blast from a near miss earlier in the patrol had warped it."

The admiral nodded. "Well, it has earned you promotion to lieutenant and I am also recommending you for command of your own ship."

Billy was non-plussed and stammered his thanks as he took his commission from the admiral's hand.

It was the new year before the Admiralty got around to approving Billy's command and he found himself back in the admiral's office.

"Good news, the Admiralty has approved your appointment. You will take command of HMS *Prize* immediately. She is being fitted out at Ponsharden near Falmouth. She is a topsail schooner that we captured from the Germans at the start of the war. At the time she was sold off but has been given back to us to use as a Q-ship."

Billy sailed to Falmouth on a regular navy destroyer that was on its way to Plymouth. The captain made the unofficial stop as a favour. The *Prize* was a majestic three-masted schooner that had been built in Groningen in the Netherlands. Originally christened the *Else*, she was the first ship captured by the Royal Navy in 1914 and thus renamed HMS *First Prize*. The first thing Billy did was request that they shorten her name to the *Prize*, but that would take time to implement.

The *First Prize* was hauled out onto the shipyard when he found her. She was having a diesel engine fitted, which obviously could only be done ashore or in dry dock. The shipyard at Ponsharden had a history of working on packets and other sailing ships and were expert at this kind of work. The master shipwright was Samual Trevilian, a Cornishman to his thick woollen socks and with an accent to match.

"We will fit your guns on the bow and stern," he told Billy, whom he took a shine to as soon as they met. "We'll hide the bow gun with a deckhouse that folds down, and the stern gun will be down in the hold on a hydraulic platform that lifts her up when needed."

Billy thought that ingenious. "What about the engines?"

"Two four-cylinder Kelvin sleeve valve engines running on paraffin and making about fifty horsepower each, and two propellers. They also power the generator for the Marconi radio set. Where do you want your machine gun mounts? We can fit them anywhere. You have two Lewis guns as well as a Maxim."

Billy chose positions for the guns that would maximise their firepower on either beam. They didn't need disguising, as he planned to have the crew mount them at the last minute.

Before his ship was refloated, Billy received his new crew, comprising twenty-six men and officers. He had them parade beside their ship.

"This is the *First Prize*, a Q-ship. For those who haven't sailed on one before, that means she has been made to look like a merchantman, to lure a submarine in close enough so we can sink it with our guns. From now on, you dress as regular merchant sailors. There is to be no saluting, you address me as skipper, and the executive officer as first mate. Stokers are engineers and the rest of you are hands. If you don't have suitable gear, there are a couple of excellent second-hand shops in Falmouth where you can get some."

He looked them over.

"But just because we dress like merchantmen doesn't mean we act like them. No fighting in the pubs when ashore, and when aboard we keep navy discipline. Am I clear?"

"Yes, Skipper!" the men cried — with the occasional "sir!"

First Prize was refloated and commissioned on 25 April 1917. She had orders to sail from Falmouth/Ponsharden on their first patrol, which would end at their new home port of Milford Haven. She sailed out past Pendennis Castle, heading south, then turned west past the Lizard and on into the Atlantic. Billy decided Milford Haven could wait and, as per his instructions, made for the Scilly Isles — five days later, she was attacked.

Edgar von Spiegel von und zu Peckelsheim, commander of the *U-93*, responded to his lookout's hail of, "Sail on the horizon. Red 40," by taking a bearing on the speck of white.

"Steer course 1, 6, 2. Full ahead."

The speck grew from a topsail to a full set and then a hull, which he identified as a schooner, probably Dutch-built, and as they closed even more at sixteen knots, he saw she was British.

"Action stations, gun action."

The gun crew arrived on deck and prepared the 88-mm gun.

"We will commence the attack at 1,000 metres."

At a closing speed of close to twenty-three knots, it only took fifteen minutes to close the range and get off a warning shot.

"Panic party away!" Billy ordered, and the men made a good show of abandoning ship. As soon as they were clear, the submarine opened up with intent, staying at a 1,000-yard range. Billy stayed with his forward gun crew as the shots poured in. Two men were blown overboard by the blast of a shell on the side away from the submarine and the boat picked them up. Through it all, the *First Prize* stood firm: she had been built strong, and after twenty minutes of taking a pounding, the submarine closed in.

"Take us around astern of her," Von Spiegel ordered.

The *U-93* made way and traced a long arc to bring her up on the smoking and listing ship, her gun taking pot shots as she moved.

"We will finish her off."

* * *

"He's closing for the kill. Get ready!" Billy ordered from where he lay behind a gunwale near the forward gun crew. He could see the submarine through a scupper. A groan behind him reminded him that at least one of the gun crew was wounded.

The men in the aft hold manning the gun were up to their knees in water but the hydraulics were intact, and they were ready with the gun loaded. Messages from Billy were passed by a volunteer.

Billy waited. The submarine was being cautious and stalking them like a cat does a mouse. They came up astern and Billy used the starboard engine to nudge them around so both guns would bear. Then they were off the port quarter and just 300 yards away.

"Raise the White Ensign! Let them have it! FIRE!" he ordered.

Then the foredeck deckhouse collapsed with a crash and the gun swung around, the gun layer furiously winding the traverse wheel. At the stern, the aft 12-pounder rose majestically from the hold, already pointing in the right direction. They fired almost simultaneously. The forward gun's shell hit the conning tower; the aft gun destroyed the deck gun. All three machine guns were mounted on the port side and opened up: the noise was tremendous. They kept firing until the *U-93* disappeared into a convenient bank of mist that had come up from the direction of the Scilly Islands.

The men of the *Prize* cheered; they had won. Billy spotted men in the water and hailed the panic party as they closed to reboard. "Pick up those survivors," he told them.

When they returned to the *First Prize*, they had pulled three out of the water. One was the captain of the U-boat, who had been blown out of the conning tower by the first shot. It seemed they had sunk her, and now they turned their attention to getting the *First Prize* home. She was badly damaged and everyone, including the prisoners, had to lend a hand in the repairs.

Billy was confident they could get back to their base in Milford Haven, so he set a course for there; two days later, they met a destroyer off Kinsale, which took them under tow.

The *U-93* was badly damaged but still afloat and able to make headway. She had lost her skipper and was now under the command of the navigation officer, as the executive had also been killed. He set a course for their home base of Sylt, an island on the border between Germany and Denmark. It took them nine days to get there.

When they got home, the name *First Prize* was officially changed to *Prize*, and Billy was summoned to London. He was to report to the Admiralty.

He duly arrived on time and reported to the clerk in the waiting room, who checked his name against a list. "Lieutenant Sanders, let me see. Oh yes, you are to report to the First Sea Lord."

A messenger guided him through the building to an office on the top floor. The door was large and made of dark, aged oak. The messenger knocked and the door was opened by a flag lieutenant.

"Lieutenant Sanders, sir," the messenger announced.

The flag lieutenant beamed a smile and shook Billy's hand then steered him into the office. It was smaller than Billy had expected, but still grand; there was a dark wooden desk, a meeting table and chairs and a fireplace. Admiral John Jellicoe rose from his desk and came around to greet him with a handshake, having first returned Billy's salute.

"Sit down, me boy."

Farnborough

Billy took the chair he was offered and they sat at the meeting table. The lieutenant — who had introduced himself as Knightsbridge — poured three glasses of port. During this preamble, Billy was wondering what the hell was going on. Then Jellicoe started the meeting.

"First of all, congratulations on your action against the submarine ... aah ..."

"*U-93*," Knightsbridge said, filling in for him.

"*U-93*, yes ... an extraordinary effort that showed great fortitude and bravery."

Billy blushed. "Thank you, sir."

"It's earned you a promotion to lieutenant commander."

Billy was surprised at that, to say the least, but Jellicoe hadn't finished.

"And I am very pleased to be able to tell you that you are being awarded the Victoria Cross. It will be gazetted, but the details of the action will be kept secret."

In fact, the published details were simply:

In recognition of his conspicuous gallantry, consummate coolness, and skill in command of one of H.M. ships in action.

Jellicoe sat back and let all that sink in. Then he smiled and said, "Your lieutenant will get a DSO and two others get the DSC. The rest of the crew get the DSM. You can tell them yourself upon your return."

Jellicoe took a sip of port before he continued. "Now to your future in the navy. How would you like to command a destroyer? You can pick which one you get."

It was almost all too much — promotion, a medal, a VC! And now the offer of the ship of his choice ... Billy cleared his throat. "Actually, sir, if you don't mind, I would like to stay on the *Prize*."

Jellicoe looked genuinely surprised. "Well, if that is what you want, of course you can stay, but destroyer commands do not come up every day."

But Billy wouldn't be swayed; he wanted to stay where he was.

Billy arrived in Milford to find repairs well under way with the *Prize* in dry dock. New hull plates were being riveted into place, to repair the holes punched by the 88-mm cannon shells. Her rigging would be replaced as it had been heavily spliced to get them home. Billy didn't spare himself and was there for the installation of every rivet and rope.

"You should take a break," said Simon Harris, his number two, after a particularly trying day.

"She has to be right!" was all that Billy said in reply.

By late May they were back at sea, carrying out a three-week patrol off the north-west coast of Ireland. Nothing much happened until 12 June.

"Skipper! Submarine on the surface at 0, 2, 0."

Billy quickly found it and ordered them to maintain course and speed. But the commander of the *UC-35* was bold; he charged into the attack and commenced fire at 1,500 yards. Some shells landed in the sea, but some hit — and one hit the side opposite the bridge.

A shell fragment sliced through the thin wooden wall and struck Billy. He staggered and leaned against the wall on the other side of the bridge, where blood spread and stained his jumper on one side.

"Skipper!" the helmsman said.

"Stay at the wheel!" Billy barked, and moved back to where he could see the submarine.

When she was close enough for him to read the *UC-35* written on her bow, he gave the order to open fire. The submarine immediately dived as it turned away — it wanted nothing to do with an armed ship.

Simon returned to the bridge after the action to find Billy sitting in a chair, their medic binding a pad over his wound.

"Is it serious?" he asked.

"A piece of shrapnel cut through his side," the medic replied. "Luckily, it's only a flesh wound — a few stitches when we get home, and he'll be fine."

They returned to Milford Haven, repaired the *Prize* again — and its lieutenant commander — and went on patrol at the end of July for a two-week cruise in the Western Approaches. They did not see any submarines, and if any saw them, they stayed well clear.

All this time, the strain of constantly being on alert was wearing down the crew and its skipper. However, they got a boost when the announcement of their awards was made in the *Gazette*. A signal from HQ congratulated them. Billy made a request to be relieved of his command, citing "overstrain", but it was not approved in time to affect his next patrol.

In early August the *Prize* embarked on yet another patrol, this time into the Atlantic under a Swedish flag and accompanied by submarine HMS *D6*. Billy briefed his officers.

"You all know we have a shadow, who is staying as close to us as she can during daylight hours. The idea is, as soon as we spot a U-boat they submerge, and we update them on the target's position, course and speed using discreet signals in our rigging. They will then move to a position where they can torpedo it. I think it's a long shot doing things this way, but we have our orders."

By now — it was 13 August 1917 — Billy was exhausted. He was having trouble sleeping and had lost his appetite. But once again, the call came and he had no choice but to respond.

"Skipper, submarine on the surface. Red 0, 1, 0 — 3,000 yards."

The *D6* was on their port side and Billy flashed them the alert. They submerged, but Billy feared the submarine had spotted them.

"We will attack with guns. Action stations."

With the engines on full ahead and the wind in their favour, the *Prize* sped towards the submarine and opened up on her at 600 yards. The submarine, the *UB-48*, immediately submerged, having received confirmation that the vessel was one of the British trap ships.

Oberleutnant Wolfgang Steinbauer, the captain of *UB-48*, identified the *Prize* as the ship that had attacked the *U-93*. He had a copy of the report from that U-boat's navigation officer in front of him, and the description was very detailed.

"We will stay close to that ship; I want it. Edgar von Spiegel was my captain before I got this boat."

It was a practically moonless night; the moon was in its final phase, after which it would disappear altogether. So, when he raised periscope to look for his target, he could see nothing.

"Dammit, it's as black as hell up there."

He knew which quarter of the compass they would be in, so he kept looking, scanning back and forth across the quadrant. Then, suddenly, his eye picked up a flicker of light.

"There they are! Some fool has opened a porthole or lit a cigarette. Steer 1, 3, 1. Ready torpedo tubes. Depth two metres."

Now he had located her, he could see her outline against the stars.

"Range 1,000. Target course 0, 1, 0. Relative speed five knots."

He waited until he led the target by the correct distance, then yelled, "Fire one." This followed a few seconds later by, "Fire two."

"Torpedoes running, first will be on target in eight seconds," his torpedo officer said.

Steinbauer watched as a huge explosion, followed shortly by a second, lit up the sky.

In the D6, Lieutenant Robert Filkin heard the explosions and his heart sank. He knew what a torpedo sounded like. He came up to periscope depth and scanned the area, but by then the *Prize* had gone.

They surfaced at dawn and looked for survivors. They found wreckage and a single body. The *Prize* had been lost with all hands.

Sanders had been awarded a DSO for his action against the *UC-35* on 12 June and he never knew. The man was a hero: he also received the British War medal, the Mercantile Marine War medal and the Victory Medal at the end of the war.

In June 1918, his VC and DSO medals were presented to his father by the Governor-General of New Zealand, the Earl of Liverpool, at Auckland Town Hall.

PART TWO: THE GERMANS

All at Sea

Felix Graf von Luckner — the *Graf* signified that he was a count, a title passed down by his great grandfather, Nicholas, who had been ennobled by the King of Denmark in the eighteenth century — was the younger of two sons of Heinrich and Maria. According to their father, his elder brother Ferdinand was the perfect son, and followed his father into the cavalry. His half-sister, Anna, would be married off by the time she reached twenty and declared a perfect daughter.

Felix, in contrast, was not content with life. He found most things boring, except things that coincided with his interests. He was sent to a variety of private schools, where he consistently failed his exams. His parents despaired for his future. In fact, their worries were unfounded — Felix was actually more intelligent than most children and substantially stronger, due to his love of the wilderness. His exam failures were not because he didn't know the subject matter, but because the subject matter didn't interest him.

His first love was sailing. He had a small, and very fast, dinghy that he had built himself and sailed on the river Elbe. His second love was exploring, and he would often disappear into the forest that lay to the south-east of Dresden. So, it did not surprise his family when he disappeared just after his thirteenth birthday in July 1894 on what they assumed was yet another hike into the hills. His parents did not begin to worry until he had been gone for several days, at which point his father searched his room for clues to his likely location. That was when they found the letter:

> *Dear Mother and Father,*
>
> *First of all, I wish to assure you that I love you both and that my actions have nothing to do with the family. They have everything to do with my frustration and claustrophobia at living in Dresden. I am going to join the merchant marine and see the world. I will return when I wear the uniform of an officer of the Imperial Navy. I will make you proud, Father.*
>
> *Your loving son, Felix.*

And that was it. They checked his wardrobe, to find that all his sailing clothes were gone. A search by the local police concluded that he had sailed down the river Elbe — the dinghy was missing — and that by now he must be in Hamburg. His father set out to find Felix, but he was too late.

Felix sailed his dinghy from its storage place near the Augustusbrücke, downstream on the Elbe. He had some money, and had taken a joint of ham, a pot of mustard, a loaf of bread and a cheese from the family home. He knew that the Elbe flowed all the way to Hamburg and the sea, and that it was a journey of some 400 or so kilometres. He had calculated that he could sail 160 kilometres a day. At night, he would pull over to the bank and sleep. His plan was to find a ship in Hamburg and sign on as a deckhand.

After two days it started to rain. This soaked him and, as his little boat had no cabin, his rucksack and food. He had to bail the boat out more than once. It was a cold, wet and hungry Felix who arrived in Hamburg and docked his boat at a place where leisure craft were stored. He set off to find a ship, but soon discovered he was on the wrong side of the river, since all the docks were on the southern bank.

He found a bridge and crossed over into a veritable maze of docks and shipyards. Warships for the Kaiserliche Marine and commercial ships were being built on the many slipways and dry docks, but what interested him was the plethora of ships from all over the world loading and unloading cargo.

The first ship he tried turned out to be a Venezuelan cargo steamer and the captain was an evil-looking man who leered at him in a very disturbing way. Frederick left that ship in a great hurry. He was more careful with his next choice. She was German, and registered in Hamburg. He walked up the gangway.

"Excuse me, I'm looking to sign on as a hand. Can I speak to the captain?"

The mate who met him at the entry looked him up and down and recognised his accent.

"And what does a boy from Dresden know about sailing and working a ship?"

"I sailed from Dresden to here. I'm strong and can work and learn."

"Did you, now?" the mate said, wondering if he should believe him. "Well, whether you did or not, we haven't got any open berths. Try the *Niobe*. Old Vlad is always looking for hands."

* * *

Felix was not put off by these challenges. He walked along the dock until he spotted the name *Niobe* — registered in Kaliningrad, according to the name on her stern. He stood back and looked at her. She was a brigantine, a two-masted sailing ship flying the Russian Ensign. He shrugged and walked to the gangway. He shouted up: "Ahoy, the *Niobe*!"

A rugged red face appeared over the gunwale. "What do you want?"

"I'm looking for Captain Vlad."

"I'm Vladimir Petrakov."

Felix said, not understanding because of the man's accent, "Oh, I'm sorry — I was told to look for *old* Vlad."

The man looked at him, trying to decide if he was being mocked. But the boy looked at him seriously.

"Hmph. Well, you found him. Now, what do you want?"

"I want to sign on as a deckhand."

The man stomped down the gangway. He was only four foot eleven, with broad shoulders and heavily muscled arms. "You don't sound like a local," he said.

"I sailed here from Dresden in a boat I built myself," Felix explained, with a hint of pride.

Vlad laughed. "Ha! Freshwater sailor, eh?" Then he grabbed Felix's arms and ran his fingers down them to his hands, which he examined. "Rope callouses, good muscles," he muttered. "How old are you?"

"Sixteen," Felix lied. He was exceptionally strong for his age, so he thought he could get away with that.

"Your parents know you're here?" Vlad didn't sound like he cared.

"I left them a note."

Vlad walked around him, while Felix stood still and waited.

"You have brothers and sisters?"

"Yes, a brother and a sister. I'm the oldest," he lied.

"Are those all your belongings?" Vlad prodded the backpack.

"Yes."

"Come with me."

Vlad stomped up the deck and led him down into the depths of the ship. There were hammocks slung in the crew quarters, which they passed through to get to a storeroom. Vlad unlocked the door and went inside; Felix followed. After a bit of rummaging, Vlad presented Felix with two pairs of white linen trousers, a couple of striped shirts and a neckerchief. An empty seabag followed, and a rolled-up hammock. Finally, Vlad placed a sheathed knife on the top.

"You have a belt."

He walked out and waited until Felix followed him, then shut and locked the door.

"You will sling your hammock there," he said and pointed to the end of the row.

"Am I ..."

"Get changed and report to me on deck."

Looks like I got a berth, Felix thought happily. What he didn't know then was that his berth was unpaid.

Felix came up on deck — after studying and copying the knots the other hammocks were tied up with — and looked for Vlad. He found him in a small deckhouse on the quarterdeck, near the open wheel. He sat at a table with a book in front of him.

"What's your name?"

Felix feared that his parents may be searching for him so came up with a false name on the spot.

"Phylax Lüdecke." Felix thought this name was close enough to his own for him to recognise, but different enough to be a cover.

"Felix, all right," Vlad said, having misheard. "I'm signing you on as a cabin boy. We're sailing to Australia."

Felix was happy to be aboard a ship but wanted to know more about sailing, so he stood his ground.

"I want to learn about sailing."

Vlad looked up at him. "You do, do you? All right, I'll add *apprentice seaman* to *cabin boy*. Your sea daddy will be Aksel Fisk. He's a bosun's mate and will teach you everything you need to know about the ship. I'll teach you navigation. Sign your name here."

"Can I ask, where are the crew?" Felix said as he signed.

"Shore leave. They'll be back tomorrow. We'll be taking on a cargo of farm tools and metal goods for Fremantle, a trip that takes eighty days or more."

When the sign-up process was complete, Vlad dug out a book and handed it to Felix.

"This is the chart room, and that is a book on navigation. If you want to learn about it, you must read that. Now bugger off and leave me in peace."

He was lucky the book was in German and not Russian. Felix found a sheltered spot on the deck and settled down to read. It was the driest book he had ever read, full of mathematics about spherical navigation; shooting the sun, moon and stars; latitude and longitude. The sun came out, and he got hot and dozed off. He awoke with a start when someone kicked his foot.

"You want to eat?" a bearded man said.

His stomach growled; he hadn't eaten since yesterday evening.

"That'll be a *yes*, then." The man grinned. "I'm Grüber, the cook. Come with me."

Grüber turned and stomped away, and Felix was surprised to see he had a wooden leg. He got up and followed. They went down to the galley, where a large pot of sailors' stew bubbled. A metal bowl was thrust into his hands and a large portion ladled into it. A thick chunk of fresh bread followed. Grüber gestured that he should sit at a table with long benches down either side. He handed him a spoon.

"Look after the plate and spoon. If you lose them, you pay for them. Same with the mug."

A mug of beer was placed in front of him then. Grüber joined him with his own meal. It was hearty and tasty, full of slightly gristly meat, potato, onions, carrots and mushrooms. When they had finished and Felix had used the crust of his bread to mop the dish clean, Grüber said, "You can come with me this afternoon to get supplies for the voyage."

Grüber could move surprisingly fast despite his peg leg, and Felix had to work hard to keep up. A full belly helped and gave him the energy required. They made their way along the road behind the warehouses on the docks, calling in at different shops as they went. Each shop seemed to specialise in one thing or another. Dried pulses and fruits came from one, preserved meats from another, ship's biscuits from yet another. Live chickens, a pair of goats and a pig. Beer, schnapps, wine, lime juice, flour, potatoes, dried herbs, salt. They bought everything needed to keep a crew of twenty-seven fit and healthy during a long voyage.

Then there were the private stores. Things that sailors would buy to give themselves, and maybe their mates, a treat. Felix chose a block of chocolate with his scant resources. Grüber shopped from a list provided by the skipper and Felix got to carry it. The smell of fresh roasted coffee beans was wonderful.

Soon they were back at the ship, and by late afternoon carts started to arrive and unload their purchases. At first, Felix thought he would be loading and storing it all on his own, but several of the hands returned in time to make it a team effort. In fact, a steady stream of hands, some more sober than others, arrived during the evening and he was introduced to them all.

A few of the hands were Germans but most were Russian or Nordic. As the most junior crew member, Felix was given the job of caring for the livestock. That involved mucking out the pens they were kept in and making sure they were fed. The pigs were the messiest; they ate all the leftovers and scraps from the kitchen, but their shit was runny. The chickens provided eggs and were fed from a supply of maize, and the goats were fed hay. He was told that when the feed ran out they would be slaughtered and eaten, so he tried not to get attached to any of them.

The next day, 5 August 1894, the cargo arrived. Cart after cart of crates were brought alongside and hoisted up and into the cargo holds. Felix discovered what hard work was that day. He was detailed to the team that pulled the rope that hoisted the cargo up using a pulley system. His hands blistered and bled despite his callouses. He didn't complain, but Boris Götz, the first mate, spotted the problem and gave him a pair of leather working gloves. That night Aksel, his sea daddy, helped him with his hands. Aksel was a Norwegian from a long line of fishermen.

"They will take a while to harden up, but we can speed things up," Aksel said, and prepared two bowls. One had salt water in, the other neat rubbing alcohol. "This is going to hurt." He took a cut-throat razor and ran the blade through a candle flame, then used it to slit open any unburst blisters. "Place your hands in the salt water, then take them out and put them in the alcohol. Do that ten times."

Felix gasped as he placed his hands into the brine.

"Hold them there for a count of twenty," Aksel said.

Tears poured down Felix's face as he counted while shuddering.

"Now into the other."

If he thought the salt hurt, that illusion was dispelled as soon as raw flesh hit alcohol. He opened his mouth and a squeak came out.

"The words you are looking for are 'Jesus, Fucking, Christ,'" Aksel informed him. Felix grinned. He wasn't about to be beaten. He did the whole treatment and was surprised how it hurt less each time. The next day he still wore gloves, but the blisters were hardening up nicely. He repeated the treatment every evening for a week.

They set sail and Felix started to learn. He learned how to knot and splice; the names of all the ropes in the rigging; how to push a capstan; how to climb the rigging and set sails; how to trim and haul; and how to steer. He was a fast learner and while he was at it, learned Norwegian from Aksel. The skipper taught him how to shoot the sun with a sextant and how to work out their position. His hands hardened, his shoulders broadened and he grew; he was still exceptionally strong and amused the men by bending coins with his fingers.

The *Niobe* specialised in the Australian run, and stopped off to water along the way. Felix wrote to his parents telling them of all the places he visited. He didn't tell them about the time he fell overboard in the middle of the ocean.

He was working aloft, helping to reeve a replacement block, when he lost his grip and fell. He was lucky as he was on the leeward side and therefore the heel of the ship sent him into the sea. He surfaced and heard the men shouting "man overboard", but the ship kept going and he thought for a moment that they would leave him behind. Then a trio of huge albatrosses started to circle him. One swooped down and grabbed at his waving hand. Felix gripped its leg and hung on as the huge bird flapped furiously to get away and almost lifted him out of the water. He hung on for grim death and eventually saw the ship heave to and a boat drop from its davit. The bird continued to struggle, and he had to let go just as he saw the boat approaching.

"You're lucky," a crew man said, after they had hauled him aboard. "Vlad wanted to leave you behind, but Boris wasn't having any of it and defied him. We saw the birds circling and figured you were under them."

Felix would remember Boris as long as he lived.

They arrived at Freemantle in Western Australia at the end of October. Felix, holding a grudge against the captain now and keen to explore this strange new world, jumped ship and spent the next seven years wandering the continent.

Homeless and without any money, he found the Salvation Army and sold their newspaper, *The War Cry*, to make some money so he could eat. They looked after him and let him sleep in their mission. Felix was not a religious boy, but he was thankful for their charity.

After a month, he got bored doing that and made his way south along the coast to Cape Leeuwin, hitching rides on carts. There was no plan, he just wanted to explore. When he got there after three days, he found a settlement and started looking for work.

The kindly lady shopkeeper of the only store in town told him, when he went in to spend the few pennies he had on bread and cheese, "Old Henry is looking for an assistant at the lighthouse, why don't you try there?" So, he walked to the lighthouse and banged on the door. A pretty girl a couple of years older than him answered. She saw a grubby boy with a tanned face, who was interesting as he spoke with a pronounced accent.

"What do you want?" she asked.

"The lady in the shop said the keeper is looking for an assistant."

She smiled at him and yelled over her shoulder, "Dad, there's a bloke here who wants to be your assistant."

Henry stomped up behind her. He was bearded with a weathered face which made him look older than he was. He looked Felix up and down.

"What's your name, boy?"

"Felix, sir."

"German?"

"Yes, sir, from Dresden."

Felix had grown and put on muscle during his time on the ship. Henry held out his hand and when Felix took it, he squeezed hard. Felix grinned and squeezed back, matching him.

Henry nodded. "You'll do."

He was given a room and told to bathe. When he said he only had the one set of clothes, Henry dug out some old ones of his and tossed them to him. The girl spied on him as he took a cold bath outside on the porch.

The work was easy, mainly consisting of tending the oil-fired light and running errands. It left him time to go fishing with a hand reel from the rocks for herring, skippy and tailor. He explored the local area and watched the ships rounding the cape. The regular diet and exercise saw him mature into a fine figure of a young man.

The daughter, Sarah, was seventeen; meanwhile Felix was going through puberty at fourteen. He was experiencing some new sensations, and Sarah was interested in helping him explore them. It was two days after his fifteenth birthday when her father caught them together. Sarah had led him by the hand into one of the storage sheds and shown him the difference between boys and girls. He was energetically learning about copulation when Henry walked in on them.

To avoid a shotgun wedding, Felix left the lighthouse in a hurry — taking food and the cash he had saved from his earnings — and headed inland. He was on the road to Alexander Bridge on the Blackwater River when he met a professional kangaroo hunter. Jim, as he called himself, took a shine to the young man and taught him to shoot. They travelled from homestead to homestead on horseback, shooting kangaroos and other animals that competed with the cattle or sheep for food. It was a good life; they went wherever they wanted to go, when they wanted to go there. It came to an end when Jim was killed. He got into an argument with a stockman in a bar and the two fought. The fight ended with a knife between Jim's ribs and the stockman being hanged for murder.

From there Felix rode to Jerramungup, where he joined a circus as a strongman. The circus moved from town to town, and he developed a show that included bending coins with his fingers and metal bars around his neck. The circus included a professional boxer who would take on all comers for a prize purse. The boxer, a former sailor called Bruce, taught Felix how to box. It turned out that Bruce had ambitions to become the manager of the act and retire from fighting. So, naturally, once Felix became proficient, he became the professional boxer taking on all comers. He soon got a reputation for having a seriously dangerous right hook, which knocked out eight out of ten opponents in the first round.

However, the call of the sea could not be denied, and he became a fisherman for a while out of Port Augusta. The boat, a copy of a Brixham trawler and called the *Sally B*, was a fast, deep-sea fishing boat. She was seventy feet long on the deck, with a heavy displacement, straight prow, fantail stern and a low freeboard. She was a weatherly ship, able to take whatever the ocean threw at her; gaff-rigged, she had the power to get to the fishing grounds quickly and then tow big trawls. She was one of a twenty-four-boat fleet that fished the Great Australian Bight.

Felix eventually tired of fishing and the call of the deep caught up with him again. He signed on to a ship bound for Mexico as a deckhand. Once again, when the ship reached its destination, he jumped ship to explore this new and fascinating country. On a whim he joined the Mexican army and served in the Imperial Guard of President Diaz until he was thrown out for being insubordinate.

Being strong, Felix had no trouble getting work as a railway construction worker after he demonstrated smashing a boulder with a sledgehammer. He stuck at that for a few months, at which point he decided he needed a change of scenery and went to Santiago, Chile, where he got work as a barman and eventually became a tavern keeper.

After some time, Felix was arrested and charged with stealing pigs, (pleading guilty as charged) and spent a short while in prison. He got out and made his way to Jamaica, only to break his leg in a riding accident and end up in hospital. He only had a little money, which soon went on medical bills, and he was thrown out on the street. Now aged nineteen, he decided to go back to Germany and got a berth as a stoker on a cargo steamer bound for Hamburg.

At the age of twenty, in 1901 Felix entered a navigation training school in Hamburg, where he passed the examinations for his mate's ticket. He gained experience on a number of ships sailing between Germany and the Mediterranean and the SS *Pinmore* in 1902 that sailed the Atlantic routes. In 1908 he signed up for the Hamburg–Südamerikanische Line on the steamer *Petropolis* as first officer, where he served for nine months before enlisting as a volunteer in the Imperial German Navy for a year to gain even more experience. In 1909, he returned to the merchant navy.

Heligoland Bight

Felix was in Dresden for Christmas in 1911 when he met Petra Schultz, who was from a fairly wealthy family in Hamburg. Herr Schultz owned a chain of men's outfitters. Petra was, in Felix's eyes, the most beautiful girl he had ever seen. She was living in Dresden, caring for an elderly aunt. His parents, though pleased to see him, were reserved about his enrolment in the merchant navy. His father, being a military man, did not understand why he had chosen to leave the Imperial Navy after his one-year enlistment. His mother was just pleased to have him home and even more pleased when he started walking out with Petra.

"Do you think that the Balkans will cause a problem?" Petra asked as they sat together in the parlour of his father's house.

The question caught Felix off guard. "Why do you ask? I'm surprised you're interested in that."

"Oh? Because I'm a woman?" She swatted his arm with her hand. "I heard your father and a friend talking about it."

He pulled her to him and kissed her, then thought about it. According to the newspapers, Serbia, Greece, Bulgaria and Montenegro were forming the Balkan League. Their ambition was independence of all their peoples from the Ottoman Empire, and they seemed to have the backing of Russia.

"Well, as you are so serious, I think the alliance will fall apart. Those countries can never get along for any length of time."

"Then what will happen?"

"They will probably start to fight each other."

Felix was right. In 1912 the alliance won independence — then fell apart. In mid-1913 the Bulgarians fought the Greeks and Serbs over Macedonia. The Ottomans and Romanians allied with the Greeks and Serbs, and they jointly defeated the Bulgarians. This all destabilised the region even more and tensions grew between Serbia and the Austria–Hungary alliance that had allegiance to Germany.

Felix changed the subject. "Will you marry me?"

Petra had not seen that coming and looked at him in surprise. Her mouth opened and closed several times before she managed to say, "Yes."

They were married in the town hall two weeks later.

In April 1912, before he returned to Hamburg, Felix received a letter from the Kaiserliche Marine. He opened it with Petra.

"My God, I've been recalled to the navy as a leutnant zur see!"

"Why? When do you have to leave?" she cried, appalled at the idea.

"As to why, I have no idea. We're not at war. As to when, I'm instructed to report to Wilhelmshaven naval base immediately."

Petra was not happy about this at all — she had envisaged that her husband would give up the sea and take a senior post in her father's company.

His own father was pleased; to him, being a leutnant zur see in the navy was far more prestigious than being the first mate on a steamer. He presented Frederick with a gold pocket watch in commemoration.

Petra had news for him before he left. "Felix, I think I'm pregnant."

Felix was delighted; he picked her up and swung her around. However, duty came first.

"Go home to your parents in Hamburg, we'll be closer there."

She agreed, albeit reluctantly.

Felix dug out his uniform and took the train to Wilhelmshaven. There, he made his way to the naval base, which was near the outer harbour. He reported to reception and was directed to an office on the first floor, where he was met by a kapitän.

"Graf von Luckner?" the kapitän said, and shuffled through a pile of dockets. "Aah, here you are."

Felix stood rigidly at attention and the kapitän looked up at him. "At ease, man." When Frederick relaxed, he passed him a sealed envelope. "Those are your written orders, but in a nutshell, you are to report to the gunboat SMS *Panther*. She is moored in the outer harbour and will sail tomorrow."

Frederick was disappointed. "A gunboat?"

"More of a ship, as she has a crew of 130, and has had a prestigious career so far. Get along, they are waiting for you."

Frederick had heard about the *Panther*, and he dredged up the story from his memory as he walked. The previous year she had been sent to Morocco, to bully the French into ceding territory in French Equatorial Africa in return for the Germans staying out of France's attempt to colonise Morocco. It was a typical bit of gunboat diplomacy and had been quite successful.

The *Panther*, when he saw it, was far from a mere boat. She was an Iltis-class gunboat of around 1,200 tons displacement. At sixty-seven metres long and almost ten metres wide, she had two triple-expansion steam engines driving two propellers. She had two 10.5-cm SK L/40 guns and six 3.7-cm cannons. His orders said that Felix was to be her navigator.

The *Panther*'s captain was Kapitänleutnant Heinrich Zients. Felix reported to him in his cabin.

"Welcome aboard, leutnant. How do you like our ship?" the kapitän said.

Frederick was very careful when he answered. "She's a fine ship, Kapitän, with a fine record."

Zients smiled knowingly. "You'll go far, but for now get your gear stowed then report to the chart room."

Unpacking his gear he wondered about his new boss. He was typical navy in his manner and looked like he would follow orders to the letter. As soon as he was ready, he reported to the chartroom to find Zients waiting for him.

"We're heading back to the Mediterranean tomorrow. Plot us a course that keeps us out of British waters."

This was easy; he had done the route many times in merchant ships. Then he had a thought: *Where will we refuel?* He checked the capacity of the bunkers and rate of usage to calculate the range. Then he read the kapitän's standing orders and their notes, the guidelines from the Admiralty and the orders for this cruise. He looked for a refuelling depot ship in the Mediterranean and found one stationed in the Bay of Naples. He plotted the course and took it to the kapitän.

"Very good. How much coal will we have left when we get to Naples?"

Frederick knew he was being tested. "Approximately a quarter of a bunker if we stay at nine knots, sir." That was within both the German Admiralty guidelines and compliant with the standing orders.

"Take us out of port — we are singled up," the kapitän said, referring to the moorings.

"Sir?"

The kapitän gestured for him to proceed. They were tied up to the dock on their port side. Felix gave a long blast on the ship's horn then ordered, "Cast off forward!"

He went to the engine telegraph and set it to *stand by*. Once they acknowledged, he rang for *dead slow ahead* on the port engine and *back slow* on the starboard. The bow slowly swung away from the dock, pivoting on the stern mooring, and when it was approaching where he wanted it to be, he set the telegraph to *all stop*. The ship settled back a little as the stretch in the cable pulled on it.

"Cast off aft."

The confirmation that they were free of the land came and he ordered *slow ahead both*; the telegraph bell rang in acknowledgement.

"Midships."

He went to the starboard wing of the bridge and checked for any ships or boats that could be in the way then steered her out into the channel.

"Good, you seem to know what you're doing," the kapitän said. "You have the bridge. I'll be in my cabin."

The first leutnant left with the kapitän. He was in charge.

The Mediterranean was quiet. The only excitement was a letter from Petra telling him he was a father to a daughter, Inge-Maria. It contained the usual information — weight, length, colour of hair — however, the tone of the letter troubled Felix; it was somewhat cold and impersonal.

In June 1914, two things happened that changed everything. He received a letter from an advocate serving him divorce papers, and the Austrian Archduke Franz Ferdinand and his wife Sophia were shot in their car in Bosnia by Gavrilo Princip, a nineteen-year-old Serbian revolutionary. This put Austria–Hungary at odds with Serbia and her ally, Russia. The Germans promised to support Austria–Hungary if they declared war on Serbia, which they did on 28 July 1914.

This was further complicated when Russia mobilised its forces in support of Serbia, which dragged France into the war as they had a treaty with Russia. Not wanting to fight on two fronts, Germany declared war on France two days later with the intent of knocking them out of the war quickly. Germany had to go through neutral Belgium to get to France and when they massed on the border, the Belgians called for help. Britain declared war on Germany on 4 August.

The *Panther* was recalled to Germany and attached to a cruiser squadron that made occasional forays out into the North Sea to keep the British Home Fleet on its toes.

"Running a screen again tonight," Kapitän Zients said as they prepared to sail on 28 August 1914.

"It will be quiet as usual, I expect," Felix replied. They had seen no action to this point.

They had been out every night for a month acting as a scout for the escorting cruisers of the nightly destroyer and minesweeper patrol. They would range ahead of the cruisers, which were escorting the patrol out to the operation area. Once the destroyers and minesweepers were in position, the cruisers would return to port, leaving the destroyers to patrol. This night, 28 August, the *Panther* had orders to accompany the minesweepers on their patrol. In all, their little fleet consisted of six light cruisers, nineteen torpedo destroyers and twelve minesweepers.

They completed their patrol near the island of Heligoland in the Heligoland Bight and were rendezvousing with the cruisers to go home when they spotted three British submarines on the surface.

Commodore Reginald Tyrwhitt was on the light cruiser HMS *Arethusa*, commanding the 3rd Flotilla of sixteen L-class destroyers. The *Arethusa* was a brand-new ship, and untried. She had two 6-inch guns and six 4-inch guns of a new design.

"What's the time?"

"04:00, sir," a voice said.

"Are the submarines in position?" Tyrwhitt asked.

"Yes, sir, we just received confirmation," the communications officer said. Radio was not reliable, but it was their only option in the dark of the early morning as signal lamps would give the game away.

"Willie's in position with the first behind us," Captain Dicky Forester said, referring to Captain William Bunt commanding the 1st Destroyer Flotilla from HMS *Fearless*, another light cruiser.

"Sunrise in thirty minutes," a lieutenant called.

"Steer 1, 8, 0," Tyrwhitt ordered.

A signal flashed from the cruiser *Mainz* and four destroyers broke away from the main group to attack the British submarines. The *Panther* was told to extend the range of her patrol to the south. Felix was on deck and watched as the false dawn lit the eastern horizon.

Then there were the first rays of the morning sun. It was beautiful above the light mist.

"Visibility two kilometres," the lookout called.

Felix took a deep breath of the morning air; all was good. Then the radioman reported, "Sir, I've picked up a signal from *G194*. She's spotted a force of British destroyers and a cruiser west by north-west of Heligoland."

"Lookouts, keep your eyes open!" Felix called.

"Admiral Hipper has ordered *Frauenlob* and *Stettin* to defend the destroyers," the radioman further explained.

Back in the port of Ems, word had reached naval command, who ordered the light cruisers SMS *Strassburg*, SMS *Cöln*, SMS *Ariadne* and SMS *Straslund* to start raising steam, along with SMS *Kolberg* on the River Jade and SMS *Danzig* and SMS *München* on the River Elbe. They had to be ready to sail when the tide was high enough for them to exit the river.

Felix scanned the horizon with his binoculars. He swept past a darker patch of mist. *What was that?* He scanned back over it and shouted, at the same time as the lookout, "Submarine dead ahead."

The kapitän came on deck; Felix brought him up to speed. As they closed, Felix could see that there were more submarines to either side of the one they had first spotted.

"It's an ambush," Zients concluded, then ordered, "Action stations! We will try to draw their fire, send a signal to the admiral."

During action stations, Felix had command of one of the 10.5-cm guns. He was at his station in time for the kapitän to order the big guns to fire.

"Target the nearest submarine and open fire." He watched as the layer adjusted the azimuth angle and the range was set.

The gun roared, but the shell fell short. It didn't matter; what they wanted was to get the submarine's attention. They did that all right, as the submarine's deck gun opened up with their 12-pounder. Their shot also fell short. The *Panther* closed the gap, and they fired again; this time they had the range and straddled the submarine. The submarine also had the range and fired with more skill and luck, hitting the *Panther* just aft of the bridge.

Back in the north, Tyrwhitt in the *Arethusa* ordered four destroyers to attack the SMS *G194*. The gunfire was heard by the other German destroyers who were heading north, who promptly began turning south for home. It was too late; they were spotted and the British destroyers opened fire. The rearmost destroyer, the *V1*, was hit, and then the minesweepers *D8* and *T33*. A request was sent to the coastal batteries for support but there was a light mist, and the gunners couldn't distinguish one ship from another at that range.

Tyrwhitt had his destroyers chase the remaining German destroyers east for thirty minutes, but the Germans reached the cover of the batteries on Heligoland, and they had to turn away. Then the German cruisers arrived, and the 1st and 3rd Flotillas had to break off and retreat to the protection of *Arethusa* and *Fearless*.

Felix was approached by an oberbootsmann. "Sir, can you come to the bridge? Both the kapitän and oberleutnant are wounded."

That was worrying; if they were out of action, Felix was in command.

When he arrived, he found both officers being treated for shrapnel wounds to their backs. Neither was in a fit state to command. A glance at the rear of the bridge explained everything. A ragged hole showed where the blast from the shell had ripped its way through.

"Is the radio still working?" he asked.

"No, sir. The radio room and kapitän's day cabin were destroyed. The radio officer and radioman are both dead."

"Was a message sent about the submarines?"

"Yes, sir, it was," Fähnrich zur See Gustav Zimmer replied.

Another shell exploded, close enough to send water over the bridge. A second submarine had joined in the fight.

"Steer north, full ahead. We'll rejoin the fleet and report," Felix ordered.

The fähnrich zur see looked relieved. A final pair of shots was sent as the *Panther* turned and the crew cheered.

"Did we hit him?" Felix asked, as he and the fähnrich zur see trained their binoculars south and saw that the conning tower of one of the submarines had been damaged.

The *Arethusa* was engaged by the *Frauenlob* and was totally outgunned because her new design 4-inch MK V guns kept jamming after being fired, a fault that put two out of action and slowed down the rate of fire from the rest. Given that, and the inexperienced crew, the *Arethusa* took a lot of damage, including having another 4-inch gun knocked out.

Tommy Wilson, the gun layer of the forward 6-inch gun, took careful aim, ignoring the sounds of shot hitting his ship. He shouted "SHOOT" and the gun roared and recoiled. He kept his eye to the sight and yelled in joy as he saw the bridge of the *Frauenlob* explode. He had just killed thirty-seven men, including her kapitän. After a moment, during which a chain of command was re-established on the German ship, it turned away and sped off towards Wilhelmshaven.

It was 08:12 and Tyrwhitt decided to sweep from east to west to find the German destroyers. He spotted a gaggle of six, which turned to run away. Then one of them turned back. It was a suicidal rear-guard action.

In the meantime, Vice Admiral David Beaty with the battle-cruisers HMS *Lion*, HMS *Queen Mary* and HMS *Princess Royal*, and Commodore William Goodenough with the 1st Light Cruiser Squadron, had arrived unannounced as their radios could not get through to the destroyer squadrons. Goodenough sent HMS *Nottingham* and HMS *Lowestoft* ahead to try and close the trap.

The SMS *V187* had spotted the cruisers *Nottingham* and *Lowestoft* ahead of her and turned to try and sneak through the destroyers, but was identified and engaged by eight British ships, which surrounded her. The rain of fire they endured was relentless. She fought bravely and never surrendered. The *V187* sank under heavy fire and torpedo hits, her remaining guns still firing. The German crew abandoned ship, and the British started to pick up survivors by launching boats. Then the SMS *Stettin* arrived, and the British were forced to retreat.

The British submarine *E4* spotted the *Stettin* and launched a torpedo from the surface. She missed, but it got the attention of the cruiser, which tried to ram *E4*. The submarine dived and made its escape.

Rather than return to port, Felix decided to stick around and pick up survivors as his kapitän and first officer were not critically wounded. *Panther* was now a spectator to what was in fact the opening sea battle of the war.

"Our cruisers are coming out with Admiral Maass on the Cöln. They will chase the British off," Felix stated confidently.

He was wrong. At 11:30 the *Mainz* was engaged by the 1st Destroyer Flotilla who had linked up with the *Arethusa*; she was badly damaged. Then Goodenough and his battlecruisers arrived, just as the *Strassburg* and *Cöln* joined the fray. *Strassburg* managed to escape but *Cöln* was trapped. The *Ariadne* tried to help her, but she fell to the big guns of the battlecruisers. *Cöln* was sunk.

By 13:30 it was all over, the British ships withdrew after picking up survivors. The *Panther* searched, moving slowly through the mist listening for any cries, but only found a few from the *G194*, whom they picked up before returning to port.

Escape from Wilhelmshaven

On his return, Felix was praised for his action in rescuing the sailors despite his ship being damaged. The *Panther* was put into dock for repairs and her crew reassigned. Felix had two weeks' leave, which he took in Dresden. His mother and father were at home alone as his half-sister had married and his brother was on detachment.

"Where will they send you next?" his father asked him.

"I'm to report to SMS *Kronprinz Wilhelm*. She's a battleship."

"Do you want that?"

"Not really. I've also put my name down for special operations. There's more freedom to act there."

"What are these *special operations*?" his father asked.

"They're arming merchant ships to make them commerce raiders. They get to roam the ocean and sink enemy merchant ships."

What he did not know was that these overtly military ships were generally unsuccessful, as their guns could be seen from a distance, and they didn't have the speed or range to catch a fleeing merchantman.

His one regret during his leave was that he could not visit his daughter. She was in Hamburg with her mother and by the time he got there he had to report aboard.

Felix reported to the *Kronprinz Wilhelm* in Hamburg in June 1916 and was involved in the Battle of Jutland. He commanded a gun turret, but had little to do as the ship was far from the centre of the action and came out unscathed. On their return to Wilhelmshaven, he was called to the executive officer's office.

"Von Luckner, you have a change in orders." He was handed an envelope.

Felix was surprised, but he opened the envelope, which was sealed with wax impressed with the symbol of the Kaiserliche Marine. He frowned as he read it.

"It says I'm to report to Wilhelmshaven, special operations."

The executive scowled; this would leave him an officer short. However, there was nothing he could do about it.

"Pack your things and be off the ship by the morning. We sail at 08:00."

The dismissal was short and to the point.

Felix packed his things and left the ship that evening. Impatient to learn what he was being assigned to, he went to the train station as his orders had included a travel voucher. He asked at the ticket office and found there was a train to Bremen that would get him halfway to Wilhelmshaven by midnight.

He read a book for the first two hours of the journey and then dozed until the train pulled up in a cloud of steam in Bremen. He found a station master and asked, "When is the next train to Wilhelmshaven?"

"The early train leaves at six from platform two," the man replied.

"Is there a hotel nearby?"

"There's one just outside the main entrance."

Felix found that hotel and got a room, paid for out of his own money as the travel voucher only covered the train. It was small but clean and he slept until five, automatically waking in good time for his next task, in the way that sailors can.

The train took six hours to get to Wilhelmshaven and he grabbed a bite to eat before looking for the address given in his orders.

The building, when he found it, was as nondescript as they came. There was no guard outside and just a plain door with no plaque or sign telling what it was. He double-checked the address. He was in the right place, so walked up to the door and pushed it. It swung open and he stepped into a hallway with a desk manned by a civilian receptionist. There was absolutely nothing *navy* about the place at all.

The receptionist looked at him and smiled. She was blonde and had striking blue eyes. "May I have your orders?" She had a Bavarian accent.

Felix stepped forward and dug them out of his jacket pocket.

"Thank you. Aah, you are Leutnant Graf von Luckner. Please go to the second floor, second door to the right."

She handed his orders back to him and when he hesitated, trying to decide whether to ask why the building was so nondescript, she shooed him on his way.

He found the door and knocked.

"Come."

He opened it and stepped inside to be met by a kapitän, who saluted without getting up from his chair. Felix handed over his orders again.

"Good, you are here in time," the kapitän said.

Felix was confused now. "Can you tell me what I'm just in time *for*?"

"Oh, of course! You don't know, do you? Your ship, she just arrived for refitting."

Felix almost dared to think the impossible ... *Is this a command?*

"I'm to join a new ship?"

"Well, she's a new old ship, and you will be her commander."

Felix's pulse rate increased by a couple of beats. "Where is she?" he asked, his voice quivering just a little.

"Down in the Bauhaven. We want her out of sight while we do the refit."

The Bauhaven was an enclosed dock where security could be maintained that before the war had been used for leisure craft.

The kapitän lit a Meerschaum pipe and settled into his chair. He pointed to another chair with the stem. Felix sat down.

"Plenty of time to see her, but first I want to tell you what you'll be doing. The merchant raiders idea has been a bit of a flop, so we've come up with an alternative. Stole the idea from the British, to be honest, as they've been making decoy ships for centuries. We'll take a ship that's as far from being a warship as possible and arm her with hidden weapons so, under false colours, she can get close enough to her targets to sink them. It's a perfectly legitimate *ruse de guerre*."

It took several moments for that to sink in and when it did, Felix asked, "Why was I chosen to command it?"

"Well, first, you volunteered. Second, you have experience of merchant sailing in both steam and sail ships. Third, you speak Norwegian. And last but not least, you have your master's ticket, so you are qualified to command."

Felix could not deny any of that.

"Your crew members are being selected under the same criteria. Most of them speak Norwegian or Swedish and all have similar experience."

"How many men?" Felix asked.

"Fifty-seven men and five more officers. Oh, I almost forgot! You have been promoted to kapitänleutnant, congratulations. Now, do you have civilian clothes you can change into?"

In Felix's view, this had all been very un-German, un-navy and informal, and he still wondered if it was a joke.

That ended when he saw her.

She was beautiful. A three-masted windjammer, steel-hulled and of around 1,500 tons. She was called the *Pass of Balmaha*.

"We impounded her. She was captured by one of our submarines in 1915 and was flying the British flag. The captain swore they were Americans and that they had been forced to fly the flag by a British cruiser. There was a prize crew aboard, apparently. After her refit, she'll be renamed and classified as an auxiliary cruiser."

Felix took in her lines; she would be fast. "Does she have an engine?"

"Yes, they considerately fitted auxiliary diesel engines at some time."

Felix was thinking of the British blockade. She should be able to pass for a Norwegian ship. He pictured her in his mind flying the Norwegian flag. Yes, that would work.

"We better make sure everything is well hidden if we're to run the blockade."

The British had mined vast areas of the approaches to the German ports, forcing merchant ships to stick to safe lanes that passed through neutral waters. All the safe lanes were patrolled by British cruisers and destroyers.

***

The refit was comprehensive. The crew helped the dockyard workers to convert hold space into hidden lounges and living quarters to accommodate the men who would sail and fight her, as well as accommodate any prisoners they captured. Extra storage rooms and refrigerated units for food, and bigger water tanks, were also created.

The main guns would be mounted on either side of the forecastle. When he saw the large 10.5-cm SK L/45 guns on shore, Felix realised they would have to go the extra mile to conceal them. The guns weighed close to 1,500 kilograms and were 4.75 metres long. He needed the gun crew to have access so they could man the guns before the big reveal. Steel deck cabins were erected on the foredeck that looked like storage lockers. These were low and covered the new sunken deck that carried the guns. A piece of the hull was made into a drop-down panel, and the on-deck structure folded away when the gun was in action. There were two heavy MG 08 machine gun mounts either side of the bridge, hidden under hinged wooden panels.

The crew were trained to disguise the gun housings with ropes and other bits of deck debris, which made the ship look a bit untidy but worked very well. Felix was asked what he wanted to call her and after some thought chose the *Seeadler* — the *Sea Eagle*. By now it was getting close to the time for her to sail and his next decision was crucial. Her cargo.

Felix discussed it with the kapitän, and they decided on making her a Norwegian wood carrier and loaded her accordingly. Of course, the cargo was only superficial and, while they were running the blockade, helped hide the modifications.

* * *

The fateful day arrived, 21 December 1916, and the *Seeadler* was to set sail. Felix called his crew together.

"We'll be sailing on the tide. From now on, we're a commercial ship and only one sailing watch at a time will be on deck. No naval terminology will be used. I'm the skipper, and the executive officer is the first mate. Other officers are mates and to be referred to by their trades or as *mister*. You're all used to dressing as working sailors" — that caused a laugh — "now you need to behave like them. If we're searched, the off-duty watches and gunners will stay silently in their accommodations. The false cargo should keep you hidden, but any noise will tip off the British that something is amiss."

He dismissed the men, the majority went below to the hidden lounges and only the watch needed to sail the ship stayed on deck. Felix ordered the auxiliary engines started and used them to manoeuvre from the dock. Then, as he had a favourable breeze, he raised the jibs and topsails to sail up and out of the canal. Against all expectations, he then turned east.

"Are we not heading to the Atlantic?" the first mate, Wolfgang Beckert, asked.

Felix had been ordered not to tell anyone of his plans before they sailed, and now they were at sea, he called his officers together on the bridge.

"I first have to apologise for not telling you my plans before we sailed. I was following orders. Now we're at sea, I can reveal them to you." Felix smiled. "As you know, we're posing as Norwegians. We'll follow the Danish coast north to Norway and take the passage through the Shetland Islands west into the Atlantic. We'll hug the coast and follow the prescribed lanes to avoid the minefields. If we're stopped by the British — and I fully expect we will be — you are to be friendly.

We are neutrals, after all. Once we're in the Atlantic, I plan to sail south-west into the mid-Atlantic, where we'll start to hunt. We'll maintain our disguise at all times until we show our true colours to our victims. At that point, we'll show our teeth and order them off their ship. I want everyone taken off, including any livestock, before we sink them. Prisoners will be held until we can either rendezvous with a German ship and offload them or we dock in a friendly port."

Felix watched their faces to see their reactions to the rule about prisoners. Some were obviously pleased, others looked puzzled, most were neutral, but one looked annoyed.

So, Leutnant Giehl, you think differently. I'll be watching you.

They sailed up past the vast minefields the British had laid across from the north-west tip of the Netherlands, east to Heligoland and north to the Skagerrak, shutting off that entire square of the North Sea. This drove them into the arms of a pair of British ships as they exited the passage into the Skagerrak. Felix calmly told his men, "Heave to. Back the foresails. Prepare to accept boarders."

The lead ship — a light cruiser, HMS *Essex* — sent a boat across while keeping them under her guns.

"Calmly now, speak only Norwegian and be friendly," Felix said to his men.

A lieutenant came aboard, with a pistol in a white holster on his hip, followed by a squad of marines carrying rifles. Felix stepped forward, a smile on his face and his hand outstretched in greeting.

"Captain Hans Nilsen. Welcome aboard, Lieutenant." He spoke in heavily accented English.

The lieutenant saluted, then shook his hand saying — in Norwegian — "Lieutenant Rye, His Majesty's Ship *Essex*."

"You are Norwegian?" Felix said, exuding hearty surprise.

"My father is, my mother is English." The lieutenant became all business. "We need to inspect your ship."

"Of course! Can I show you around?"

"That will not be necessary, my men can manage." Rye turned to the NCO in charge of the marines. "Carry on, Corporal."

The marines spread out in pairs, looking at things on the deck and peering into ventilators. The lieutenant turned back to Felix. "I need to see your papers."

"Of course, come with me," Felix replied. He had expected this and prepared accordingly.

He took the lieutenant down into his cabin that sat in the traditional place in the stern. He could see the second ship, a destroyer, through the transom window. It had manoeuvred into place behind them.

"He's wasting his time — we only have small auxiliary engines," Felix said.

Rye shrugged. "Standard operating procedure."

Felix handed over the ship's registration, his captain's papers and the cargo manifest.

"You're taking a cargo of wood to Scotland?"

"Yes, good Danish pine."

The papers had been carefully forged to support their cover story and even aged to make them look used. Rye was writing the main details in a notebook.

"How long have you been captain?" Rye asked.

"For three years and ... ahh ... four months," Felix replied, making a show of counting the months.

That confirmed the date on his papers.

"Can I offer you a drink?" Felix asked.

"I'd love one, but I'm on duty."

Felix pulled a bottle of akvavit out of a desk drawer.

"Then please accept this as a gesture of friendship."

Just then there was a knock on the door, and the corporal stuck his head through. "All done, sir. Everything is correct."

"Thank you, Corporal. Get the men back in the boat."

Rye turned back to Felix. "Well, Captain Nilsen, it looks like you can get back under sail."

Felix smiled. "Excellent! Here, take the akvavit."

Rye took the bottle and put it in the satchel he carried his notebook in. The two men walked to the ladder.

"Fair winds, Captain. I hope you have a pleasant voyage." Rye shook his hand and climbed down into the boat, which shoved off and chugged back to the cruiser.

Wolfgang sidled up next to Felix.

"He swallowed it?"

"Hook, line and sinker." Felix grinned and waved a farewell to the boat. "Did you slip the corporal a bottle as well?"

"I did."

Felix waved at the cruiser one last time before he ordered, "Make sail."

The British ships dropped astern as they sailed away towards the coast of Norway. A course of north by north-west took them to the island of Utsira, where they would turn west towards the Shetland Islands. Felix was aiming for a point between Fair Isle and Shetland to pass into the Atlantic, and a series of long tacks was needed to get them there.

"Why not take the route south of the Orkneys?" Leutnant Giehl asked.

"You want to sail through the British Home Fleet?" Felix asked.

"We could assess their numbers and report it back to command," Giehl replied stubbornly.

Felix looked at him. His eyes were full of zeal and not a lot else; he did not speak Norwegian, and Felix wondered why he had been chosen for this mission.

"Our mission is to sink merchant ships, thereby denying the enemy of much-needed supplies. Tell me, how does counting battleships fit in with those orders?"

"But …"

Felix ran out of patience.

"No *buts*. I am the captain of this ship, you are one of the gunnery officers. You will obey my orders and not question them. Is that clear?"

Giehl snapped to attention and saluted. "Yes, sir!"

"And that includes the ones about saluting and calling me *sir*. Dismissed."

Felix shook his head as Wolfgang — who knew Giehl's history — came over to him.

"His father pushed him into volunteering for special operations, then got him assigned to us. He thought it would see him promoted faster."

"Who is his father?"

"Kommodore Wilhelm Giehl. He's retired and is a friend of the grossadmiral. Our boy is his youngest son."

That explained everything! Giehl was young for a lieutenant. Patronage had got him onto Felix's ship. Well, if the boy wanted glory, Felix would give it to him.

"Put him in charge of the boarding party, make Städler his number two."

Städler was an older, steady oberbootsmann who was not easily pushed into doing things in ways his kapitän didn't want.

The Atlantic

A day and a half later, they passed Shetland to the north and headed into the Atlantic Ocean. The main mast lookout spotted smoke on the horizon to the south that could signal more British warships.

"One of the advantages of having a sixty-five-metre-high mast is we can see them before they see us!" Felix noted.

Once past Shetland they turned to the south-west, to a point south of Iceland. There, they turned west. They saw no ships and when they were due south of Kulusuk in Greenland, at 58°67'N 36°67'W, they tacked south.

Christmas and New Year passed without a single ship being seen and they sailed for more than 1,000 sea miles before …

"Ship ho! A point off the starboard bow," the lookout cried.

Felix shot out of his day cabin and peered through his binoculars. Wolfgang laughed. "You forgot your shoes, Skipper."

Felix looked down at his stockinged feet. He shrugged.

"I can't see her yet, change course towards her."

He stepped back into his day cabin and found his shoes. When he returned to the bridge he could see a smudge of smoke on the horizon. He checked the mizzen mast, where the Norwegian flag fluttered.

"We'll approach as if we want to exchange news, so fly a time signal flag. When we're too close for them to run, we'll show our true colours and guns. Fire a shot across her bows. As soon as they strike, the boarding party is to go across. Mr Giehl, you will scuttle her as soon as all the crew and livestock are off. Take a demolition charge with you in case their seacocks are stuck."

He treated Giehl to a look that said *obey your orders*.

The boarding party men were issued with Gewehr 98 rifles from the armoury and Giehl carried a Luger P08 that his father had given him.

They came up on the ship and signalled that they wanted to exchange news and wanted the time, requests that were not unusual among ships that had been at sea for a long time. Their target was a cargo steamer flying the British flag. They were a kilometre away and closing. Felix steered a course so he could come up a beam of her.

"Action stations!" Felix ordered and the guns were manned.

They came alongside.

"Heave to, back the fore sails." As soon as both ships were level, Felix ordered,

"Run up our colours, drop the panels."

Their disguise dropped with a series of clangs and the guns swung around. A warning shot was fired across her bows.

"Surrender and I will take you all off," he called through a speaking trumpet.

He could see that the ship was call the *Gladys Royle*. There was obviously some discussion on board.

"Fire a second shot."

Still the ship continued to steam along.

"Marine, fire your rifle at their bridge wall. Try not to hit anybody," Felix ordered, and heard Wolfgang chuckle behind him.

The shot rang out and the bullet whined away as it ricocheted off the wood of the bridge. The flag came down and a cloud of steam showed she had stopped her engines.

"Boat party away."

The crew of the *Gladys Royle* took to their boats and rowed across to the *Seeadler*. Their captain was first aboard. He was not happy.

"What are you going to do with my ship, you pirate?"

"Kapitän Felix Graf von Luckner, Imperial German Navy. And you are … ?" Felix replied calmly.

"Captain Wilbur Stokes of the *Gladys Royle*."

"Welcome aboard, Captain. We will make sure everybody is off the ship and then sink her. What is she carrying?"

"We have 300 tons of Argentinian beef."

Felix turned to Wolfgang. "Signal the men to bring back a carcase or two. We will eat well for a few days."

The signal was sent by semaphore flag.

"Mr Hartmann will show you and your crew to your quarters," Felix told Stokes in English. Then he turned and said in German, "Search them. I do not want a single pocketknife in their possession."

The boarding party started back to the *Seeadler*, a pile of beef carcases amidships. They came aboard and Städler was carrying something in his jacket. He approached his skipper and pulled out a tabby cat. "You said to include the livestock."

Felix reached out and stroked the cat's head. "Take him down and return him to his shipmates." He turned to the now proud-looking Giehl, who stood very straight, waiting for his kapitän to notice him. "Report."

"We searched the ship, and as per your orders brought the cat you have already seen and her papers. We set a charge under her propeller shaft as her seacocks had been welded shut." He checked his watch. "It should go off in three minutes."

"No one left aboard?"

"No, sir."

"Excellent, good job."

The cook was delighted with the sides of beef they had brought with them and was busy planning how to break them down for storage in their small, refrigerated room when the charge went off with a dull thud.

The *Gladys Royle* started to settle by the stern and a blast of steam showed when her boiler went under. She took her time but finally, after an hour, her bow slid below the waves. Felix allowed her officers to witness the sinking.

"Make sail, resume our previous course," Felix ordered. He had his first success of the cruise. His first 3,268 tons.

They ate well that night, as the cook had decided that thick rump steaks were the order of the day, served with pan-fried potatoes, onions and sauerkraut. Beer was drunk and the *Seeadler* was a happy ship. The off watch slept well, and the prisoners — who were fed the same as the crew — soon settled in, surprised at their accommodation.

The next morning, 10 January 1917, they spotted another ship. This one refused to identify herself and refused to heave to after they raised the German Ensign and exposed their guns.

"Fire a warning shot," Felix commanded.

The gun boomed and the shot exploded in the air on the other side of their target.

Still they were ignored, and she sailed stubbornly on.

Felix became impatient and ordered, "Fire into her."

The gunners, freed to do their jobs, opened up and soon the ship had been hit four times. She struck her flag, hove to and lowered her boats.

"Captain, come over to my ship," Felix ordered through a speaking trumpet.

No one got into a boat. There was no sign of life.

This was making Felix cross. "Boarding party away," he snapped.

Giehl, who was aware of his kapitän's mood, jumped to it.

Felix watched and waited as the party chugged across and boarded without any opposition. They disappeared into the ship, which they could now see was called the *Lundy Island*. The boarding party reappeared at the side and got back into their boat with only one prisoner. Felix's mood changed from angry to intrigued — but he had to wait for an explanation until they got back to the *Seeadler*.

The prisoner was the ship's captain, who identified himself as Captain Bannister. He admitted that the crew had abandoned ship as soon as they had fired the first shot by taking to their boats on the other side of the *Lundy Island* to the *Seeadler*.

Felix noted that Bannister looked more worried and afraid than he should.

"Then why did you stay?"

Bannister looked around him, as if seeking an escape route, then he sighed.

"Well, to be honest, I was captured before by a German ship and gave my parole to the captain."

"Which you have obviously broken," Felix said.

"Yes — you can understand why I didn't want to be a prisoner of war again."

Felix nodded.

"It makes no difference to me. If you end up in Germany, you may have to answer for it, but here you're just another prisoner."

The captain looked relieved.

"Take him down to the prisoners' quarters."

The manifest showed that the *Lundy Island* was carrying sugar.

"Sink her," Felix ordered.

The gunners enjoyed the target practice and sent her to the bottom. The crew could be anywhere by now and Felix didn't want to waste time searching for them. So they resumed their course.

The weather picked up, and with that the visibility lessened. They continued southwards. The prisoners were allowed time on deck to exercise and Felix started spending time with the captains. He told himself that it would improve his English, which he spoke with a noticeable Australian accent.

"Don't worry about the cold," he joked as they walked together around the deck. "We'll soon be in the tropics."

Bannister took to Felix, as he was a likeable character. "So, your family has no history of being at sea?" he asked as they strolled along the slanting deck.

"Not really. My father is a cavalry officer."

"You didn't want to follow in his footsteps?"

"No, I find the army and horses boring."

Bannister smiled. "A bad day's sailing is a hundred times better than work," he quoted.

"Ha! I see. One of your English sayings. I find English a rather strange language. So many words sound the same or are even spelled the same but mean very different things."

"Yes, English is full of those — which makes puns a target for comedians."

"German humour is different."

"Tell me a German joke."

"*Wenn der Bauer zum Waldrand hetzt, war das Plumpsklo schon besetzt.* If a farmer rushes to the woods, the outhouse is already occupied. Or another is, I only believe in one rule: if it rains in May, April is over!"

Bannister took those in and laughed somewhat politely.

Felix was on a roll. "A man goes to the doctor and says, 'Doctor, I poop every morning at seven. What should I do?' The doctor tells him not to worry, that most people would love to be that regular. 'But wait,' the man says, 'I wake up at seven thirty …'"

That got a genuine laugh, and the two exchanged jokes until the time for exercise was over.

As they sailed south, the weather got progressively warmer. They were out of the hurricane season and only had to cope with the occasional day of rough weather. Felix pulled out a chart of the equatorial Atlantic and showed Wolfgang what he intended to do.

"When I was sailing as a merchant seaman, I sailed these waters between Africa and Brazil. It was always busy with ships of many nations carrying all sorts of cargo. My plan is to sail within a box that runs parallel to the Brazilian coast that's around 1,500 kilometres long by 500 wide. We should find plenty of targets there."

"I agree, there should be ships from many of our enemies there. It should make rich pickings."

It was eleven days from their last capture and the end of January when they spotted a ship that was very similar to the *Seeadler*. She was a three-masted barque sailing north, flying a French Ensign and heavily loaded.

"Raise the French Ensign and signal, *We have letters for home*," Felix ordered, then called the ship to action stations.

The ruse worked and the two ships hove to just 100 metres apart on a relatively flat sea. As soon as they had both stopped, Felix ordered, "Raise our ensign." As it fluttered out in the wind the gun ports crashed down, and a warning shot flew through the *Charles Gounod*'s rigging. She lowered her colours instantly.

Felix used the diesel engines to bring them in alongside as the two ships were of a similar design and height and the boarding party could jump across. The crew soon came aboard and the crew of the *Seeadler* went through the now-familiar routine of searching them. Felix allowed them to bring their sea bags with them and looted the stores. Her manifest showed she was loaded with corn. A few well-placed shots sent her to the bottom.

Felix read her captain's logbook. It was full of useful information about ships they had met, where they were from and their intended routes.

Very useful, he thought.

There was a three-day intermission and then, on 24 January 1917, they spotted a schooner sailing north-west. She flew the Canadian Ensign, and they chased her down without using deception as they were much faster than she was. The *Perce* was brought alongside after a burst of fire from the machine guns brought her to a halt. The crew was taken off and Felix was surprised to see a young woman among the men.

Felix gave Giehl an extra order: "Find her cabin and bring all her possessions with you."

The ship carried general cargo, which they looted for anything useful.

"Sink her," he said, and the machine guns went to work as the schooner only had a thin hull. When they had finished, he approached the woman.

Seeing him, the Perce's captain stepped protectively in front of her. Felix stopped, made a short bow and introduced himself: "Kapitän Felix Graf von Luckner."

"Captain Rodney Olafsson and my wife Janita," the captain said.

"Yours is an Icelandic name. Your wife, is she Brazilian?" Felix said, taking in her coffee-with-cream-coloured skin and beautiful dark eyes.

"I'm Canadian. My grandfather came to Canada from Iceland. She's Brazilian — we married while I was ashore."

"Well, you must dine with me. Wolfgang, do we have a private cabin where Captain Olafsson can sleep?"

Wolfgang looked the couple over and saw how protective Olafsson was of his new bride. The man looked ready to fight — and that could mean trouble.

"They can have mine," Wolfgang said. "I'll move in with Mueller."

The couple had dinner with Felix and Wolfgang and the cook went the extra mile to make a stew with some of the beef they had captured. Felix was the perfect host and told them, "I was married but my wife could not stand me being at sea, especially when I was called on by the navy. I'll put you on the first neutral ship we see. That makes life less complicated for me and will let you enjoy your marriage."

The Olafssons were grateful to him and would tell the story of the gentleman pirate they had met for the rest of their lives.

There was another pleasant interlude until 3 February, when they spotted a four-masted barque. She was the *Antonin* and was French. Heavily laden with a cargo of saltpetre from Chile, she stood little chance against the swift *Seeadler* and succumbed without any kind of fight. The crew, several passengers, a dog and three goats were taken off before she was scuttled.

Saltpetre was a valuable commodity for the war effort, and denying it to the French and their allies was a big win for Felix. It was a critical component of gunpowder and used to preserve meat, both of which the allies needed to progress the war.

"We are becoming more of a passenger ship than a cruiser," Wolfgang joked as the latest set of inmates were taken to their quarters. There were more women, and they had to partition off part of the quarters to keep them separate

"There will be more. We will just have to avoid liners," Felix laughed.

Their next victim on 9 February was an Italian sailing vessel, the *Buenos Ayres*. She was carrying saltpetre as well. She was sunk with just two shots and added another thirty men and a cat to their prisoner list.

The accommodation was filling up and they were getting through supplies at a high rate, forcing Felix to think about resupply. He didn't want to take the *Seeadler* into port because he had so many prisoners aboard and that would expose him as a belligerent and get him interred.

Farnborough

The solution came when a familiar profile appeared. Felix studied her before telling his men, "I know that ship. Make all sail, get after her!"

The *Pinmore* had spotted them and was piling on all sail. Felix grinned, the chase was on. "She's fast — I sailed on her in 1902 — but she's not fast enough. Start the engines!"

With the aid of the engines, they overhauled the British ship and put a shot across her bow. She dropped her sails and came to a stop. This time Felix led the boarding party, which was larger than usual. He met the captain at the side. He didn't know him, but did recognise a couple of the mates. The ship had a mascot — a spider monkey called Brian, who sat on one of the mate's shoulders.

"Take your crew over to the *Seeadler*," he told the captain as more than a boarding party came aboard.

"What are you going to do with my ship?" the captain asked, sensing something unusual was going on.

"I'll sail her to Rio for supplies," Felix replied. He examined the papers that one of his men had retrieved. "I'm now Captain Reeves," he said — with an Australian accent that was stronger than ever.

They dumped almost half the cargo by the time Rio came into sight, so they would have room for the quantity of supplies that they needed. Funds were not a problem. Every ship they had taken had contributed to the pot and they had enough money for all their needs and more. Fresh meat was a priority, along with vegetables, fruit and flour. Crates of beer were procured and Felix topped up his private wine store.

Felix had chosen his crew carefully, picking men that spoke English or Norwegian. They flew the Red Ensign. Felix still spoke English with a slight Australian accent, and on one occasion was approached by another ship's officer as he finished a purchase.

"G'day, mate. I heard you speaking. You're an Aussie?"

The man was large and bluff, with blond hair and a ruddy complexion. Felix grabbed his hand and shook it vigorously. "I am, where you from?" The man returned the shake with equivalent pressure. "Sydney, but I ain't been there for many a year."

Felix thought quickly. "I'm from Albany, it's been a while since I've been home, too."

That was far enough away from Sydney for the other man not to profess to have mutual friends.

"You were a whaler?" Albany was a famous whaling port.

"Only for a bit. Couldn't stand the smell. What's your name? I'm Bruce," Felix said.

"Pete. Fancy a beer?"

"Always, mate."

The two moved to a bar and ordered beers. Felix drew on his experiences to fill in the gaps in his history. After the third beer and a fair amount of talking, he was running out of material. He was rescued when one of his men found him.

"Skipper! There you are. I've been looking all over for you."

"What's up, Stan?" Felix said, relieved.

"The chap we're buying the pork from wants paying before he'll deliver."

Felix drained his glass.

"I'm coming. Pete, it was great to talk to a fellow Aussie, but duty calls. Fair winds, mate."

They shook hands and Felix made his escape.

They sailed the *Pinmore* back to the rendezvous and transferred the stores. Felix went back aboard and opened the seacocks himself to scuttle her. It was the least he could do for the old girl.

Resupplied, they continued to patrol the box, as Felix called it. A couple of easy days passed before they spotted another ship. She was a Danish three-masted barque and therefore a neutral. She was carrying a general cargo and was bound for Copenhagen, so they let her go unmolested.

It wasn't until 26 February 1917 that they spotted a three-masted barque and gave chase. They caught her, so she struck and dropped her sails. The boarding party rowed across and sent the crew over to the *Seeadler*. A message came with them that the ship was carrying pig and chicken carcasses. Felix now understood what the engine he could hear throbbing away was for. It must be a donkey engine they used to run the refrigeration plant. Well, any meat was welcome, and he sent another boat over to fetch what they could. The *British Yeoman* was sent to the bottom.

That evening they stopped another barque flying the French flag, *La Rochefoucauld*. The captain wailed about pirates and being stopped again. Felix heard him and took him aside.

"You were stopped before?" he asked.

"Mais oui! A British cruiser stopped us. They were looking for a German pirate, the *Seeadler*."

So, the British had heard they were here! That did not worry Felix too much. Locating them would be like finding a needle in a haystack. The chances of the cruiser coming on them by chance were remote, and if it happened, they should spot it well before they got into range. In any case, Felix had sunk in excess of 20,000 tons of shipping in two months and had no intention of stopping now. And besides all of that, the *La Rochefoucauld*'s captain's log listed another three barques from France, and their routes, which he could pick up easily.

The evening of 5 March 1917 was a pleasant moonlit evening, with no clouds and a steady breeze. Perfect sailing weather. A ship came into view and according to the log they had captured, she should be the *Dupleix*, another French barque. They sailed alongside her and flashed the signal *Stop immediately! German cruiser.* The ship came to a halt with her foresails backed and a rowing boat came across. Felix met the occupant as he climbed the side and came aboard.

The man laughed and said something in French. Felix replied in English.

"Welcome aboard the Imperial Navy cruiser *Seeadler*, Captain. I expect this is a surprise, but I can assure you that I wish you and your crew no harm. Tell your men to abandon ship and come across."

"Mon Dieu!" the man said, as he realised she was not what he had assumed, namely a French ship playing a prank on them.

The captain was returned to his ship with the boarding party, and once he and his crew had left, the ship was scuttled.

On 11 March, six days later, they came upon another barque. This time she was British, the *Horngarth*. They chased her down and Wolfgang spotted that she had a radio antenna. He traced the cable, which was poorly disguised, to the rear of the bridge.

"Take out the radio cabin, there," Wolfgang ordered.

The gun crew complied. It served as a warning shot as well.

They sank her after removing the crew as usual, then discovered that the shot that had been fired to disable the *Horngarth*'s radio had burst a steam pipe, which had killed a sailor called Douglas Page.

Felix's perfect record had been ruined.

Felix had a problem — overcrowding. He was, by now, carrying nearly three hundred prisoners and their pets.

He turned to Wolfgang. "We have to get rid of them and I don't want to return to Germany or try to land at one of our colonies. The British know who we are, and we'll be interned before we know it. The next ship we take, we offload the prisoners and send them to Rio."

However, it wasn't until 21 March 1917 that they got the chance to stop a ship that was big enough. The *Cambronne* was French and carried a cargo of timber. They stopped her and threw the cargo over the side. Then they removed her topgallant masts and took any spare sails and spars.

"Move the prisoners across."

Felix had to reassure the captains that he would not blow them out of the water as soon as they boarded her. He put Captain Mullen of the *Pinmore* in charge, leaving him with charts and a sextant.

"If I was you, I would head for Rio. It's the closest port and is neutral," Felix told him.

Mullen liked Felix and thought that in other circumstances they could be friends.

"My thinking as well," he said. "You know the British are looking for you?"

Felix laughed and lit his pipe. "Oh, I'm well aware of that. I hear they call me Der Seeteufel [the Sea Devil] and my crew Die Piraten des Kaisers [the Emperor's Pirates]."

Mullen smiled at the nicknames. "You have gained notoriety in a short time."

Felix shrugged. "We have had our successes."

Mullen snorted a laugh, then shook his hand. "Thank you for your hospitality. I'll be going now."

Felix watched them sail away. Without the topgallant masts they would be slow, and he gave them plenty of time to get away.

Now it was time to leave the Atlantic.

The Pacific

April 1917

The British merchant cruisers *Otranto* and *Orbita*, along with the armoured cruiser HMS *Lancaster*, proceeded south from their patrol near the Falkland Islands. They were heading down to Cape Horn as they had received intelligence that the *Seeadler* was moving into the Pacific.

"We need to catch that beggar. He's the most successful raider the Germans have got!" said John R. Segrave of the *Lancaster* and commander of the squadron. "He's sunk the best part of 30,000 tons of shipping in three months." This was only a slight exaggeration. "My intention is to set a trap at the cape, where our steam power will be most effective against his sail."

The British were unaware that the *Seeadler* had auxiliary diesel engines, but even they wouldn't save her against a cruiser with a top speed of twenty-three knots and carrying 6-inch guns. The trap was well planned, and they were in position well before the *Seeadler* reached the cape.

* * *

Meanwhile, Felix was blissfully unaware that the British knew so much about him. In fact, radio messages had been sent before some ships were sunk and their description had been circulated. Once they knew what they were looking for, British spies in Hamburg soon found out what the ship was called and who her captain was. Thereafter, British agents in Brazil and Argentina were on the lookout for them and any ships that made it into port were asked if they had seen them.

"We'll move over to the Pacific and try our luck there," Felix told Wolfgang.

The weather was fine as they sailed down the Argentinian coast and the men were enjoying the cruise, now they had got rid of their passengers. The ship stank less without 300 men farting and sweating below decks, and they had cleaned the lounges and berths with vinegar and soda. They had plenty of food and ammunition and no excuse to go home.

The one place Felix expected trouble was between the Falkland Islands and the Argentinian coast. They had stopped to rewater at Montevideo in Uruguay and had stocked up on supplies at the same time. Now he had to decide whether to try and go through the Strait of Magellan or round the Horn. Argentina and Chile were both neutral, but that posed its own problems. Almost all of South America was neutral — but that meant that warships could not enter any of their ports and receive aid or supplies. He had taken a risk with Uruguay and had flown an American flag when he entered the port, knowing his hosts were aligned with the United States.

"On balance, we should go around rather than through. If the British find out that we're using the Strait of Magellan, they'll tip off the Chileans, who will have no choice but to impound us," Felix said.

So — international waters it would be. The British trap was set.

* * *

They approached Cape Horn hoping for an easy passage. It wasn't to be. As they passed around the east side of the Isla de los Estados, a storm came from the west on the Roaring Forties.

"God damn and blast!" Felix swore as they were forced to turn south. Tacking against the Roaring Forties and the current through Drake Passage was hard enough, but with the storm shifting the wind to the north they had no choice but to turn south by south-west.

He did not know how lucky he was.

On the *Lancaster*, Segrave felt the full force of the storm and cursed for a different reason. "Of all the bloody luck. This will push him south, and around us." He shook his head. Luckner was a very lucky sailor. "Order the squadron to turn south, we might get lucky." But in his heart Segrave knew the chances of spotting the *Seeadler* were slim to non-existent.

Felix wore a coat with a fur collar and gloves as they were pushed to sixty degrees south. The days were shorter here and the temperature much, much lower. His on-watch men were hammering ice from the rigging. The good news was, they had gone as far south as they had to. The storm had passed, and they were able to turn north-west and sail as close to the wind as they could to enter the Pacific. At that latitude the waves circumnavigated the globe without the interference of any land. That allowed them to become huge rollers, which the *Seeadler* had to sail up and over. It wouldn't be until the 48th parallel south, when New Zealand and Australia exerted an effect, that the wave heights decreased.

They entered the Pacific proper on 18 April 1917 and steered north up the Chilean coast. There, in early June and east of Easter Island, he met a German cargo ship. The two captains got together for a drink and to share news.

"Kapitän Holst, your good health," Felix said as they shared a schnaps in his cabin.

"And yours, Graf Luckner."

They downed their shots in one and Felix poured them another.

"What news? We have been at sea for months," Felix said.

"Things have gone badly. America has joined the war. Those idiots in the submarine corps sank an American liner that was full of celebrities and important people. Instead of apologising, the Kaiser just declared open season on any ships supplying aid to Britain and its allies."

"That is indeed bad news. They have many soldiers and a large industrial base," Felix said.

"It gets worse. Bolivia, Brazil, Guatemala, Haiti, Honduras, Cuba, Nicaragua and Panama have all severed ties with Germany — with several actually declaring war alongside America."

Felix blew out his cheeks. He had no idea that the submarine war was having such a disastrous effect. "Well, I can only do my part as ordered," he said, fatalistically.

"Yes, but watch yourself. The British know who you are and have put a price on your head."

In response to the news, Felix turned his attention to American shipping. He sailed north to more productive waters and started to hunt. On 14 June 1917 they spotted a small schooner, the *A.B. Johnson*, which was carrying a cargo out of San Francisco. The *Seeadler* caught her and sent her to the bottom. She was only 529 tons.

Just four days later they found the *R.C. Slade*, another schooner. She led them on a chase, but they finally overhauled her and she was forced to strike her colours. She was a mere 673 tons.

By this time, the US Navy had joined the hunt for Felix. He wasn't doing that much damage, but he was a raider and was in their backyard — something the Americans would not tolerate.

On 8 July the *Seeadler* spotted the *Manila*, another schooner. They gave chase but by now their hull was dirty and in dire need of cleaning. Even so, they caught and sank her — but the chase had been longer and harder than Felix wanted.

Felix and Wolfgang consulted the charts, looking for a suitable place to careen the *Seeadler*.

"We need to get away from the Americans — their destroyers are everywhere," Wolfgang said.

They had been playing a game of hide and seek with them for weeks now, and had a couple of close calls.

"How about the Society Islands?" Felix suggested.

"The where?"

"Society Islands — they are part of French Polynesia. Here just north-east of the Cook Islands and about 236 kilometres from Tahiti."

"That will put 6,500 kilometres between us and the Americans," Wolfgang estimated.

It was decided. They set sail.

The first island — or rather, atoll — that they came upon was Mopelia, also known as Maupihaa. It was a coral atoll and about 10 kilometres in diameter. Unfortunately, the *Seeadler* drew too much water to enter the sheltered lagoon, so they anchored outside. As it had been a long, hard journey, Felix decided to treat his men and their forty-six prisoners to a picnic on the sands, taking them across in the ship's longboats.

They were having a good time, and the party was well under way, when disaster struck. No one was paying attention to what was going on to the north, when a squall — a very big squall — bore down on the *Seeadler* out of an otherwise clear blue sky. The first Felix and the others knew of it was when they were engulfed in a downpour driven by 100-kilometre-an-hour winds.

This lasted no more than a few minutes, but the damage had been done. The *Seeadler* was aground. Felix called out, "Get everything we can from the ship. Provisions and guns are the priority."

The atoll had water, which was a major saving grace, and there were three Polynesians in residence who harvested coconuts to make copra for Tahiti.

Wolfgang managed the men and salvaged enough material from the stricken ship to build shelters for all of them. Within a week they were comfortably settled, with enough food to last them months.

"We are Germany's latest colony," Felix joked to his men. "We will christen it Cäcilieninsel." He had in mind the song "Cäcilie" by Strauss when he named it. The village they created was named Seeadlerburg, after their ship.

They lived comfortably, but Felix was too impatient to wait for a ship to come from Fiji to collect the copra harvest and rescue them. After a few months he spoke to Wolfgang about it, his patience exhausted.

"I think I'll take one of our longboats, set a mast and sail to Fiji via the Cook Islands. I can find us a new ship and come back and collect you."

"What will you do if you're confronted by the British?"

Farnborough

"Why, we'll be Norwegian survivors of a shipwreck!" Felix said, and laughed.

Felix was as good as his word and he and a hand-picked crew of six took one of the longboats and converted her into a sloop. "I name this boat the *Crown Princess Cecilie*," Felix declared on her launching.

He had a compass and supplies, a crew he could trust and nothing to lose. They set out and headed towards the Cook Islands. Luckily, the weather was fair and the wind favourable.

Three days later they reached Atiu island, a New Zealand colony. The New Zealand resident who administered the island came to greet them as they came ashore.

"Hello, we don't see many people turning up here in longboats."

Felix improvised; he was feeling playful and he had a supply of American dollars. "We are Dutch-Americans sailing across the Pacific for a bet. Can we get some supplies?"

The resident didn't really believe them, but had no soldiers or police to back him up so he gave them supplies to enable them to reach one of the bigger islands in the group. They chose Aitutaki. Again, the island resident was unconvinced by their story that they were shipwrecked Norwegians, but had no means of detaining them. Felix sensed his suspicion and got them off the island as quickly as possible.

Their next waypoint was Rarotonga, which they approached in the dark. Then: "Skipper, there's a ship ahead!" Wolfgang said.

Felix stood and peered into the dark. Sure enough, there was the outline of a large ship.

"Looks like an auxiliary cruiser," Felix said.

"It must be either British or a New Zealander," Wolfgang said.

Felix decided to avoid landing and steered a course for Wakaya, one of the Fijian islands. They had sailed 3,700 kilometres in an open boat — an exceptional feat.

Most people on the island accepted Felix's story that they were shipwrecked Norwegians, but he didn't convince everyone. There was one sceptic in particular who kept his views to himself while he watched and listened to the sailors and their captain. He was British — Barry Kingston, a former sailor who had been around the world at least twice. He had spent time in Norway and knew the coastal part of the country well.

Barry waited until one of the sailors was on his own in a bar and asked, "Where did you sail out of?"

"Oslo."

"That's a long way from here."

"It is."

"A nice port, set there on the coast. Lots to do."

"Yes, never boring."

That was all he needed to hear. Barry headed to the police station on the island of Ovalau and reported what he knew.

"You think they're Germans?" Inspector Collins said.

"I asked one of them where they came from, and he said Oslo. I said, 'That's a nice little port on the coast,' and he agreed."

"Well?" Collins said.

Barry sighed. "Oslo isn't on the coast. It's at the end of a bloody great fjord and any genuine Norwegian would tell you that."

Collins assembled a squad of men and sailed to Wakaya. On 21 September 1917 they confronted Felix and his party at their boat.

"You are under arrest," Collins said.

"Why?" Felix asked.

"Under suspicion of being enemy agents," Collins said, then nodded towards the inter-island ferry they had used to get there. "She's armed with a 6-pound gun and will blow you out of the water if you try to escape."

Felix knew the game was up. He had guns but they were hidden at the bottom of the boat. He raised his hands in surrender.

Collins heaved a silent sigh of relief. It had all been a bluff; his men weren't armed, and the ferry didn't have a gun.

Felix and his men were taken to the internment camp on Motuihe Island, off of the North Island of New Zealand.

While all of this was going on, the remainder of Felix's crew back on Mopelia had received a visitor. The French trader *Lutèce* anchored off the reef to rewater. Leutnant King, whom Felix had left in charge, had heard about Felix's capture on the BBC World Service on their radio and knew he would not be coming to rescue them.

"Get a team together and arm them," he told Rolf Reitenbach.

They used one of their longboats to sail out to the *Lutèce*, which they boarded and captured. King sent the crew to shore and brought all the German sailors aboard, leaving the prisoners on the atoll. They renamed her *Fortuna* and sailed for South America.

Left behind, the master of the *A. B. Johnson*, Captain Smith, decided to take the remaining longboat and one other sailor, and sail to Pago Pago for help. He duly arrived there and told the authorities of the *Seeadler* and what she had done. He also reported that Felix had sailed before them in a similar boat. As Felix had already been captured, this confirmed his identity for the New Zealand authorities, which sealed his fate.

The remaining prisoners were rescued a week later.

King and the rest of the *Seeadler*'s crew were not so lucky. They struck some uncharted rocks off Easter Island and had to scramble ashore. The Chilean authorities promptly arrested them and interned them for the rest of the war.

Felix may have been captured, but he was far from beaten and started to plan his escape. The building in which were being held was not really a prison. It was intended to be an internment camp for Germans resident in New Zealand when the war broke out. Consequently, the security wasn't really all it should have been.

"Wolfgang, have you noticed how the commander of our prison gets to shore every night?"

"You mean that nice little launch?"

"Yes, the *Pearl* — she's fast, and I bet she has a decent range, especially as he has her refuelled here once a week."

Wolfgang grinned. "What's your plan?"

"We're going to set up a Christmas play!"

Felix went to the commander and asked for permission to produce a play "to celebrate Christmas".

"That's an excellent idea, what can I do to help?" the commander replied.

"I could do with some supplies," Felix said.

Felix used the provisions to plan their escape and on 13 December he and his men made their move. The *Pearl* had been refuelled and the guards were as lax as usual.

"The armoury first," Felix said, and led the men to the blockhouse.

A single guard was on duty, and he was lighting a cigarette when two of the crew members jumped him and knocked him out. They took his gun, then forced the lock on the door.

"Get a machine gun," Felix said, taking a pistol and ammunition for himself. A Vickers and a tripod were taken and then they moved down to the dock. No one saw them, and within minutes they had the engine started and motored out of the harbour. Luckily the boat had a compass, and Felix set course for the Coromandel Peninsula. "See that?" he said when they arrived, as a ship hove into view.

"Yes, it's a scow — but we don't have a lot of choice," Wolfgang said while tapping the fuel gauge.

It was indeed better than nothing. The *Moa* was a ninety-ton scow with a flat bottom, normally used for transporting cargo to and from ships in the harbour. They seized her at gunpoint.

"Where now?" Wolfgang asked Felix.

"The Kermadec Islands. There's a castaway depot there. All we need is a map and a sextant."

"A map we have — there's a school atlas aboard — but there's no sextant."

"That's all right, von Zatorski will make one," Felix said with irrepressible confidence. "Throw the cargo overboard, we'll go faster without it." Van Zatorski did indeed make one and the other five crew threw the cargo over the side.

The Captain of the *Iris*, an armed cable ship, was alerted to the escape and ordered to apprehend them. The skipper was a clever man and guessed where Felix would head. She was much faster than the *Moa* and arrived at the Kermadecs on 19 December. She spotted the *Moa* just after the latter arrived on 21 December. After a brief chase, the *Moa* was captured and the Germans surrendered.

Epilogue

"So, what happened to all these brave souls after the war ended?" you may ask.

Harrington Edwards (*Taranaki*) returned to submarines commanding HMS *E5*, which was lost after striking a mine.

William Mark-Wardlaw (HMS *Prince Charles*) was promoted to commander in 1919, served through World War II and died in 1952 at his home in Reading, Berkshire.

Ernest Jehan (*Inverlyon*) served on HMS *Sarpedon* as the executive officer then commanded HMS *PC-55*. He retired from the navy in 1920.

Godfrey Herbert (HMS *Baralong*) retired from the navy after serving on Bayly's staff at Queenstown. He became a car sales manager for the Daimler division of the Birmingham Small Arms Company, where he was promoted to director. In World War II he commanded the armed merchant cruiser *Cilicia* on convoy duty off the coast of West Africa and retired again in 1943 to settle in Mozambique. He married and had two daughters. He died in what was then called Rhodesia (now Zimbabwe) in 1961.

Andrew Wilmot-Smith (HMS *Baralong*) was promoted to the rank of commander after the war. Little else is known of his post-war life.

Harold Auten (HMS *Zylpha*) was married in 1917. He left the navy after the war and moved to the United States of America, where he wrote a book called *Q-Boat Adventures* and produced a film about the *Stock Force*, in which he played himself. He continued in the film industry, in time becoming a vice president of the Rank Organisation. During World War II he was a commander and acting captain in the RNR and served as a staff officer, organising transatlantic convoys. He received the Legion of Merit in the USA and was made a Commander of the Order of Orange-Nassau by the Royal Netherlands Navy. He died in 1964, at the age of seventy-three.

Gordon Campbell (HMS *Farnborough*, HMS *Pargust*, HMS *Dunraven*) attained the rank of vice admiral by the end of his career. He commanded HMS *Tiger*, a battlecruiser from 1925–27 and served as an aide-de-camp to King George IV. He was active politically and served as the Member of Parliament for Burnley. In World War II he was recalled to the navy and served as the commander of anti-invasion measures around Padstow in Cornwall.

William Edward Sanders — Gunner Billy (HMS *Helgoland*, HMS *Prize*) — may have died in action but his legacy lives on. His medals are on display at the Auckland War Museum. He is commemorated with a plaque in the church at Milford Haven, the home of the *Prize*, on another in Auckland Town Hall and there is a scholarship in his name for children of members of the Royal Navy or mercantile marine to the University of Auckland. Sanders Avenue and the William Sanders Retirement Village in Devonport are named after him.

Felix Graf von Luckner (SMS *Seeadler*) left the German navy after he was repatriated, became a freemason and wrote a book about his adventures which became a bestseller in Germany. He moved to Malmö in Sweden and married Ingeborg Engeström on 24 September 1924. In 1926 he raised the money to purchase a sailing ship he called the *Vaterland*, and set out on a worldwide goodwill mission. He was, by all accounts, an entertaining speaker and was lauded for his seamanship and the fact he did not kill anyone intentionally. Henry Ford gave him a car and San Francisco made him an honorary citizen. In World War II he refused to join the Nazi party or denounce his American ties, and he saved the life of a Jewish woman in his hometown of Halle. He was captured by the 414th Infantry Regiment, who placed him under guard to protect him from the local Nazis — who planned to execute him without trial. He moved to Sweden after the war, back to his wife's hometown of Malmö, where they lived until his death at age 84 in 1966. He is buried at Ohlsdorf Cemetery in Hamburg, Germany.

There is no doubt that the captains and crews of the Q-ships were brave. One could argue that they were fanatics, whether in their beliefs and conduct or in their determination. It is true that more submarines were sunk by regular Royal Navy warships and that, after the war, the Q-ships were deemed overrated. More than two hundred were commissioned, of which sixty were sailing ships.

I think the attitude of most players in this book can be summed up in the worlds of von Spiegel, spoken after he and his crew were picked up by the *Prize*.

"After the war we can be friends," von Spiegel told Sanders. "I am fighting for my country and you are fighting for yours. That is right and proper for both of us."

I will close with a quote from Winston Churchill.

The use of these vessels [...] afforded opportunity for some of the most brilliant and daring stratagems in the naval war.

THE END

Author's Notes

British money in 1919
Farthing = a quarter of a penny
Halfpenny or ha'penny = half a penny
Penny = one-twelfth of a shilling (or one two-hundred-and-fortieth of a pound)
Threepence or thruppence = three pennies
Sixpence or tanner = six pennies
Shilling or bob = twelve pennies or one twentieth of a pound
Florin = two shillings
Half-crown = two shillings and sixpence or one eighth of a pound
Half-sovereign = ten shillings
One-pound note = twenty shillings

Imperial weight
One ounce (oz) = 28.35 g
One pound = 16 ounces = 0.45 kg
One stone = 14 pounds

One hundredweight = 8 stone or 112 lbs = 50.8 kg
Large sack = 16 stone

Tons burthen

The estimated cargo capacity of a sailing ship, calculated by the formula:

Tonnage = (Length x Beam x Depth) / 94

Imperial volume

One fluid ounce = 28.4 ml
One pint = 20 fluid ounces = 0.56 l
One gallon = 8 pints = 4.54 l

Fahrenheit to Celsius

32 oF = 0 oC
Thus, Celsius = (Fahrenheit −32)/1.8

Drinking age during WW1 in the UK

The age a person could legally buy beer between 1914 and 1918 was fourteen years old in a pub or off-licence. When they reached sixteen years old, they could buy spirits and wine.

Queenstown is now called Cobh.

Hexanite was a German explosive of sixty per cent trinitrotoluene (TNT) and forty per cent hexanitrodiphenylamine (HND). It was developed in the early twentieth century in response to a shortage of TNT.

A slide rule

Photo by aldoaldoz on Freeimages.com (and yes, I did use one at school!)

Military honours
The Victoria Cross = the highest award for valour for operational personnel
The George Cross = the highest award for non-operational personnel
DSO = Distinguished Service Order
OBE = Order of the British Empire
DSC = Distinguished Service Cross
DCM = Distinguished Conduct Medal

German naval officer ranks
Grossadmiral (GAdm) = admiral of the fleet
Admiral (Adm) = admiral
Vizeadmiral (VAdm) = vice admiral
Konteradmiral (Kadm) = rear admiral
Kommodore (Kdm) = commodore
Kapitän (Kpt) = captain
Korvettenkapitän (KKpt) = commander
Fregattenkapitän (FrgKpt) = commander

Kapitänleutnant (KptLt) = lieutenant commander
Oberleutnant zur See (Obltn.z.S) = lieutenant
Leutnant zur See (Ltn.z.S) = lieutenant (junior grade)
Fähnrich zur See (Fhr.z.S) = midshipman

The Lume & Joffe Books Story

Lume Books was founded by Matthew Lynn, one of the true pioneers of independent publishing. In 2023 Lume Books was acquired by Joffe Books and now its story continues as part of the Joffe Books family of companies.

Joffe Books began in 2014 when Jasper agreed to publish his mum's much-rejected romance novel and it became a bestseller.

Since then we've grown into the largest independent publisher in the UK. We're extremely proud to publish some of the very best writers in the world, including Joy Ellis, Faith Martin, Caro Ramsay, Helen Forrester, Simon Brett and Robert Goddard. Everyone at Joffe Books loves reading and we never forget that it all begins with the magic of an author telling a story.

We are proud to publish talented first-time authors, as well as established writers whose books we love introducing to a new generation of readers.

We won Trade Publisher of the Year at the Independent Publishing Awards in 2023 and Best Publisher Award in 2024 at the People's Book Prize. We have been shortlisted for Independent Publisher of the Year at the British Book Awards for the last five years, and were shortlisted for the Diversity and Inclusivity Award at the 2022 Independent Publishing Awards. In 2023 we were shortlisted for Publisher of the Year at the RNA Industry Awards, and in 2024 we were shortlisted at the CWA Daggers for the Best Crime and Mystery Publisher.

We built this company with your help, and we love to hear from you, so please email us about absolutely anything bookish at feedback@joffebooks.com.

If you want to receive free books every Friday and hear about all our new releases, join our mailing list here: www.joffebooks.com/freebooks.

And when you tell your friends about us, just remember: it's pronounced Joffe as in coffee or toffee!

www.ingramcontent.com/pod-product-compliance
Ingram Content Group UK Ltd.
Pitfield, Milton Keynes, MK11 3LW, UK
UKHW020106110625
6334UKWH00009B/87

9 781839 016158